HARD TIME

'What are you doing here, Travis?' Dave demanded.

Paul stood directly in front of him. 'I came to see you,' he said. 'I need a favour.'

The guard smirked. 'I hear you're Spalding's bitch, now,' he said. 'What do you want from me?'

'I want to get into the solitary block,' Paul said. 'I want to talk to John.'

'The nonce.' Dave sneered. 'Why? Want to get some tips on how to pleasure Spalding?'

'I just want to talk to him,' Paul said. 'Through the cell door – it doesn't have to be face to face.'

'And why should I –' Dave never finished the sentence. Paul had reached forward and cupped his hand over the bulge in Dave's uniform trousers.

HARD TIME

Robert Black

First published in Great Britain in 1999 by
Idol
an imprint of Virgin Publishing Ltd
Thames Wharf Studios,
Rainville Road, London W6 9HT

ISBN 0 352 33304 9

Cover photograph by Colin Clarke Photography

Typeset by SetSystems Ltd, Saffron Walden, Essex
Printed and bound in Great Britain by
Mackays of Chatham PLC

For my beloved Richard.

Thanks to John R, Paul B and the Rev. David W.

Special thanks to my friend Mike, whose support and creativity helped make the book happen.

The Terrence Higgins Trust

SAFER SEX GUIDELINES

These books are sexual fantasies – in real life, everyone needs to think about safe sex.

While there have been major advances in the drug treatments for people with HIV and AIDS, there is still no cure for AIDS or a vaccine against HIV. Safe sex is still the only way of being sure of avoiding HIV sexually.

   HIV can only be transmitted through blood, come and vaginal fluids (but no other body fluids) passing from one person (with HIV) into another person's bloodstream. It cannot get through healthy, undamaged skin. The only real risk of HIV is through anal sex without a condom – this accounts for almost all HIV transmissions between men.

Being safe
Even if you don't come inside someone, there is still a risk to both partners from blood (tiny cuts in the arse) and pre-come. Using strong condoms and water-based lubricant greatly reduces the risk of HIV. However, condoms can break or slip off, so:
* Make sure that condoms are stored away from hot or damp places.
* Check the expiry date – condoms have a limited life.
* Gently squeeze the air out of the tip.
* Check the condom is put on the right way up and unroll it down the erect cock.
* Use plenty of water-based lubricant (lube), up the arse and on the condom.
* While fucking, check occasionally to see the condom is still in one piece (you could also add more lube).
* When you withdraw, hold the condom tight to your cock as you pull out.

* Never re-use a condom or use the same condom with more than one person.
* If you're not used to condoms you might practise putting them on.
* Sex toys like dildos and plugs are safe. But if you're sharing them use a new condom each time or wash the toys well.

For the safest sex, make sure you use the strongest condoms, such as Durex Ultra Strong, Mates Super Strong, HT Specials and Rubberstuffers packs. Condoms are free in many STD (Sexually Transmitted Disease) clinics (sometimes called GUM clinics) and from many gay bars. It's also essential to use lots of water-based lube such as KY, Wet Stuff, Slik or Liquid Silk. Never use come as a lubricant.

Oral sex
Compared with fucking, sucking someone's cock is far safer. Swallowing come does not necessarily mean that HIV gets absorbed into the bloodstream. While a tiny fraction of cases of HIV infection have been linked to sucking, we know the risk is minimal. But certain factors increase the risk:
* Letting someone come in your mouth
* Throat infections such as gonorrhoea
* If you have cuts, sores or infections in your mouth and throat

So what is safe?
There are so many things you can do which are absolutely safe: wanking each other; rubbing your cocks against one another; kissing, sucking and licking all over the body; rimming – to name but a few.

If you're finding safe sex difficult, call a helpline or speak to someone you feel you can trust for support. The Terrence Higgins Trust Helpline, which is open from noon to 10pm every day, can be reached on 0171 242 1010.

Or, if you're in the United States, you can ring the Center for Disease Control toll free on 1 800 458 5231.

Prologue

Paul Travis was set down for sentencing on 20 May, at the Inner London Crown Court. The preliminary hearing had been a laugh – he'd taken a posse of mates along, and his girlfriend, Jill. Hanging about before they were up, he'd cajoled her into the gents' toilets, into a cubicle. His legs straddling the seat, he'd unbuttoned his trousers and pulled them down his thighs. Then he'd hitched out his cock, already semi-erect and bowing against the tightness of his white briefs, and stroked it slowly to full hardness. His other hand he'd placed on the top of Jill's head and pushed her downward. She'd bent her knees and opened her mouth, running her lips around his swollen bulb. He'd trained her well, and he watched with satisfaction as her head came forward, rolling back his foreskin. He'd felt the light nick of her teeth around the hard ridge, the way he liked it; felt himself bumping against the roof of her mouth as he began to thrust gently forward, building a rhythm, his hands closing around the back of her head, pulling her to him as he thrust into her.

He'd heard footsteps in the toilet area beyond the cubicle door, movement, voices. Mr Page, his brief: talking to some other lawyer, by the sound of it. He'd smiled to himself and let out a low moan. Fuck them. Jill's fingers had been probing around his balls, her nails pinching at his ball-sac, pulling at the dark hairs that grew under there, pulling at the thick trail of hairs that grew under his perineum and up into his arse-crack. She'd worked a finger into his arsehole, wiggling it. The nail had ripped at his inner wall, and he winced. He liked that, too. She knew exactly what he liked.

The lawyers had still been in full flow at the urinals. Jill had slipped another finger inside Paul, then another. He had been close to coming, his cock wet with her saliva, thrusting into her cheek as she probed his arse with her fingers. His pelvis had banged against the cubicle wall. Outside, the two lawyers had lapsed into silence. They must have been listening: he hadn't given a fuck. He'd let out a sustained groan as his orgasm hit him. His cock had sprung from between Jill's lips, spasming and pumping, his juices slooshing and spurting out, covering her face. She'd caught the last of it in her mouth, and he'd shuddered as he'd held her head; then he'd hauled her to her feet and pushed his tongue between her lips, tasting his own spunk on her breath. He liked the taste of his spunk.

The hearing had been a doddle. His barrister had spun out this song and dance about what a good pupil he'd been, until only a couple of years ago, about how he'd fallen into the wrong company and gone off the rails, and how he planned to go back to college and study to be a sports trainer. Bullshit, all of it. The poor guy had had to work hard out there. Paul had stood in the dock, grinning and watching his mates horsing around in the public gallery, mumbling insolently at the judge and his counsel when they spoke to him. He'd been able to tell the judge was pissed off; his barrister, too, judging by how little he'd said to him afterward. His mates had thought it was a great grin, though. They'd carried him on their shoulders down the steps of the building, as if he'd walked free.

That had been over a month ago. The judge had deferred sentencing for social enquiry reports. He'd been assigned a social worker, whom he'd seen only once. When he'd tried to get back in touch with her, the previous week, she'd told him it was too late to do anything for him.

He was alone, this time – or as good as alone. Jill had dumped him – she said he'd never understood her; that he'd gone out with her only to impress his mates. Maybe it was true – she was the best-looking girl around these parts, and Paul reckoned he was one of the better-looking blokes. His father was Jordanian, his mother a Londoner – he'd inherited her fine bone structure and his rich coffee complexion and thick, dark hair. He'd been described by an old girlfriend as looking 'like a young Robert De Niro'. He liked that. Jill had been more blunt – 'a piece of Moroccan rough', she'd called him. He liked that, too. It fitted the way he put himself about. It was Jill's loss.

His mates hadn't come with him, this time. He hadn't wanted them to. His barrister went through the motions – Paul could tell he was going down, almost from the moment the bloke opened his mouth – and the judge passed sentence. 'This court takes very seriously matters involving violence against the person. You and person or persons unknown set upon an innocent man, knocked him to the ground and proceeded to viciously kick his body, before robbing him of his money and running off.'

Paul couldn't tell him that the bloke they'd smacked was anything but innocent – he was a small-time dealer who owed nearly a thousand pounds to a mate of Paul's. That's all Paul was doing – helping out a mate. The fucking mate who'd then shopped him to the police. He hoped his proper mates would give the cunt the kicking of his life. None of this came out in court.

'This was an act of callousness and cowardice and, even taking into account your previous good character –' Paul had suppressed a chuckle, there '– I feel I have no choice but to award a custodial sentence. You will serve eighteen months in prison. Take him down.'

Simon Muir had spent the night before his sentencing crying and remembering better days. He remembered the beach at Eilat, where he and Mehmet had spent their last night together. They'd walked, hand in hand in the sunset, across the endless stretch of dark-golden sand on the edge of the sea.

'The colour of your hair,' Mehmet had said to him. They made a striking couple, everyone said – Simon with his burnt-gold hair, like sheaves of cut corn, his pale, delicate face and slender body; Mehmet dark and hairy and muscular, a strong Arab face and a grin that could melt snow.

They'd met when Simon had been a student, touring Israel with friends one summer. Mehmet worked over the border in Jordan. Twice a day he had to cross the border illegally, running the gauntlet of armed guards, just to earn enough to feed himself and keep a roof over his and his brothers' heads.

Simon had wondered how he could stand it – the barbed wire, the guns . . . He'd have done anything – suffered anything – to get him out of there. Or so he had thought.

He'd been back countless times – and just once managed to snatch a few days in Eilat with him. A few days of paradise.

Walking along the dunes, the dry, soft sand collapsing beneath their feet . . . Simon struggled, breathless, to the high summit of a dune. Mehmet was waiting for him, regarding him with his lazy, half-lidded eyes. He collapsed forward into Mehmet's waiting arms.

Mehmet hauled him upright, and planted a long, slow kiss on his mouth, his tongue slipping forward between Simon's teeth. He removed Simon's clothing without ever breaking contact with his lips – shirt, shorts, sneakers. Simon lay in the soft sand, his cock hardening, gazing up at his Palestinian lover. He watched Mehmet strip. He was lean and lithe and muscular. His arms and chest were lightly scarred: trophies of his hard life. A light down of dark hairs peppered his chest. His circumcised cock rose defiantly from a thicket of black hair which stretched under his balls, all the way to his hole.

So different from Simon . . .

He dropped down on top of Simon, and they kissed again,

harder this time. Their arms clutched at each other; their legs intertwined; their hard cocks strained and rubbed together.

Quite suddenly, Mehmet grinned a grin of pure devilment and pitched to one side, dragging Simon with him. Naked, they began to roll down the dune. They quickly gathered speed, laughing, kissing, clutching tight to each other, the world spinning, their hard cocks buffeting together.

They slowed and were still, breathless in the sand. Mehmet slid down Simon's body, blazing a trail with lips and teeth, nipping at his nipples, running his tongue in a hard, straight line, deliciously down the centre of his chest to his bellybutton, pausing for a moment, then on down into his golden pubes.

Mehmet slipped his full lips over the head of Simon's tall, pale cock and slid them down the shaft. He began steadily to masturbate him with his mouth – long, cool strokes, the occasional sharp-sweet nip of teeth, slowly gathering in speed and passion. Simon could see Mehmet wanking his own cock as his mouth worked Simon's.

Simon pulled out and changed position. As Mehmet again sank his head over Simon's cock, Simon opened his mouth wide and closed it over Mehmet's chunky, circumcised prick. Naked on the sand, they blew one another, clutching at each other's thighs and buttocks, probing each other's arses with frantic, passionate fingers.

They came together, each thrusting his cock deep into the other's mouth, each drinking the other's hot seed.

Their last night together. The sand stretched like a shadow before them in the fading light. The sea, to their left, became ghostly with the dark. They walked along the water's edge, the spent waves lapping over their bare feet, naked, hand in hand in sweet silence.

That had been the last time he'd seen Mehmet: he'd planned his crime without him – he'd known Mehmet would never have gone along with it, even though he was doing it all for him – and carried it out in secret over the next eight months. During that time, he'd salted thousands out of the launderette of which he was manager. The plan was simple – use the money to leave England for ever, for he and Mehmet to find a place where they could live, far from England, far from Palestine, unhindered by immigration authorities, border guards and all the rest. Their place in the sun.

At six in the morning Simon had tried to cut his wrists open. There wasn't a sharp enough knife in the flat. He'd taken all the paracetamol he could find, along with the remains of a bottle of gin, and thrown up.

The sentencing passed in a dream. His counsel had to tell him afterward what he'd got. Two years. Two fucking years.

The Once-Reverend John Williamson spent his final night of freedom at prayer. He felt strangely calm. The sense of relief which had attended him ever since this whole thing had blown open hadn't left him: if anything, it had grown. He could take the harsh words, the lurid headlines – Sick Vicar In Choirboy Sex Scandal – the graffiti and broken windows. He could take the defrocking – that too had seemed something of a relief when the bishop told him. He was even learning to accept that Pamela and the girls were no longer a part of his life. She still loved him, she had lied, but for the sake of their daughters she felt she had to begin a new life.

It was all in the open now, and he was glad. The secrecy had troubled him more than anything else, and – praise God – that was over.

He had crept back into his old church – he still had a key – and knelt at the altar rail, looking at the moonlight pouring through the stained-glass window, at the eerily illuminated glass Jesus, his arms open in a gesture of welcome, of forgiveness, of comfort against the night.

Again and again the image of Toby, singing in the choir, serving at the altar, ghosted into his mind. He didn't think about what they'd done together over the past year – he never dwelt on the details – but the boy's purity, the boy's innocence and curiosity and energy haunted him.

What he found hard was the contempt Toby now exhibited towards him. He could understand it: pressure from parents, the authority, the church itself, to denounce what they'd done – but still it hurt. This was Toby. Toby, who he'd loved more than anyone else ever. More than God. Toby, who'd cried when John had admitted to him that he wasn't the first, who'd said he loved John and would stand by him, no matter what. Toby, who had now accused him of rape, of coercion – of all manner of abuses, both physical and psychological.

They had been lovers; nothing more or less. John Williamson was thirty-eight; Toby Green was nineteen. But they had been lovers. And now he was going to jail for it. The day of his sentence was a bitter one: it was Toby's birthday. He'd hoped – in vain – to see Toby in court that day. He thought with regret about the birthday celebration they might have had – the one he'd planned.

Eight years, his counsel had told him to expect. The judge gave him ten.

One

'Travis, Paul James. Date of Birth: 13–5-77.'

A uniformed prison guard stood on either side of him. One played idly with the truncheon which swung from his belt; the other read from a clipboard.

'What?'

'Is that your name?'

'Yeah.'

The other guard leant in close. He was in his mid-twenties, sandy-haired, stocky and muscular. His face was unshaven, and Paul could smell beer on his breath. 'This one's got attitude, George,' he said.

'Shame,' his middle-aged colleague replied.

'You've got attitude, boy,' the guard whispered into Paul's ear. 'You'd better watch that. There's blokes in here'll cut your head off because they've got nothing better to do and there's fuck-all on telly.'

His lips were brushing Paul's cheek now. He was tense; his fists were clenched, his arms trembled slightly. He wanted to take a swing at this bloke. Save it, a fading voice inside his head was crying. You've no chance against these two.

Paul was tired and angry. He'd sat in a cell at the court for six hours, before being dragged out and thrown into a meat wagon, driven up the motorway for another two hours, and dumped here. H. M. P. Cairncrow, back-of-fucking-beyond.

'Walk through the metal detector,' George, the guard with the clipboard, said flatly.

Paul did as he was told.

'Now strip,' said the other guard.

'What?'

'You heard me.'

'We need to be sure you're not carrying anything in,' the guard with the clipboard said, not looking up.

Paul was still in his court clothes. He removed his shoes and socks, jacket and shirt. Naked to the waist, he looked around. 'Where do I put these?' he asked.

The guard shrugged. 'On the floor.'

Paul dropped the bundle.

'Now your trousers,' the guard said. 'And your pants.'

Paul loosened his belt. His trousers fell to the floor and he stepped out of them. He looked quickly down at the tight white briefs which bulged around his cock and balls, stark against the pale brown of his skin, at the black pubic fuzz which spilled over the waistband and curled like thin smoke up over his bellybutton, dissipating about his chest and nipples.

'Like looking at yourself, do you?' The guard was watching him intently. His partner, George, was still studying his clipboard.

'Lot to get through today, Dave,' George muttered, still not looking up.

'Got to be thorough, George,' Dave said. He turned back to Paul and snapped the elastic of his briefs. 'Now take them off,' he hissed.

Clenching his teeth, Paul lowered the briefs. His cock flopped and swung slightly. He stepped out of the pants and stood naked in front of his gaolers.

'Raise your arms,' Dave said. Paul obeyed.

'OK. Spread your legs.'

'What?' He wasn't fucking going to do this.

10

Dave plucked the truncheon from his belt and jammed it hard into Paul's bare back. 'You heard me,' he said.

Paul inched his feet apart across the floor.

'More,' the guard barked. He thrust an open hand between Paul's legs, running it up and down between his calves, grazing the underside of his balls.

'Now squat,' he said, pressing down with his truncheon on Paul's shoulder, forcing him to the floor. 'Lean forward.'

Paul heard a rustling noise behind him. Grinning, the guard was pulling on a latex glove. Paul swallowed hard. Sure, he'd put the occasional finger up there when he was a kid, when he'd just started wanking. Sure, he liked Jill poking around up there. But this – this was . . .

He gasped and clenched as he felt a latex finger pressing on his ring, working its way inside.

'You'd better not fight me, boy,' Dave hissed, and pushed his finger in hard, probing around the walls of Paul's arsehole.

Paul closed his eyes. He couldn't believe this was happening – this bloke, this vicious stranger, who suddenly had complete power over his every waking hour, wanted to do this to him . . .

'Booked your holiday yet, Dave?' George asked casually, scribbling a note on his clipboard.

Paul gasped in disbelief. This was nothing to them. Part of the job.

'Not yet,' Dave grunted.

Paul felt the guard's finger withdraw. He let out a long breath – then tensed again. He felt the pressure of Dave's hand – two fingers, this time – forcing their way inside him.

His cock, which had been small, clinging to a pair of shrivelled balls, twitched involuntarily. It began to slacken and swell. To his horror, it was growing. Half-hard, he squatted like an animal, being played with by this uniformed sadist.

'Nothing up here, George,' Dave said casually. Slowly, he withdrew his hand. 'Hang on. What's this?' He'd noticed Paul's cock. He swung his arm up, and Paul felt a sickening blow to the back of his head, which sent him reeling across the tiled floor. 'Dirty little prick,' Dave spat. 'Get into your uniform.'

Paul picked himself up, and George tossed him a pair of trousers and a shirt: both grey, both drab. He scrabbled into them, stooping over to hide his hard-on, pulling the trousers up fast.

'Go through there, please,' George said blandly, unlocking a door – metal, of course: all the doors he'd seen were metal, and all locked – and pushing it open.

Paul stumbled forward into a large room, its bare walls painted the same bland, pale green as the rest of the place, with nowhere to sit. Men – there must have been about thirty of them – stood about, staring into space, or glaring savagely around them, or not lifting their eyes from the floor. All were dressed in the same uniform grey. Paul looked around their ranks, and wondered how many of them had been put through the initiation he'd just had. Could he tell from their faces? Could they tell from his? He felt as if the burning in his arsehole was somehow written all over him.

He couldn't tell. There were too many other emotions written on those faces. Muscular, scowling thugs, all muscle, tattoos and scars, scanned the crowd like predators. Paul locked eyes with one of them, held the killing gaze for a second, then dropped it. He swallowed hard. For the first time, he felt scared.

Others in the room looked petrified. One, a slender, blond pretty-boy with big, round girl-eyes – almost certainly a batty-man – was sniffing, trying to stifle tears. Others looked furtive and scared. One or two just stared about, wired like space cadets, as if they didn't quite know where they were.

One guy stood out. Not just because his face was cut and swollen. The bloke – he must have been in his late thirties – stood perfectly still. Beneath his bruises, his face was peaceful. Serene. He looked as if he was in fucking church.

They must have waited there for another hour and a half. The tension didn't ease. Eventually the door opened again. Two new guards walked in. 'All right,' one barked. 'Single file, turn to your left, follow the officers. Move.'

They did as they were told, some reluctantly, some numbly, along a corridor and through three sets of locked doors. Finally, they filed into a room with rows of seats, all bolted to the floor, facing a podium and a large TV screen. Guards – at least twenty – lined the walls. The prisoners sat, and a uniformed figure rose to address them.

'Inmates,' he said, 'welcome to the Cairncrow Hilton. Some of you have been inside before; others are new to our strange little world. So, for the benefit of our newcomers, I'm going to run through some of our quaint customs. I am Senior Officer Craigie. This is D wing – your new home. I control this wing of the prison, which means I control you. The governing principle of this wing is, you obey me and my men to the letter, and we all get on OK. I am trusting you to do this, for all our benefits. If you betray that trust, my men and I will make you wish you were dead. It's that simple.'

His accent was Scottish. He must have been in his late thirties, swarthy skin, his nose hawklike, his face deeply lined, a cruel smile and penetrating blue eyes. He looked like he worked out, too. It was obvious that he'd given this speech a hundred times.

'I am required to warn you about the dangers of drugs and unsafe sex. Now, basically, you and I know it's pointless me trying to stop you taking drugs, so all I will say is, if we catch you in possession, we'll break your balls. As for sex, you'll find more condoms in there than in the gutters of King's Cross. Use them. Oh, yes, and if you find yourself sexually harassed, tell one of the guards.'

He seemed to be half smiling as he said it. Paul looked around the room; the guard Dave, and many of his colleagues, were smirking openly.

'Now, we have a little induction video for you to watch. Just to make you feel at home.'

He stepped from the podium and the lights dimmed. The TV screen flickered into life.

It took a few seconds for Paul to realise what he was watching. An uneasy murmur went around the audience. They were looking down on a bed, a top bunkbed in what appeared to be a cell. A young man lay, naked, spread-eagled on the mattress, his fists gripping the bars of the headboard. He was slender – a pretty-boy – with a long mop of curly brown hair, a pale, freckled face and slightly turned-up nose, and a half-hard cock which lolled about his thighs.

Another man came into view – older; tall, stocky and muscular, with a goatee beard and a crew cut. He too was naked. Crude prison tattoos covered his arms and chest. His dark prick, long and thick and slightly bent, its livid bulb wreathed by a drawn-back foreskin, was in his hand. He climbed up the bed-frame and dragged the youth towards him, forcing his thighs apart as he did so. His bare feet braced on the lower bed, he manoeuvred his prick between the youth's cheeks and pushed forward. His cock began to disappear inside the boy. The boy groaned and clenched his teeth.

Paul looked around at the guards, who were grinning and smirking. Some of them had their hands thrust into their trousers, obviously working their cocks.

The captive audience was restless. A man sitting close to Paul sprang to his feet, shouting. 'Oh, man, this is sick. This ain't happening, man!' He began pushing his way to the end of the row.

Two guards closed in, their truncheons in their hands. 'Fucking sit down,' one of them growled.

The man kept coming, muttering and moaning to himself. A fast, hard truncheon stab to the stomach stopped him in his tracks. He doubled over and buckled at the knees in front of the guards. Both began laying into him with truncheons and boots. Whimpering, he turned and began crawling between the seats, over the feet of his fellow prisoners, back to his position.

On screen, a third man had joined in the drama. He was black – he looked African: his skin like ebony, his limbs lean and rangy, his face handsome. He had climbed up the other end of the bed and was kneeling over the youth's face, his inner thighs on either side of the lad's head. He leant forward and angled his long prick towards the youth's mouth, pressing the head between his lips, forcing his teeth apart, driving downward. The youth appeared to gag on the great shaft; the black guy grinned and drove down harder.

The bed rocked and creaked as the two men pumped into the younger man. His body shook and juddered as the two cocks, both of them thick and long, one a pale brown and the other jet black, drove into him. The black guy had his great prick totally buried in the young boy's mouth – two great black balls slapped against the pale, freckled face and a thick mat of pubic hair bristled against his lips and nostrils.

His own prick was no longer soft. It jutted upward from his belly, quivering and lightly leaking its juices. He brought a slender hand around to his balls and started squeezing and pulling at them. He ran his fingers up the length of his cock, then let them tighten around the shaft. Slowly, then faster, he began wanking himself.

The ballet was speeding up, punctuated by the grunts of the tattooed slab-of-muscle as he drove forward into the youth's arse. His face was drawn into a snarl of barely restrained fury as he fucked. He lost it for a moment when his wildly swinging prick popped out and skidded around the lad's cheeks. He reinserted himself and resumed his machine-gun rhythm, his untidy brown bush slamming against the lad's hairy balls. He looked close to orgasm.

The first to come was the youth himself, sending a great slew of semen arcing into the air, raining down on the black guy, peppering his chest and face, clinging in chains and droplets to his hair.

The tattoo-man came next, ripping his cock free and squeezing and tugging at the head as it discharged its heavy load. Finally, the black guy's cock, its head buried between the lad's lips, spasmed and shot. The youth's mouth filled with come; it spilt out of his lips and ran across his cheeks. He licked his lips as the black guy withdrew.

The picture on the screen cut to static.

Craigie was again standing in front of them. 'That,' he said, 'was unsafe sex. No condom.'

'That was also a camera hidden in a cell,' the bloke next to Paul muttered.

'If I hear that anyone's been fucking without a condom,' Craigie continued, 'I'll bust his arse. I don't want any diseases on my wing.'

'That's bad,' the bloke next to Paul whispered. 'Normally they don't give a fuck about condoms in prison. It means the guards intend to fuck us.'

'So, remember the rule,' Craigie said again. 'Obey me – obey us – in all things, and we will live as one big, happy family, just the way it was on the TV film. Otherwise, this place will be hell on earth for you: that, I promise.'

Shocked into silence, Paul filed out of the room with his fellow inmates. They were marched along corridors and allocated cells. Most people seemed to be sharing. Paul looked along the thinning line. The cry-baby was still there, and so was the other guy – the weirdly calm one with the beaten-up face.

'Williamson,' a guard said, 'you have the privilege of a cell to yourself. Quite right for a man of the cloth.'

The weirdo was pushed through a door, which was slammed shut behind him.

'Travis, Muir: you two gay-boys are in here.'

A double cell. Shit. Paul watched as the cry-baby stepped forward and through the door. Swearing to himself, Paul followed him. The door was shut behind them.

'Bastards.' The cry-baby was still crying.

'Oh, for fuck's sake!' Paul spat. 'Can't you pack it in?'

'I'm sorry,' his cell-mate said. 'I can't help it. This is a nightmare.' He broke down into great sobs.

Awkwardly, Paul reached out and patted him on the shoulder. 'Look,' he said. 'We're all freaked out by this. We're all a bit scared. It won't be so bad. You don't want them to see you like this tomorrow. You'd better sort it out.'

A voice suddenly boomed down the stone-and-metal corridor – 'Lights out!' – and instantly they were plunged into darkness. Paul's cell-mate let out a sort of shriek. Paul swore under his breath.

'I'm sorry,' the lad said. 'I hate the dark.'

'That's OK,' said Paul. 'I'll take the top bunk.'

He thought, somehow, that the top bunk denoted seniority, and he couldn't be seen to be bottom dog to this wuss. He hauled himself on to the bed. Images from the film they'd seen flickered across his mind.

The lad seemed calmer now. In the darkness, Paul introduced himself, and so did the lad. Simon. Simon was twenty-two – a year older than Paul – but he seemed so much younger, like a child, totally unequipped to deal with the world in which they now found themselves.

'Try to get some sleep,' Paul said, knowing that he at least would be awake half the night.

Two

Simon Muir lay bolt awake all night, motionless, trembling, listening to the creak of the bunk above him, to the sounds of his new roommate tossing and turning, to the distant, disturbing clangs and shouts which echoed about the corridors. He'd cried himself out. His eyes stung from crying; his throat was dry. The night was endless, and the day to come held horrors he had yet to imagine.

He thought of Eilat, of Mehmet, and stroked his cock for comfort.

His cell-mate, Paul, didn't look unlike Mehmet, he thought. His complexion wasn't quite so dark, but he had the same thick black shock of hair, the same deep-brown, lazy lake-eyes and sensuous, dark lips.

He wondered if Paul was . . .

No. He remembered with a shudder the advice given him by a friend of a friend, an ex-inmate himself. No one in prison is gay, he had said. It's a manhood thing. It doesn't matter what they're doing, or who they're fucking: if they find out you're gay, you've got problems.

He thought about the day that had been: the strip search, the video. He didn't understand. If they weren't gay . . .

How could he possibly pass as straight? He'd never been able to fool anybody, even at school. He thought of the country school bully-boys. He thought about the men he'd seen yesterday, clustered into that cramped room. The same savage, uncomprehending look in the eyes.

He was going to die in here; he suddenly felt sure.

The dawn crept through the small, barred window of the cell, and shortly afterward Simon heard the ringing of warders' voices, the turning of keys, the clanging open of metal doors. The sounds were getting nearer. Simon dreaded their advance, the opening of his door, the madness of the little world beyond it.

The door opened. Already he could hear the dull clamour of the prison day.

Paul, above him, stirred. 'Christ,' he said, 'what the fuck's the time?'

'Eight o'clock,' Simon replied.

He watched Paul drop nimbly, naked, to the floor. He was slim yet muscular; a hefty cock, uncircumcised, bounced up off a generous pair of balls as Paul hit the ground, then settled again. Paul threw on his grey shirt and trousers.

'What happens now?' he wondered aloud.

'I suppose it's breakfast time,' said Simon.

'Breakfast time? Look, this isn't a fucking hotel, mate. What d'you expect, fucking croissants and jam?'

'I . . .' Simon felt a great well of emotion building inside him. 'I . . .' He couldn't help it; a great sob burst from him, followed by another, and another. 'I'm sorry,' he tried to say, but the words wouldn't come out.

Paul swore, and stomped out of the cell.

Ten minutes later, a trembling Simon crept along the corridor, not knowing where he was going. No one had told him anything about daily procedure. He was following a noise – a low, terrible rumble which he assumed was the focus of the morning's activities. The noise came from behind a set of double doors. He pushed them open and emerged into a canteen. Rows of tables were lined with inmates – untidy, grey lines, rank upon rank.

He scanned the room for Paul. He was sitting on a crowded table to Simon's left. There was no space near him. With a sinking heart, Simon made for the least crowded table. A figure sat at one end; about eight people were sitting immediately down the table from him, but the rest of the space was free. Simon picked a seat near enough to the gathering not to seem unfriendly, but far enough away not to have to speak to them. He sat, and wondered what would happen next.

There was a sudden hush at the table. Slowly, the character at the far end rose to his feet and strolled towards Simon. He was smiling, to Simon's relief. He looked in his early twenties, quite beautiful, blond – blonder than Simon. This guy's hair was white; his skin was deathly pale. His eyes were red. He was an albino.

He sat down next to Simon.

'Hello,' he said quietly. 'What's your name?'

'Simon,' said Simon.

'Well, Simon, you know, you've got a lot to learn in here. For instance, you're supposed to pick up a plate and a fork and spoon over by the door there, then go to those hatches and collect your food.'

Simon felt foolish. It was so obvious.

'Would you like me to collect it for you?' his new friend asked. 'I don't mind, as it's your first day.'

'Uh . . . thank you,' said Simon. He was disorientated by this sudden show of friendliness. All he'd encountered so far were varying degrees of aggression, even from Paul. He'd heard no kind word spoken by anyone since the judge had pronounced sentence.

He slowly became aware that an expectant silence had fallen across the room. All eyes seemed to be on the figure who was now getting his bacon, eggs and beans for him. The congregation was frozen, watching him as he returned to sit next to Simon.

'Here you are,' he said.

'Thank you,' said Simon uneasily. Something wasn't right.

'Would you like me to feed it to you as well?' the albino asked gently.

'Wha –'

Simon was instantly aware of the metal plate rising from the table, hitting him hard in the face, the burn of still-sizzling bacon, egg yolk and bean juice, a plastic fork and spoon clattering to the ground, his chair falling backward, his head hitting the wooden floor.

Noise erupted all around him. The albino stood above him.

'Like I said, batty-boy,' he snarled, 'you've got a fuck of a lot to learn in here. Like no one sits at my table except my friends.'

He aimed a kick at Simon's stomach. Simon curled up with the pain. The albino kicked Simon's overturned chair on top of him.

'I better not see you again,' he growled. 'Or you're my bitch. Now crawl out of here, bitch.'

He jabbed Simon with his foot. Sobbing, Simon began to crawl, on his hands and knees, between the tables, towards the double doors. The breakfasters jeered him as he crawled; some kicked him as he passed.

He looked up, searching for some means of escape. Two prison officers stood at the end of the room. They could see what was happening to him. Why didn't they do something? He spotted Paul, just in front of him.

'Paul . . .' Simon croaked the name, barely daring to give it voice, already knowing what Paul's response would be.

Paul looked down, held his imploring gaze for a moment, then looked away. Simon crawled on, flinging himself through the swing doors, then lurched to his feet and back down the corridor to the safety of his cell, where he sat, shaking and crying on his bunk, wishing the world would end.

Paul appeared about half an hour later.

'Paul . . .' Simon sniffed.

'Don't fucking talk to me,' Paul snapped. 'I'm stuck in a cell with the fucking wing's newest fraggle. How d'you think that's going to make me look?'

'I'm sorry, Paul,' Simon pleaded. 'I don't know what I did wrong.'

'Well, for starters you were just you. And then you sat at Spalding's table. I was talking to a couple of blokes at breakfast. That's Spalding. He's the daddy here – and boy, he fucking doesn't like you.'

'What can I do, Paul?'

'There's nothing you can do,' said Paul, and left the cell.

Simon closed his eyes. He'd barely felt the pain of the kicks at the time, but now he was starting to ache. His face and neck were covered in congealed egg and beans.

'You better get yo'self cleaned up,' a deep voice from the door said.

Simon looked round. Standing in the doorway – practically filling the doorway – was a great slab of a man: late twenties, muscle upon muscle, tattoos everywhere. The figure tossed Simon a towel, and placed a bar of soap on the end of the bed. 'Shower block's down there, to the left,' he said. 'No one tells you shit in here, man. You got to work it out fo' yo'self.'

His accent was American. Deep South. He smiled at Simon. One gold tooth sat in his broad, beard-fringed grin.

'Thank you,' whispered Simon as the man vanished.

Gingerly he rose from the bed, picked up the soap and towel, and limped out into the corridor.

He found the bath-house with ease, hung up his clothes and stepped, naked, into the shower. It reminded him of school – the row of jets pissing hot water into the one big drain, big enough to take a good dozen people at once. A huge human sink. He remembered the school sports showers with a shudder. As a boy of twelve or thirteen they had been, for him, both fascinating and terrifying places. He had been an avid cock-watcher, of course. He'd slip in when the first rugby team were in – farm-boys, mostly, covered from head to toe in mud. He'd watch enthralled as they soaped themselves, watch their muscular torsos, nipples, hard pectorals, emerging from the layers of dirt, watch the mud turning to dark, soapy rivulets which flowed down into their pubic bushes and down over tuberous, dangling, mud-caked cocks, gradually becoming visible as the mud peeled away.

They'd often play rough games, unselfconsciously naked, cocks flapping and swinging as they towel-whipped each other around the changing room, or wrestled beneath the sluicing water jets, or even pissed over each other – elaborate piss fights would develop between half a dozen heavy-cocked athletes, under the discharge of the taps.

Simon always had to balance how long he could stay in there, how much he could watch, before his own cock gave him away. Once he judged it badly; returning from a cross-country run a good half an hour behind everyone else, he found the changing rooms deserted except for the captain of the rugby team – a boy named Chris, muscular and handsome and the first great unrequited love of Simon's life. Chris – to whom Simon was no more than an insect – grunted some kind of greeting, stripped from his rugby shirt and shorts, stood, naked and heavy in front of Simon for a moment, then plunged into the showers. His mind whirring, Simon had stripped and plunged after him.

Chris was facing away from Simon, whistling some chart tune or other as he lathered himself. Simon watched as Chris soaped his sculpted shoulders and back, watched his hands soaping his taut arse, working suds up into the crack, into the mouth of the hole, moving down to his perineum, stroking and soaping.

Mesmerised, Simon hadn't noticed he'd grown hard. He also hadn't noticed voices from the changing room behind him. The first he knew he'd been rumbled was when somebody shouted, 'Well, will you look at these two homos?'

Chris had spun round appalled. 'But I didn't know he –'

'Shit, look at his cock!' someone shouted. Chris, like Simon, had a hard-on.

'You snooping little bastard!' Chris had advanced on him, knocked him to the floor and begun kicking him, to whoops of delight from his mates.

'Let's piss on him,' someone else had shouted. 'Piss on his face!'

And Simon had felt a warm, rank cascade of piss showering over him, splashing off his eyelids, in his hair, into his mouth.

The experience had kept him hard for weeks.

The thought suddenly struck Simon – this morning, in the prison canteen, crawling about the floor being kicked, he'd had a boner throughout.

'Hello again.' That booming Southern drawl. The man was standing behind him in the shower, naked, his cock hard. 'Mah name's Gary,' he said. 'Soap mah back, will you?' He was holding a bar of soap out to Simon. 'Go on, it's OK.'

Nervously, Simon took the soap. Gary turned round, and Simon began running it over the twin pillars of muscle, across his tattooed shoulders, down his spinal column.

'Lower,' Gary said. 'Wash mah butt.'

Slowly, with a care born of fear, Simon ran the soap over Gary's hairy arse-cheeks. 'Inside,' Gary purred. Simon gingerly worked the soap down his crack. 'Harder,' he growled.

Simon's soapy fingers found Gary's ring-piece, which puckered at his touch. He worked a finger in to the first knuckle, wiggled it around and pushed it deeper. With his other hand, he began stroking the big man's perineum, squeezing his heavy balls. Finally, he reached round and gripped the thick pole which stood out from Gary's belly, knotty and veiny, long and ending in a bloated purple head. He ran his slim pale hand up and down the shaft, and played Gary's foreskin back and forth over the sharp ridge of his helmet.

Gary's cock twitched in Simon's hand. He began a little thrusting motion with his hips: slowly at first, then faster. Simon pushed another finger inside his arsehole. Gary began to grunt slightly as his hips pushed forward into Simon's fist.

Quite suddenly he spun round, twisting out of Simon's grip. He had a look akin to rage on his face. Two great hands grabbed Simon by the head and forced him to his knees, forced his head down on to Gary's huge, throbbing cock. Simon struggled to maintain his balance, and to keep from gagging.

Suddenly, he knew where he'd seen Gary before. He was the guy in the video they'd been shown – the white guy who'd fucked the young bloke in the arse so viciously.

The force of his cock in Simon's mouth sent Simon skidding back across the cataract floor, hitting the wet tiled wall. Gary was slamming into him: his cock filled Simon's mouth, choking him, making it difficult to breathe. Hot water slewed down over Simon's face. He could feel the harsh chafing of Gary's dark pubic bristles against his lips and cheeks, the hammering of Gary's great bell-end against the back of his mouth, the slamming of his own head against the tiled wall.

He thought he was being killed. His mind raced – what could he do? Gary's thrusts were getting harder and faster. He sounded like a traction engine. His cock swelled again – he was coming.

Panicking, Simon kicked out with his bare foot. He caught Gary's leg, uncertainly braced against the wet floor, and sent it skidding out from under him. Gary went down heavily. His cock tore out of Simon's mouth, disgorging its hot, salty load all over Simon's face. His sixteen-odd stone of muscle crashed down on Simon.

Gary seemed confused: wriggling like an eel, Simon scrambled out from beneath him and ran from the shower.

'I could have been a good friend to you, boy!' the Texan drawl boomed after him as he stumbled out into the corridor, trying to climb into his trousers as he ran. 'They leave me alone, Spalding and his babies. Boy, oh boy, are you way up shit creek now!'

Three

The prison was exactly how John Williamson expected it to be. He'd read about this place in the newspapers – an old, worn-out Victorian bastille, failing as a penal institution, taken over by some private company. Supposedly overhauled – buildings and procedures renovated.

Supposedly.

He had prayed on the prospect of imprisonment, and been granted for his trouble a number of disturbing – and disturbingly accurate – dreams.

Coming inside had almost been a relief. At least the prison dreams stopped. He'd been beaten up by the guards during the body search – they'd kicked and truncheon-whipped him until he was virtually insensible, until his vision blurred, and all he could see was vague shapes of light dancing behind his eyes like angels among the shadows. The pain didn't bother him. It was less than in his dreams. He barely felt it, once the angels began their dance.

That first night he'd slept soundly, and dreamt of Toby. Toby, with his brown eyes, wide and wondrous; his slim, practically hairless body; that light-brown hair, always dishevelled; and his grin of pure mischief.

He'd dreamt vividly of Toby's birthday, exactly as he'd planned it; exactly as he'd longed for it.

They drove to one of John's favourite fishing grounds, on the River Nene in Northamptonshire, and found a secluded stretch of bank, erected a tiny, postage-stamp army-green tent and fished through the day.

As the afternoon lolled on – far sunnier than it deserved to be in May – Toby sprawled back on the riverbank and stripped his shirt off.

'Come on, John,' he teased. 'Get some sun on you.'

Why, in his dream, he should have felt embarrassed, John didn't know, but that was what he felt.

'It's not like we haven't seen each other before,' Toby cajoled.

Self-consciously, John removed his shirt. Immediately, Toby shuffled his shoes and socks off, unbuttoned his trousers and pulled them down and off. He lay there, stretched in the sun, naked but for a pair of grey boxer shorts.

'Come on,' he said. 'Don't be a woman.'

John's prick was already beginning to swell when he pulled his own trousers down over his clerical-white Y-fronts. He lay back on the grass, looking at his young lover.

Toby reached across and played with the little gold cross that hung around John's neck. 'You're beautiful, man – You know that?'

John smiled in his dream. Dark-haired and swarthy-skinned, he'd been considered pretty as a child, handsome in his youth, ruggedly handsome when he became a mature man. Landing his wife had been the catch of a lifetime – money, class and beauty, and he only a vicar. But hearing it, here and now, from this boy, it meant more to John Williamson than perhaps any praise had before.

He stroked Toby's cheek ever so lightly with his fingertip, let it trail down his neck and on to his chest, coming to rest on one nipple. He could see the grey boxer shorts tenting out at the front, standing up. His own cock had worked its way out of the slit in the front of his pants and was standing proud and ruddy.

In a quick, fluid movement, Toby sprang to his feet and pulled his shorts down. His cock, small but beautifully sculpted, sprang against the waistband and quivered in the air. 'Let's go skinny-dipping!' he cried. 'Race you!'

John hauled himself to his feet. The boy was already haring down the slope. He saw him leap like a madman into the air, arms and legs flying about him, cock like a steel bolt, and land, laughing, in a fountain of water. John plunged into the river after him.

Toby swam like a fish. John had been an accomplished swimmer, in his day. They raced and wrestled; John tried to catch and hold Toby, whose wet skin made him as slippery as an eel, and who could move just as fast. John bear-hugged; Toby wriggled and slipped from his grasp, diving under the water and swimming through John's legs.

The river was empty. John looked around, slightly panicked. Toby was nowhere to be seen. He couldn't be under water this long. He shouted his name.

There was a shimmering under the water, and John felt a familiar soft warmth close about his cock. Toby's dark shape, broken into ripples, was anchored to his swollen knob; his tongue played over its bevelled tip, and his fingers tickled John's balls.

Breathless and laughing, Toby surged upward out of the water. 'Couldn't hold my breath any more,' he gasped, then started laughing again.

John pulled the boy to him and kissed him hard on the lips. It was a kiss of pure exhilaration, joyous and life-affirming. He swung Toby around in the river and laid him down in the mud at its edge.

'Ugh, mud,' Toby said, giggling.

'My present to you,' John teased. 'Happy birthday, darling.'

They kissed like men, now: tongues delving deep, lips lapping. John's hands clutched Toby's hair, combing it into tumbling fronds with his fingers; Toby's hands ran the length of John's back, caressing, kneading his buttocks. John slid his body up Toby's and pressed the lad's face to his chest. Toby clutched him tight around the trunk and clung, squeezing him to him. John felt the hardness of Toby's cock pressing against his groin; he felt his own tumescence against the boy's belly. He began pushing with his hips, grinding his cock along Toby's pale flesh as Toby pushed upward from below, rubbing himself against John's hard body. They rolled in the mud as their bodies, their cocks, strained together.

Slowly, Toby the eel was slipping back down into the water. His lips traced a path down John's chest and stomach, again seeking his cock. John looked down: Toby was almost entirely under the water again. Only his bobbing head was exposed, a water nymph, its delicate mouth closing around John's prick. Slowly John began moving it back and forth, gently fucking the boy in the face.

He picked up speed, savouring the feeling, the slight grazing of Toby's teeth against his helmet, the warm wetness of his lips and tongue.

Suddenly, Toby was gone again: his head vanished once more under the water. John felt a pressure on his buttocks and pivoted forward on to his stomach in the mud. Toby's head was between his cheeks, his tongue licking up and down the crack of John's arse, finding his hole, probing wetly, dancing in and out. John squirmed in pleasure, pressing his hard cock into the river's soft edge, feeling the mud squeezing around it, caressing it.

Toby lifted his head, and John slid down into the water, letting it wash the mud away. He pulled Toby down, and laid him on his back in the shallowest water, then turned and knelt above his head, facing his cock. John bent forward, taking the delicate erection between his lips, playing the tight foreskin back and forth across the bulb beneath. Toby arched his neck back and took John's cock once again between his lips. There, in the setting sun, in the fast-flowing water, they sucked one another long and gentle, gathering in force and passion, until Toby started bucking with his pale hips, thrusting upward into John's mouth, while John drove down hard into the youthful face beneath him.

They came together, shuddering as each drank the other's hot semen. Then they lay motionless in the lapping, shallow water, each feeling the other's cock softening in his mouth.

At last, John rolled to one side.

Toby smiled at him. 'I love you,' he whispered.

The sun had risen harshly outside the tiny, barred window of John's cell. Everything in the little stone room – the narrow bed, the metal toilet and basin – stood in the starkest relief, the most heartbreaking contrast to the forbidden pleasures of the night. He'd still been tingling from the intensity, the lucidity of the dream, when he went in to breakfast.

He'd seen the incident in the canteen – that poor young man being so brutally victimised – and had for a moment thought to intervene. Something had held him back – and that troubled him. His Christian duty was clear. He thought about the video they had been shown yesterday. What sort of place was this? He had always had an implicit faith in the prison system – a belief that most of the horror stories one heard were media-inspired nonsense. Suddenly, he wasn't so sure.

He spent much of the day sitting in his cell, half daydreaming, half praying. He was no longer sure there was much difference. The clamour of the prison seemed very distant. In the middle of the afternoon, he was interrupted by a guard, who knocked on his open door, almost respectfully.

'Craigie wants to see you,' the guard said flatly.

'Now?'

'Now. I'm to take you there.'

He followed the guard through the wing into a large room with plush furniture and paintings on the walls. Craigie was sitting in an armchair, sipping a drink.

'Reverend Williamson,' he said, rising to his feet. 'Sit down. Join me in a drink.'

'No, thank you,' John replied.

Craigie shrugged. 'One of those teetotal Christians, are you? Smoke?'

'No, thank you,' John said.

'Well . . . sit,' Craigie said.

John sat in a chair opposite him. Craigie lit a cigarette, and stared hard at him. John waited for him to speak. He remained silent.

'You wanted to see me?' he said.

'I just wanted to look at you,' said Craigie. 'I read about you in the papers at the time.'

'I think everybody did,' said John.

'I suppose you're a bit of a celebrity,' said Craigie. 'Not a Brady or a Sutcliffe, of course, but a change from what we usually get in here. Most of them out there are just your bog-standard toe-rags and villains. Insects. You're different. You're an educated man. You've published books. I'd heard of you even before they caught you fiddling with that lad.'

'It wasn't like that –' John tried to interject.

'What was it then? Love?'

John was silent, suddenly loathing the man in front of him.

Craigie seemed to be chewing on a thought. His face clouded, then he smiled. 'Incredible,' he said. 'Everyone else in here is here because of greed, or hatred, or stupidity, or because they knowingly and calculatedly broke the law. You couldn't help what you did. You've been banged up for love. Good God . . .'

His grin broadened, and he began to laugh. John stared at the carpet.

Suddenly Craigie stopped. The look on his face was cruel. 'Maybe that's why they do it to you,' he said. 'You nonces. Maybe that's why they beat you and jug you and sometimes rape you. Because you're in here for love, and that lot couldn't love if you paid them.'

John didn't respond.

'You know how difficult life could get for you in here if they find out, don't you? About you, I mean. About you and that lad.

31

And there are no secrets in a place like this. Still – I suppose if you can manage to keep a low enough profile you just might –'

'Is there some point to all this?' John suddenly snapped. 'Is there something you want?'

Craigie shrugged his shoulders. 'No,' he said. 'Not really. I just wanted to look at you, that's all. Have you ever kept tropical fish? My wife and I do. And sometimes it's nice just to scoop one out in a jar and watch it up close, trapped, before letting it back into its artificial little world. You know, I had a lovely shoal of neon tetras, a couple of years ago. Magnificent. Tiny things – they'd glow when they shoaled. Trouble was, something in the tank was eating them. Every day, the shoal got smaller and smaller, until in the end there were none left. High profile, you see. Glowed. Drew attention to themselves.'

He got up and strolled to the door. 'It's like that out there. Some survive; some don't. I just like to watch.'

Four

The pool table in the rec room wasn't level, and several of the balls were missing. Those were Paul's kind of odds. He'd been on, most of the morning.

There was fuck all else to do, it seemed, between breakfast and lunch, except hang about the pool table or slouch in front of the big old television which stood at the far end of the room and provoked endless fights over what rubbish to watch. One hour a day, it seemed, they were allowed into the high-walled exercise yard. Paul didn't bother.

He was keeping his eyes open; making mental notes. Who were the obvious underdogs; who the psychos were; what the power structures among the inmates seemed to be.

Most of the blokes hanging about around the pool table were Spalding's boys. They had the run of the place. Paul got talking over pool to one of them – a lanky Scot with a straggly brown mane, streaked with the distant remains of blond highlights. He was called, amazingly, Jock.

'There's things you need to know,' he said, 'if you want to get on in here. The screws won't tell you shit.'

Many of the inmates had jobs, Jock told Paul – cleaning or kitchen work, mostly. Others sat classes. You had to do one or the other to get your six quid a week – the only legitimate money you were allowed to have. Unofficially, practically anything could be used as currency – tobacco, phone cards, drugs, sweets . . . practically anything there was a demand for.

Spalding and his friends didn't work. They could afford not to.

Many of the inmates, Jock said, passed their time quite anonymously, just quietly doing their time – the older blokes, mostly – unaffected by and largely ignoring the power games which seemed to be going on around them. Then there were the precious few who could somehow lay their hands on drugs or other supplies; they enjoyed a special status. Even Spalding showed them respect. Paul suspected they paid him a tribute. Finally, there were the fraggles. The lowest of the low; the punch-bags and bitches of anyone who happened to be feeling pissed off or horny.

He thought of Simon. He was probably used to this shit. If he'd grown up anywhere like where Paul grew up, he should be totally immune to it, by now. Once, on the landing outside the Travis flat, a bloke had been beaten shitless on the vaguest rumour that he might have been queer. Paul's mum and dad had reckoned he deserved it. At the time, Paul had agreed with them.

Now, though . . . He thought of Simon's imploring face, looking up at him from the canteen floor.

He instantly suppressed the thought. They were in jail now. He had to look out for himself.

'Another game?' he asked Jock.

Paul didn't see Simon for most of that day. He hadn't been at breakfast, he hadn't been in the cell, and he wasn't at lunch.

Paul hung about the recreation area all day. There was nothing else to do. As the afternoon dragged on, he felt a sense of boredom descending on the room and, with it, a noticeable increase in tension.

He was doing well on the pool table – he'd stayed on for hours – and some of the other inmates were getting pissed off, waiting to get on. Finally one of them came over to him.

'You've been on this fucking table all day,' he snarled. 'Fuck off and give someone else a go.'

Paul studied him. He sensed that there was more at stake here than a game of pool. The bloke looked about his size. He should be able to take him.

Everybody was quiet now, watching.

'Winner stays on,' said Paul.

The bloke took a deep breath and tensed. Paul could tell he was about to go for him.

Scarcely knowing what he was doing, Paul swung his pool cue above his head and brought it arcing into the side of the bloke's face. The bloke let out a scream and toppled sideways. Paul dropped the cue and grabbed at the bloke's hair, then pulled his face hard into the ripped baize of the table.

'Winner stays on,' he said again. 'OK?'

His heart was pounding. He was breathless; exhilarated. He dragged the bloke from the table by his hair and slung him across the room. The bloke staggered away, cursing, and the babble of conversation resumed. Paul racked up the balls.

'Who's up next?' he said.

Later, heading back to his cell, a figure grabbed his shoulder. He spun around, fists clenched.

'Hey, relax,' said Jock. 'Spalding's having a little party in his cell just now. He told me to bring you along.'

Paul shrugged. 'Fair enough,' he said. He tried not to smile. He was going to be all right in here, he suddenly sensed.

Spalding's cell was at the other side of the wing. The first thing that struck Paul on entering was the size of the cell – more than twice as big as the one he shared with Simon – and the fact that there were a settee, several armchairs and a television and video in there.

'Come in,' Spalding said. He was fascinating to look at – stunning: his hair pure white, his skin like the palest porcelain, his eyes red. He looked like a vampire.

'Sit down. I've heard you're safe,' he said. 'I've heard you can look after yourself, too. Spot?'

'You what?'

Spalding grinned. 'Not been inside before, eh?' He lit a cigarette, and placed a tiny bead of hash on the glowing tip, then produced a plastic tube – a biro casing – which he put over the bead and sucked. 'It's more efficient than rolling joints,' he said. 'Sometimes stuff's hard to get hold of in here, even for me.'

He handed Paul a cigarette, a bead of hash and the tube. Paul copied what Spalding had done, and shuddered slightly. 'It's been a while,' he said.

There were six people in the room. Jock introduced the three strangers – a young skinhead called Rob, who lay insensible in the corner; a ponytailed Chinese guy called, for some reason, Blue; and a striking, sullen guy with a tight rocker's quiff who they called Vince, after Gene Vincent.

The television was on in the background as they sprawled over the furniture, smoked and chatted. Nobody paid it much attention. Eventually, Spalding got on to the subject of Paul's cellmate.

'You share with that nonce, don't you?' he asked.

'Yeah,' replied Paul, 'if you mean Simon. I don't think he's a nonce, though.'

'I know there's a nonce just come on to the wing,' said Spalding. 'And my money's on him.'

As the cell filled with smoke and the company drifted off into insensibility, Paul's attention wandered to the TV set. For the first time, he became aware that a video was running. Two women in their early twenties, long hair, legs and tits, were on a bed, naked, arms and legs tangled, tits squashing together, cunts rubbing cunts.

He noticed that Blue, the Chinese guy, and Vince, the rockabilly, both had their hands inside their flies. He felt himself getting a hard-on, and shuffled uneasily. The thin prison material hid nothing. He saw Jock glance at him briefly, then sneak his hand into his own trousers.

'Just one of my little perks,' said Spalding to him. He had his trousers open and his cock out, and was wanking openly in front of his guests. 'Enjoy.'

Paul's eyes lingered on him for a moment. Spalding's cock was long and slim, as pale as the rest of him. His thin dusting of pubic hair didn't venture far from the base of his cock. He stroked himself loosely and slowly, with an almost open hand.

Jock's prick was long and bony, with a pronounced left-hand curve to it. As Paul watched, Jock hoisted cock and balls through his fly. The twin orbs swung, loose and hairy, as Jock's great, pale fist pumped up and down the rough shaft, drawing the loose foreskin over a distended leaking head.

Jock's eyes were fixed on the TV screen, where one of the women had her tongue buried in the other's cunt. Spalding's eyes roved constantly from the screen to his guests as he strummed his cock. The other two, Vince and Blue, seemed more interested in each other. Both now had their cocks in full view. Vince's was long and straight and circumcised, Blue's smaller, thick, dark and upward-curving. Each was wanking himself with short, fast strokes. It seemed to Paul as if they were racing. Vince's left hand was tucked under his balls; his busy fingers disappeared into his flies.

Paul swallowed hard. He hadn't done anything like this since he was twelve. Self-consciously, he moved his hand to his fly. Feeling Spalding's eyes on him, he unzipped himself and reached inside for his cock. He was fully hard. He eased his cock out – he couldn't help a lightning glance at the smiling Spalding – and began squeezing the head slightly. He felt a shudder of pleasure – he was getting a charge from this weird set-up. He pulled his foreskin back over the head of his prick, hard and purple. He drew the skin forward again, back, then forward. He could sense Spalding's albino eyes following each stroke.

'Hey, Spalding,' Jock laughed, 'the homos are at it again!'

Vince and Blue, next to each other on the settee, were now half facing each other, their heads touching, each staring into the other's lap. Their trousers and pants were practically off; their shirts were open. They had swapped cocks. Each stroked the other briskly; each had a hand on the other's buttocks, squeezing cheeks, probing cracks.

'Just as long as you don't kiss,' Spalding called across to the pair. 'I can't fucking stand that.'

As Paul watched, Blue inserted a finger into Vince's dark arsehole.

'Jesus,' scoffed Spalding.

Grinning and wincing, still pulling at Blue's cock, Vince responded, sticking two fingers hard between Blue's cheeks, up into his hole.

Blue gasped. 'Cunt,' he whispered. He withdrew his finger, bunched his middle three fingers together and pushed.

'Ahh nails –' Vince gasped in momentary pain. 'Ahh –'

Only Jock was still watching the video. With one hand, he was pulling his trousers up hard, so that the open zip cut into the underside of his balls, which looked swollen and red. With the other, he tugged at his loose foreskin, pulling it together above the head of his cock – pulling it out hard – then dragging it hard back down towards the base of his cock, far back from his helmet, forward, back, with a violent motion. His bony hips squirmed about; his mouth was open, his tongue slightly extended. Only his eyes, hooked on the box, remained motionless.

Spalding's trousers and pants were around his ankles now. He sat in the biggest armchair – his throne – with his legs apart and his shirt undone, wanking and watching. He was going fast, now; his grip had tightened. His lips were moving – he was whispering something to himself. It looked to Paul like 'I'm Daddy . . .' over and over again. 'I'm Daddy . . . I'm Don . . . Me . . .'

Paul was wanking with abandon now, watching his new friends, knowing they were watching him. He pushed his trousers free of his balls and stroked them with his left hand as his right continued to piston up and down his shaft. Next to him, Jock was coming. He let out a long moan, his hips shook and he shot a series of long, white jets over the front of his grey shirt.

Vince and Blue were getting close. Each now had four fingers up the other's arse.

'Right,' said Blue, 'here goes.' He withdrew his fingers and brought his thumb up to meet them. Like a long, closed flower, petals tight, he reinserted his hand.

'Oh, God, no,' gasped Vince. 'Oh, fuck –'

Blue's fingers were inside Vince to the second knuckle. He was still pushing.

'Jesus,' said Jock. 'I think he's going for the whole hand.'

Suddenly, a spasm ripped through Vince's body, and his cock began to spurt. He thrust his hips forward, and shot his load over Blue's stomach.

Blue came seconds after him, pushing his spasming cock into Vince's bellybutton.

Paul felt his own orgasm bearing down on him. His buttocks tightened and his cock started to pump. He heard Spalding gasp and saw his juddering, chalk-white cock spit its load into the air. His eyes were still fixed on Paul. Paul erupted, shooting his seed high, so that it showered down over Spalding's furniture. He closed his eyes and slumped back.

In the far corner, Rob the skinhead, insensible throughout, dozed on.

'Mm,' Spalding said after a moment, wiping his belly with a towel, 'not bad. Except for you two.' He threw the towel at Vince and Blue, who were grinning at each other and giggling. 'I need to have a word with you two girls. Straight porn is a privilege in here. A rarity. I don't invite you to these little sessions so you can get into each other. You better sort it out.'

Lock-up was eight o'clock, and the lights went out half an hour later. Paul was inside by seven-thirty; Simon didn't appear until the last minute.

'Where've you been all day?' Paul asked gruffly.

'Oh . . . about,' Simon replied with an attempt at forced casualness, utterly betrayed by the trembling in his voice.

Paul looked hard at him. He could be a nonce – he was certainly a poof, and that was about halfway there, in Paul's estimation.

'Why are you in here?' he asked.

'Why am I?' Simon seemed surprised by the question. He was silent for several minutes, thinking. He lowered his head. 'I'm in here because I loved someone . . . too much. Loved . . . love . . . I don't know. I still love him. It got me into trouble.' His voice began to tremble. 'Oh, Paul,' he whispered. 'I miss him so much.'

He began to cry, and extended a feeble hand to Paul's shoulder. Paul twisted away. He'd heard everything he needed to. He felt sick. The only question now on his mind was whether or not to tell Spalding.

Five

By the second full day of his two-year sentence, Simon was weak from hunger and crying. He didn't dare go into the canteen, even though he was starving. He was starting to feel like a hunted animal, or a laboratory rat in some hideous experiment, some death maze. He'd spent the previous day avoiding people, as far as possible. He hung about the corridors, hid in the shadows whenever anybody passed, watched from a distance as the laundry workers went about their business. He longed to be back at the launderette he'd managed in Fulham. His friends had laughed at him – he'd fled to London, seeking the bright lights, and ended up working in a launderette. He didn't mind. He blossomed at night, when the clubs opened.

He wondered if he should get a job now – if that would somehow enable him to get acceptance. He had to do something. He felt he was going mad with fear.

He approached a guard and asked how he could get a job.

'Depends,' the guard said. 'You any good at anything?'

'I used to run a launderette,' he said hopefully.

'Launderette's full,' the guard said. 'You can clean floors. We always need floor-cleaners.'

And so Simon cleaned floors. The guard unlocked a janitor's

cupboard and handed him a mop and a bucket. 'Get soap and water from the kitchen,' he said.

Simon waited until the breakfast crowd had dispersed, then filled his bucket. The guard directed him to a corridor outside the gym, and told him to start.

He peeped into the gym. Three black prisoners, all over six feet tall, all hugely muscled and wearing nothing but shorts, did bench-presses next to each other. He stopped himself. This was no time for cock-watching. If he was spotted . . .

He worked for about twenty minutes before he was interrupted. First he heard the scuffling of feet, then a voice – 'Here he is!'

Three men were standing down the corridor from him. One of them he recognised as Spalding. The other two were strangers to him – cropped hair, hard, narrow faces. The pair suddenly lurched forward and gripped Simon by the arms.

'I've been looking for you,' said Spalding. 'Nonce.'

A fist pistoned forward, striking Simon square in the gut. He doubled over with pain. 'Get him into the gym,' said Spalding.

He was dragged through the door. 'Put him on that box,' Spalding ordered. 'That wooden horse thing.'

His two henchmen dragged Simon forward, and hoisted him up into the air, on to the box's flat leather saddle. Face down, he cried and struggled, opening his legs wide as they dragged his trousers down. He felt the material tear. His legs were forced back together and his trousers and pants were yanked down, over his ankles and shoes. Looking behind him, he saw Spalding, his trousers unbuttoned, rolling on a condom. Spalding lurched forward and vaulted on to the box. One of the thugs reached between Simon's thighs and grabbed his balls, hauling them back between his legs and up into the air. Simon scrambled to his knees, thrusting his buttocks upward to ease the pain. The other thug grabbed his hair and pulled his face hard down on to the leather bench. He felt Spalding lining the latex head of his cock.

'I'm not getting any of your queer shit,' he said, then pressed forward, letting out a long, slow breath.

Spalding's fingernails dug deep into the pale flesh of Simon's hips. Simon felt his long cock dryly penetrating him, rutting its way inward: deep – too deep. Simon cried out.

Spalding leant forward. 'You don't say shit unless I give you permission, nonce,' he snarled. 'I own you.'

He began fucking Simon hard and quickly, digging his nails in hard, pulling Simon's buttocks back on to his cock, then driving forward, pushing Simon downward, crushing his face into the bench. The leather was hard against Simon's skin – he could taste the leather of the saddle and its polished smell filled his nostrils.

He was hard. In spite of his fear, in spite of the pain, the humiliation, his cock was standing stiffly from his body. He thought again of school sports. Was he enjoying this? He could see, on the bench-presses opposite, the three black athletes gradually losing interest in their physical jerks. One by one, they allowed their attention to focus on Simon's ordeal. He could see their cocks growing. One of them began stroking himself through the red silk of his shorts, which bulged and stretched over a massive cock, bending under the strain. He slipped the huge ebony member out of the leg of the shorts and began pulling on it hard, peeling back his foreskin over a livid purple head.

The other two were also watching. One whipped his shorts down to his knees and lay on his back with his head dangling, upside down, over the edge of the bench-press, watching – upside down – Simon being dog-fucked by the godfather of the wing, and working his own dark cock with both hands, clasped as if in prayer.

The third watched for a long time, his cock struggling against his shorts, his hands still. Finally, he sprang forward, skipping out of his shorts, and mounted the front of the box, with his wide-apart legs dangling over the wooden sides and his crotch touching Simon's head.

Every time Spalding pushed into Simon, his head smacked into the black guy's huge balls.

'Help yourself,' said Spalding.

The black guy grabbed a handful of Simon's golden hair and yanked his head up. Simon found his face inches away from an enormous cock. The guy pulled him forward and pushed his face down on to his great pole. Simon closed his eyes and opened his mouth. The cock filled him, stretching his jaw to bursting point and pressing hard on the roof of his mouth, on the entrance to his throat.

He was only about halfway down the shaft. Behind him, Spalding thrust forward again, forcing him further down on to it. He couldn't take any more.

Spalding was approaching his climax. Faster and faster, he plunged in and out of Simon's burning butt. Harder and harder, Simon's face was hammered down on to the flesh-and-gristle pole that rose from the black guy's lap. Two shovel-like hands gripped Simon's head. The black guy, too, was coming. His cock erupted; hot seed filled Simon's mouth and throat, sloshing around the great cock, spilling out over Simon's face.

Without a word, Spalding withdrew. The black guy slid from Simon's mouth, and from the box. One and all stood and walked quietly from the gym, as if nothing had happened.

Sitting on the box, spunk dribbling down his chin, naked from the waist down, Simon was alone.

He was still sitting like that, rocking slightly and humming under his breath, an hour later, when Paul came in.

'Are you all right?' he asked quietly.

Of course he wasn't fucking all right. Paul's words barely seemed to be registering. He'd known what was happening, of course. Spalding had personally invited him to take part. He'd steeled himself to go. He'd got as far as the gym door, and frozen. He'd remained hidden there, watching as Spalding's thugs pinned Simon to the box, as Spalding and the other guy had taken him, arse and mouth. He'd got hard watching it, but he couldn't bring himself to go in. As they finished, he'd fled.

'Look – I looked for you earlier, to try to warn you,' he babbled. 'There's a new nonce on the wing, and the word went around that it was you. Spalding was going on about it at breakfast. I tried to warn you.'

Simon had a dazed look on his face. Paul noticed his cock was hard.

'I've got to go,' said Paul. 'I just wanted you to know that . . . it wasn't me – OK? I didn't grass you up. You do believe me? Simon?'

Simon neither spoke to him nor looked at him. Without another word, Paul hurried away. He was practically running when he reached his cell. Spalding was waiting for him inside.

'You missed the fun and games,' he said. 'I told you to be there.'

'Yeah,' Paul flannelled. 'I had things to do.'

'Pity,' said Spalding. He leant close to Paul. 'I hope you're not going to fuck me around,' he said.

'No, I –'

Spalding wasn't listening. He turned and walked out.

Well, fuck him. Paul climbed on to his bunk and threw himself down. He felt trapped. Fuck Simon. Fuck them all.

There was a tapping at the door of his cell. The bloke from the next cell walked in.

'Can I disturb you for a moment?' he asked.

Paul shrugged.

The man walked in and sat down. 'It's Paul, isn't it?' he said. 'My name's John. I want to talk to you about your cell-mate.'

'Simon? What about him?' asked Paul.

'I heard Mr Spalding at breakfast, as did you. We both know he's planning to do something –'

'He's done it,' said Paul curtly. 'You're too late.'

'Have you seen Simon since?' John asked urgently. 'Is he all right?'

'He'll live,' said Paul. 'I think maybe he enjoyed it.'

'Sometimes they kill nonces,' said John.

Paul sat up on the bed. 'What d'you expect me to do about it?' he demanded, suddenly angry.

'You've made friends with Spalding,' said John quietly. 'Talk to him. Talk to him on Simon's behalf.'

'You must be out of your fucking mind,' Paul spat. 'I've only been here a couple of days myself. I've sorted it out.'

'But Simon hasn't. He can't. Paul, you're his only friend. Will you abandon him?'

'Look, what are you?' Paul asked contemptuously. 'Some kind of vicar or something? You talk to Spalding, if you're so concerned. Leave me alone.'

John rose to his feet. 'Unless you say something, I don't think he'll survive,' he said. 'Think about that.'

Paul thought about that, and about many things. Why did he have to have the fucking nonce for a cell-mate? Spalding was already pissed off with him over this.

It was nearly lock-up time again when Simon entered the cell. He silently undressed and lay on his bunk.

'You OK?' said Paul after a while.

'Fine, thank you,' Simon replied in a whisper.

'Fine. For fuck's sake . . .'

Why did he wind Paul up so much? Why was he so fucking prissy? He should be kicking and screaming with rage, after what they'd done to him. He should be cutting throats. If he'd just fucking kick back a bit, they'd probably leave him alone.

'If you don't mind, I'd rather not talk about it,' Simon croaked. 'I'd like to get some sleep.'

They lay in silence until the lights went out. Paul felt a rage building up inside him. He was still horny from what he'd seen in the gym – horny and angry. He dropped from the top bunk, naked and hard, and stood in front of Simon's shadowy, prostrate form. His cock jutted out from his groin like a flagpole. He looked at his cell-mate for several minutes, then jumped on top of him, kneeling over his chest, his legs pinning Simon's arms.

'What are you –'

He clamped a hand hard over Simon's mouth. 'You dropped

46

me in it today,' he snarled. He smacked him across the head with an open hand.

Simon whimpered.

'I'm not your fucking friend,' Paul muttered. He hit him again. 'Fight back, for fuck's sake!' Paul growled. 'Then maybe they'd have a bit of fucking respect for you.' He smacked him again. 'Fight!'

He leant forward, his bare back raking against the wire mesh that supported his mattress above. He pushed his cock downward, and felt it bump against Simon's lips. They opened without resistance.

All right, if the little bastard wouldn't put up a fight . . .

He forced his cock down hard, jamming it between Simon's lips. He felt Simon's teeth raking over the sensitive helmet, down the hard, straight shaft. His balls smacked against Simon's chin and he felt his cock-head hit the back of the boy's throat. Simon made a sort of choking noise. Paul pulled back and thrust forward again, again, building up a rhythm. The frame of the bunk beds rocked and creaked as he drove his cock in and out of Simon. He was just fucking lying there.

'Do something, for fuck's sake!' Paul croaked through gritted teeth.

He felt a light pressure on his buttocks and back. Simon was running his hand up and down his spinal column. His strokes became firmer. Paul squirmed with enjoyment. He felt the fingers of Simon's other hand tickling his balls.

'No!' He pulled his cock from Simon's mouth. Simon heaved in a great lungful of air.

'You've got no fucking idea, have you?' Paul snarled. He fumbled about for a condom. He'd slung a packet around here somewhere.

Why? Had he been planning something like this?

He found the packet and ripped it open. Quickly, fumbling, he rolled the thing down over his spit-wet cock.

He grabbed Simon's legs and rolled him over, pulling him half on to the floor.

'All right, you feeble bastard,' he growled. 'If that's the way you want it.'

He pulled Simon's arse-cheeks apart and peered through the gloom at his hole. Lunging forward, he forced his cock between Simon's cheeks, into his tight entrance. He stabbed forward, and Simon gasped.

'Does it hurt?' Paul demanded. 'Course it fucking hurts.'

He pulled out part-way and thrust again. The bed-frame rattled; Simon clenched tightly around Paul's thick, long cock. Paul thrust again. He kept on thrusting. Simon's head was crushed against the wall. The metal bed-frame cut into his legs. Paul didn't care. He hammered home into Simon, faster and faster, harder, until he felt close to orgasm. He let out a low, hissing roar as his climax ripped through him. He felt his cock disgorging into the latex dam, pumping shot after shot.

He slumped, breathless, over Simon's unmoving form, and let his cock slide from the boy's arse, then, peeling off the condom, he climbed quietly back up on to his bunk.

He felt drained. He listened for sounds from Simon's bed, but heard none.

Simon had not uttered a sound throughout.

Simon lay in the darkness, his hand at rest on his sticky, softening cock. Memories of school collided with memories of Mehmet . . . Paul looked so like him. The memories had overwhelmed him. He'd come spontaneously as Paul fucked him. Now he lay, basking in a warm afterglow.

'You're crap. If you won't stand up for yourself, why should anyone else?' Paul's voice, in the darkness above him. 'OK, you can't fight – or won't fight. So you've got to find a role for yourself. Something people can use – that way, you'll get protection.'

Fighting . . . protection. It was all so alien to Simon. He blotted Paul's voice out, and retreated into his memories.

Six

John went to sleep that night with the sound of Simon's violation in his ears. He could tell from the sounds exactly what was going on in the next cell. He had lain there, ashamed of his hardness, fighting the urge to masturbate.

He had thought of Toby. His planned birthday, so vividly brought to life in his dream. Fishing and sunshine and canvas. He pictured them together in the night in that tiny army tent, the wind buffeting the canvas, Toby, naked and pale, utterly beautiful by candlelight. Barely enough room to move.

Toby, shuffling across the groundsheet towards him; his cock small and rock hard, wreathed by a neat brown bush. Apart from that, he was practically hairless – just the faintest dusting about the nipples.

John reached out and pulled the lad to him, hugging him tight. Toby loved their hugs. So did John. He moved down Toby's body, kissing. His lips, then his chin, his neck, his shoulders and chest. John's lips came to rest on one of Toby's rosy nipples, with their first hints of hair. He sucked hard, drawing the nipple up between his teeth. Toby giggled and squirmed. One hand smoothed its way down the lad's stomach and into his bush. John let the wiry hairs spring and curl between his fingers, felt the root

49

of his hard cock and closed his fist around it. Moving his lips to the other nipple, sucking and nipping, he began working Toby's prick with his hand.

Toby let out a long breath of pleasure. He lifted John's head from his chest, and rolled him on to his back. Ever curious, Toby always had to try everything for himself. He sank his lips on to one of John's nipples, biting hard. John laughed as he cried out in pain. Toby gripped John's thick cock and began working the foreskin. He bit down again.

Wanking and biting . . . The sudden, sharp inflorescences of pain seemed to push John by starts closer to orgasm. He didn't want to come, yet.

He pulled away from Toby and kissed him on the lips, his tongue delving deep, his hands caressing the lad's buttocks.

'You know what we said,' Toby whispered, breaking John's caress. 'About today . . . my birthday.'

John smiled. He produced a condom and handed it to Toby. 'You get to do this bit,' he said.

Toby fingered the rolled-up latex, then stretched it over the head of John's cock. The cock twitched as John felt Toby rolling the sheath down, tight over the knob, then getting easier as it hugged the shaft. When it was on, John produced a tube of lubricant.

'Which way do you want it?' he asked.

'This way,' Toby replied. He lay on his back with his wide-apart legs in the air, pressing against the canvas walls of the tent. John reached forward and gently spread his buttock-cheeks, exposing his tight, white arsehole, his unblemished, unentered chamber of secrets. Now, faced with the actuality of penetrating his lover, he drew back, suddenly scared. There was no going back from this.

Toby reached down and took his hand. 'It's all right,' he said. 'I want you to.'

John squeezed a pool of lube on to his index and middle fingers, and gently placed them on Toby's sphincter, smearing the lube around the hole. 'I'm just going to loosen you up a bit, darling,' he whispered, and slipped a fingertip inside the tight hole. 'How does that feel?' he asked.

'Nice,' said Toby.

He slipped a second fingertip in, alongside the first. Toby gasped.

'It's all right, darling,' John whispered. 'Just try to relax.'

Slowly, he pushed the fingers further in, feeling the resistance of Toby's clenched buttocks and tight passage. 'Relax,' he breathed.

Toby's breathing became slow and measured. John felt his muscles beginning to unlock around his fingers.

'I'm ready,' Toby croaked.

John withdrew his fingers, slid forward on his knees and lifted Toby's buttocks from the groundsheet. He bent his cock forward, lining it up with the boy's slippery hole, and pressed it gently inside. He felt it stretch and close around his helmet. Toby let out a sharp, pained breath.

'We'll do this very slowly,' said John. 'Tell me when you want me to go deeper.'

Toby nodded his head. 'OK,' he said.

John pushed his cock a little further into Toby – perhaps an inch or so. Toby gasped again, and John stopped. Toby nodded: John pushed a little further.

'That's it,' he said after a few more pushes. He was fully inside the younger man. Toby smiled and wrapped his legs around John's waist.

John began moving his hips backward and forward, letting his cock slide a little way out of Toby, then pushing it back in again. He kept the strokes short. Toby lay, one arm thrown across his eyes, the other clutching his hard cock; his mouth was slightly open, a smile fluctuating with the occasional wince of pain. He began squirming and twitching his hips. John speeded his strokes up. They became harder and longer, until Toby was practically bouncing on John's cock, his legs clutched tight around John's waist, his round buttocks slapping down against John's thighs.

'Here she comes,' Toby whispered, and his cock began to spurt over his smooth, bare belly.

John groaned as he approached orgasm, his cock deep in his young lover.

He'd come in a spurt which splashed down on his belly as he lay, alone, on his prison bed. Through the wall, he could still hear the rhythmic clang of the bed-frame against the wall, and the slap of rutting flesh.

He'd sunk into sleep with those sounds in his ears. He couldn't say whether they influenced his dream or not. It was bizarre – he'd barely given God a thought since coming in here. His sense of mission, that essential guiding light for all men of the cloth, was gone, he thought.

He'd never had religious dreams . . .

He was on the Via Appia – the Appian Way, the old road to Rome. A boy was with him. A shepherd boy. They were walking away from the city – the city was in flames.

A hooded figure passed them. John glanced beneath the cowl, and gasped. Clumsily he got to his knees, dragging the boy down beside him.

'Hello, John Williamson,' Jesus said. 'Leaving the city?'

'Yes, lord,' John had replied. 'But what are you doing here. Aren't you dead?'

'Of course I'm dead, John,' Jesus said. 'Dead but not gone. I'm back – and I'm going in there, John.'

'I really shouldn't do that, Lord,' John said. 'It's a dangerous place. All Rome is on fire.'

'Nevertheless, I'm going in there,' Jesus said. 'To get the holy shit kicked out of me. They're going to crucify me again, Williamson – for you, you bastard!'

And, with that, Jesus thrust his head forward and spat into John's face.

★

52

He was awake with the dawn. The dream stayed with him. St Peter. *Quo vadis, Lord. Whither goest thou?*

The message was clear. He fell to his knees and prayed properly for the first time in weeks. 'Lord,' he said aloud, 'let this cup pass from me.'

He repeated the prayer as he washed, and as he dressed, and as he walked the long walk to the canteen. The day before, he had sat with some of the older lags; now, he sat among the aggressive young bucks, close to Spalding's table. He sat, and waited.

He saw Paul come in and go straight up to Spalding.

'I did him last night,' Paul said defiantly.

'I know,' said Spalding, smiling. 'Walls have ears. Cigarette?'

John waited. He wasn't sure whether or not Simon would appear, but appear he did, towards the end of the allotted time. He scanned the room with blank, red eyes, picked up his breakfast things and crossed to the serving hatch.

The room fell silent. Simon looked long at Spalding as he received his food. Spalding stared back: Simon held his gaze. John could sense the daddy of the wing was close to exploding.

Suddenly, he hammered the long table with his fist, making its whole length shake, and leapt to his feet. He bounded over to Simon and grabbed him by the hair. He swung around behind him and a hand went to Simon's throat – Spalding had a knife.

This was the moment. John rose to his feet. 'Stop,' he bellowed. He strode across to where Spalding was holding his victim.

'What did you say, uncle?' Spalding hissed, incredulous.

'Leave him alone,' John said. 'He's not your nonce. I am.'

Spalding regarded him closely. 'Fuck off,' he spat.

'I'm the one you want, I tell you,' John insisted. 'I was a vicar. I had sex with one of my choirboys, when he was eighteen. Hurt me, if you must hurt someone.'

Spalding released his grip on Simon. 'You – fuck off!' Spalding barked at him. Simon ran like a rabbit.

John tensed as Spalding strolled around him.

'Well, I don't know what to make of this,' the albino said. He folded the knife blade away, and pocketed the weapon. 'You've got a fuck of a lot of balls, I'll give you that. You know what we're going to do to you, uncle?'

'You'd better get on with it then, hadn't you?' John said in a steady voice.

The imp of Satan looked at him for a moment longer with his malevolent red eyes. Suddenly he seemed to relax; a grin broke out on his face, and he patted John on the shoulder. John relaxed. Too late – Spalding suddenly flew at him. His forehead smashed into John's nose, which exploded in a shower of blood. John staggered back, and stumbled.

Spalding's minions were on him. They dragged him to the floor. Some punched, most kicked. Blows rained into him from all sides. All he could see was the quick flash of booted feet, and faces, far above leering down at him. Spalding, Jock, Paul, others whose names he didn't know.

The last thing he was aware of was running feet and whistles being blown. He was already starting to black out.

It was dark when John came to: the lights were already out. He didn't know where he was. He was in bed. Not his own bed; this one was almost comfortable. He could hear sounds of breathing around him. In the moonlight he began to discern other beds, other sleepers. Most sounded ill, or restless, or fearful.

He heard movement in the darkness. A figure was standing at the end of his bed.

'Who's there?' John asked.

The figure didn't answer, but strolled closer to John. The moonlight fell on his face. It was Craigie.

'Where am I?' John asked.

'You're in the infirmary,' Craigie replied. 'That was a very brave thing you did today. Immensely foolish, of course.'

'I did what I had to do,' John said quietly.

'Yes,' Craigie mused. 'You're not very good at resisting your impulses, are you? You didn't listen to my little lecture about the neon tetras. I'm disappointed. I'd expected better sport. You're not going to last a week, at this rate.'

'It is your duty to protect prisoners from this sort of thing. To protect me.'

Craigie shrugged. 'You could always transfer to another wing,' he said.

'Would it do any good?'

'Not really,' Craigie replied. 'These things invariably follow you around. Or, of course you could go on the numbers.'

'I'm sorry?' John queried.

'Rule forty-three,' said Craigie. 'It means we lock you up with all the other sickos and perverts, where the ordinary prisoners can't get at you. Usually.'

'I'm not a pervert,' said John. ' I've done nothing I'm ashamed of.'

'Then you're a dead man,' said Craigie. 'I'm sorry.'

'Did you put the word out on me?' John asked suddenly.

'Oh, yes,' said Craigie. 'I didn't reveal your name, of course. Much more fun to let the little blighters work it out for themselves.'

'What do you want here, anyway?'

Craigie began to walk away.

'You're evil,' said John quietly after him.

'Funny,' said Craigie, turning back for a moment, 'that's exactly what the newspapers said about you.'

John watched him vanish into the darkness. He took a deep breath. To his surprise, he didn't feel frightened. He touched his face – it was swollen, soft and sore to the touch. He barely felt his bruises, though. He tingled all over. He felt strangely exhilarated. He felt his calling, now – that deep sense of mission, so intense in his seminary days. He was feeling it now like he'd felt it then: it was that powerful.

He thought about the seminary. He'd learnt so much there – not just about God and the church, but about life. About the real love of God.

He'd gone there, a callow youth of twenty-one, wholly inno-cent in the wicked ways of the world and content to stay that way.

In many ways, the seminary wasn't unlike boarding school. The same communal life – all males, eating, sleeping and washing together. He smiled grimly. Like this place. He'd become friendly with a twenty-three-year-old called Ross. Nearly six feet tall, piercing blue eyes, black hair and pale skin – very Celtic-looking, very handsome. Sculpted, somewhat square features; the slightest break in his nose.

They had met on the tennis courts, late one summer. Ross was good with a racquet, and John wasn't bad. They had spent the long evenings playing, then they would shower and retire to Ross's room and drink the whisky his dad used to send him. Within a very short time of their meeting, they became inseparable friends – and the subject of gossip and jokes which made John blush.

He'd noticed, or thought he'd noticed, Ross's eyes lingering perhaps a little too long on his naked body as he soaped himself in the shower. It was also certainly true that, when they were alone in the changing room, Ross used to devise games, wheezes and excuses to keep them there, naked under the jets – chucking a soaked tennis ball around, or whatever. John had had vague suspicions about Ross, but had pretty much dismissed them.

He well remembered the night when everything changed. He and Ross had been drinking until late, as usual. John had returned to his own room, only to realise he'd left some books behind. He needed them first thing – so he trotted back down the long, quiet corridors to his friend's room.

He was quite accustomed to walking into Ross's room without knocking, and he did so now. What he saw when he entered the room shocked him. Ross was laying on his bed, naked, his legs apart. By the light of a single candle, John could see he was masturbating. His hand was racing up and down his cock. John had never seen his friend's cock like this – he'd never seen any cock like this, except for his own – and he stared, fascinated.

Ross's eyes were shut. He hadn't heard John come in. He continued wanking for nearly a minute, before opening his eyes.

'Hello,' he said softly. 'I didn't know I had company.'

'I . . .' John had groped for a response, but found none.

'Come over,' said Ross. 'It's all right.' He'd stopped wanking, but his hand still rested on his hard cock. As John approached the bed, he started up again, slowly at first. 'Sit down,' he said, wanking himself steadily. 'Kick off your shoes. Make yourself comfortable.'

Mesmerised by the sight of Ross's cock, thick and slightly curving, rising like a tower from his black pubic forest, John did as he was bidden.

Ross reached across and placed a hand on his stomach. Beneath his trousers, John too had a hard-on. He tried to alter position, to stop Ross feeling it, but Ross followed him with his hand. He began squeezing John's cock through the material of his trousers.

John's heart was racing. Ross plucked open first one, then another of his fly buttons.

'Shouldn't we . . . I mean, isn't it . . .'

'A sin?' queried Ross. 'Then we're all sinners.' He eased John's trousers down. John's cock stood high beneath his pants. Ross unhooked the elastic and pulled them to John's ankles. His hand closed around John's cock, and he began gently squeezing, moving the foreskin gently back and forth, so that the tip of John's helmet sneaked into view, then vanished again.

With his other hand he began wanking his own cock once more. His hands moved in synch; the one around John's shaft, pulling his foreskin back and forth across his painfully sensitised and swollen head, the other working high on his own helmet, rubbing and squeezing, playing his fingers over the ridge.

'Your thing's different to mine,' John had said, in all innocence.

'I'm circumcised,' said Ross. 'You know – like the Jews. Our Lord was circumcised.'

He continued to wank them both. John watched in fascination.

'Of course, the thing about being circumcised,' Ross muttered, 'you need lots of spit. He licked his hand generously, and smeared saliva over the end of his knob. 'Want some?' he asked John. John nodded eagerly.

Ross licked his other hand good and wet. 'I can taste you,' he grinned. He closed it around John's cock-head. John squirmed with pleasure. Ross firmed up his stroke, and John felt his hips moving to the rhythm. He felt a tingling, an arousal which his own secret, guilty self-manipulations had never afforded him. Ross's stroke became faster. John was feeling peculiar contractions in his balls. This was different to anything he'd felt before. He felt a moment of panic. He was going to come . . .

'I'm going to –' His cock clenched and he shot three or four spurts of come over Ross's bare chest.

'Come?' said Ross. He was still wanking. He smeared John's seed over his chest, and over the end of his cock. 'Much better than spit,' he said. He was wanking hard now. John felt an intense desire to touch him. Cautiously he extended a hand forward, tested Ross's thick, black pubes with his fingertips . . . ran them lightly across his balls . . . cupped them in his hand. He ran his fingers up on to the base of Ross's cock. His fingers closed around the great member . . .

Ross's cock lurched, his hips leapt, and he came with a low cry.

In the darkness, John smiled at the memory. They'd slept together that night, he and Ross, their sticky juices drying between their pressed-together bodies. They'd slept together for two years after that, until Ross left to take up his ministry.

The seminary. It was ironic that the very process designed to marry John's life to God and the Church had contained within it the seeds of his destruction as a vessel of the Lord. Not that he saw it that way, now. There, in the darkness of the prison infirmary, John Williamson realised that he was blessed – that he had been given the supreme gift. The thing all sinners longed for – prayed for. A chance of redemption.

Seven

John was in the infirmary a week. During that time, there was a sense of mounting expectation on the wing. People wondered what would happen when he came out. Some doubted he'd ever come out — they thought he'd be seen to long before that. Bets were taken on what was going to happen to him, and when.

Paul joined in the circus. Spalding was acting like a child waiting for his birthday. Paul was spending a lot of time in his company, enjoying the privilege of being one of the top dog's friends. He could turn the TV to whatever station he wanted, and no one complained — he could demand a fag, and get one. One guy got lippy with him, and had to be smacked; but that was all right. Paul was sorting himself out nicely in here.

He found it difficult to face Simon, ever since their violent coupling. He told himself he'd done it because the situation with Spalding seemed to require it, or otherwise that he'd done it because Simon was pissing him off.

Though you beat someone up if they pissed you off — you didn't shag them.

He became aware of Simon staring at him, watching him the whole time. Not out of fear, which he could have handled, but with a sort of curious longing in his gaze. He didn't like it, and he didn't want to discuss it.

He became a frequent guest in Spalding's cell, for cards, or Monopoly (Spalding loved Monopoly – he was always the banker, and he always robbed the bank blind), and drugs. There were always drugs. Blow, mostly, or heroin, which Paul avoided. So did Spalding, he noted, although his minions would scurry round like hungry rodents when someone started burning the foil.

One night, tapping on Spalding's door as usual, he entered to find the albino belly down on the bed, his trousers down and his arse exposed. He was on top of another bloke, face down and naked. Spalding was pumping his cock in and out of the other bloke's arse. Paul recognised him – an Indian bloke called Sanjay, about nineteen. A pretty-boy with a long, silky mane of black hair. A fraggle.

'Sit down,' gasped Spalding. 'I won't be a minute.'

Paul watched as Spalding, pale as ivory and red-eyed, heaved and clawed at Sanjay's coffee-brown back. His nails dug into Sanjay's shoulders. He bit down on his neck so hard that Sanjay cried out.

Spalding fucked him viciously. He wrapped his hands around Sanjay's shoulders and hoisted himself forward, pushing off with his toes, slamming his cock into the Indian's passage. Sanjay squirmed and whimpered and bit hard on the pillow.

'Ah . . . shit . . .' Spalding began to orgasm, his arse clenching, his body shaking as he sank his cock deep inside Sanjay.

He let out a low whistle as he rolled off him. He rose from the bed and peeled off his condom. He stood, naked in front of Paul, his cock slackening and dripping slightly.

'Good,' said Spalding. He caught Paul's eye and nodded at Sanjay. 'Be my guest,' he said.

'What, you mean . . .?'

Spalding smiled.

Paul had realised these little displays of male bonding were important to Spalding. He moved behind Sanjay, unzipped his fly and pulled out his cock. It was soft and small as he brought it close to the Indian's arse. He began pulling at it, trying to work a bit of life into it. It grew slightly, but remained effectively limp. Paul shot a glance at Spalding, who was watching intently. He carried on pulling; his prick remained limp.

Spalding sat in an armchair and motioned to Sanjay. The lad seemed to know what to do; he knelt in front of Paul and took his cock in his mouth. Paul looked down at Sanjay's mane of long black hair, swaying as the guy's head bobbed against his groin. He felt the warm wetness of Sanjay's tongue licking his shaft. The lad tightened his lips and teeth around the head of Paul's prick and pulled, arcing his neck back and stretching the still-soft member until it hurt.

Paul was getting hard now. Spalding tossed him a condom, and Sanjay returned to his position on the bed, face down, arse slightly in the air. Paul rolled the condom over his stiff cock. Sanjay gripped his own arse-cheeks and pulled them apart, offering Paul his hole. Paul mounted him, pushing his cock slowly between the Indian boy's cheeks until his balls were pressed against Sanjay's arse.

He withdrew slightly, then pushed forward again, finding a rhythm which pleased him. Sanjay wriggled beneath him – he seemed to be enjoying being taken. He raised his buttocks and slipped a hand underneath, searching for his cock.

Spalding scowled slightly – Paul guessed the fraggles weren't supposed to enjoy this. All the same, Sanjay was wanking himself as Paul drove his cock into his hole, bed creaking, balls slapping. His arse clenched and unclenched around Paul's stiff cock, and he started to grunt and moan slightly. He began moving his arse in time with Paul's thrusts, pushing up to meet his downward strokes, as if he was seeking ever deeper penetration.

Sanjay made a sort of choking noise, and his strokes of his cock became quicker. He was coming into Spalding's sheets. Paul, too, felt close to orgasm. He buried his face in the lad's luxuriant curtain of hair, and inhaled deeply, smelling the sweat on his brown skin beneath.

He let out a long breath and grabbed Sanjay's juddering hips, pulling him tightly on to his cock, pressing his pubic bush into the Indian boy's hairy arse-cheeks, his cock clenching and firing. He felt his spunk bouncing off the walls of the condom, soaking his cock-head. He clung to Sanjay as his climax subsided, then released him and let his cock slip out of the tight hole.

Spalding watched, scowling slightly, throughout. 'You fuck like a queer,' he said to Paul.

Sanjay was on his feet, and dressing. Without a word, he stripped Spalding's bed and left the cell.

'My laundry-boy,' Spalding said. 'Now, I wanted to talk to you about a little surprise we're planning for the nonce when he comes out of hospital.'

Simon kept his head down all that week. He continued with his job, cleaning corridors. He didn't like it; it left him too exposed. Anybody could come along and, whatever was bothering them that day, they could vent their aggression on him at their leisure. That's what the fraggles were – human punch-bags. There were others on the wing, not just him. He watched a kid get beaten shitless for splashing water on the shoe of a huge black guy. As the days passed, he came to expect the odd passing punch or kick.

He was beaten up twice, by different combinations of bored, vicious inmates. The beatings lacked the ferocity of Spalding's attacks – they were more style than substance; mostly aggressive posturing rather than any actual desire to seriously hurt him. He got the impression that, since John's intervention, no one was quite sure what his status was. Was he a nonce?

Spalding gave no clues. He spoke to Simon only once, when he was trying to slip through the recreation area to the drinking water.

'Don't think I've forgotten you,' Spalding said.

But Spalding did seem to have largely forgotten him. When hunger forced Simon to enter the canteen, Spalding ignored him completely – he seemed to look right through him. The whole wing knew he was preoccupied with John's return from the infirmary. Simon felt a sense of guilty relief. John seemed to have drawn the sting from the attacks on Simon. He dreaded to think what lay in store for John when he returned to the wing.

From a distance, he watched Spalding and his cronies – Paul especially – lording it over the other prisoners. A part of him enjoyed seeing his swarthy, pretty cell-mate strutting about, taking what he wanted, dishing out the odd lick. It gave Simon a sort of peculiar pride.

Paul was quite different when he was alone with Simon. Simon could see his discomfort clearly. He couldn't meet his eyes any more. Simon, by contrast, could scarcely tear his gaze away from Paul.

He looked a little like Mehmet – the same dusky complexion and dark, hooded eyes, the same lazy, half-lidded expression: perhaps that explained it. Simon particularly liked watching Paul dress and undress, in the dusky half-light of evening or the faint glow of the early-morning sun. His body was slim, like Mehmet's, but more muscular. He had less body hair than Mehmet. Apart from the thick black hair that sprouted in his armpits, around his cock and over his balls, Paul was almost hairless. A dark sprinkling around his nipples, and a thin trail from his bellybutton down to that great pubic forest, and that was it.

Mehmet, of course, had been circumcised; Paul was not. A neat, tight foreskin sat around the bulb at the end of a long, thick shaft. Sometimes, when his cock was a little hard, the bulb would push its way unaided out of its collar, peeping though as the skin retracted. Often in the evenings, after Paul had been in Spalding's cell, his cock-head would be livid and swollen, moist with spunk and still dribbling slightly. Simon would lay on his bunk and gaze up at him, his own cock hard. Sometimes, he thought of Mehmet; at other times, he didn't.

In truth, the resemblance wasn't that striking, and Paul's aggressive manner was completely unlike that of his gentle Palestinian lover. No; but there was something in the manner in which Paul had taken him – Paul's anger had seemed to Simon to be concealing something else. Need, perhaps. All Simon was sure of was that his cell-mate had begun to fascinate him.

Simon's corridor-cleaning job took him outside the laundry each morning. It was in a quiet part of the wing, and Simon enjoyed dawdling outside the door, listening to the sounds of the machines, enjoying the old familiar smells and warmth, occasionally getting to see inside when somebody entered or left.

There was a guy in there whose eye he kept on catching – a guy about his own age, a fraggle, by the look of him, who spent his day loading and unloading the machines. He was pretty – curly brown hair in need of cutting, tumbling over piercing blue eyes, a turned-up nose, a light dusting of freckles. He looked gay, to Simon.

Several times, they exchanged shy smiles when the door swung open and their eyes met, each slacking when he ought to be working. Simon thought of saying something, but there was always someone passing in or out of the laundry, and he didn't have the nerve.

He was mopping the floor one morning when the door opened. The other man was standing there, beckoning to him. Glancing along the corridor to make sure he was unobserved, Simon put down his mop and went inside.

He glanced gladly around the big room – the industrial-load washers, dryers, the huge steam-press.

'Hello,' said the lad timidly. 'My name's Tim. Who're you?'

'Simon,' said Simon, smiling at him. The first welcoming words he'd heard in here. 'It's really good to meet you,' he said.

'Cigarette?' Tim asked, flopping down on a pile of unwashed bedlinen.

Simon shook his head. 'I don't,' he said.

'Well, sit down, anyway,' said Tim, patting the pile of sheets.

Simon sat, and they talked. Tim, too, was a country boy – an orphan at some godawful rural institution – who'd fled to the city. The bright lights. It was obvious what he was fleeing from. 'It's something we all have to do,' Simon said.

Tim had been inside for two months already. 'It's hell,' he said, 'but hell's bearable.'

'Do they ever beat you up?' Simon asked.

'In the beginning, I had it rough,' said Tim. 'I'm OK now.'

'So they do stop,' Simon said urgently.

'Sometimes.' Tim looked uneasy.

'How did you get them to leave you alone?'

Tim lifted himself from the pile of sheets and began checking one of the washing machines. He looked flustered. 'They just do, OK?' he said tetchily.

'Sure, sure,' said Simon. 'I didn't mean to . . .'

'That's OK,' said Tim. 'I suppose I'm getting touchy, like them. You've seen how raw everyone's nerves are in here.'

'You're not anything like them,' said Simon.

Tim smiled at him, and ran a hand quickly through his golden thatch of hair. 'Listen,' he said, 'we'd better get back to work. Come again tomorrow, will you?'

'You bet,' said Simon.

Washing the corridors, the rest of that day, he actually found himself whistling aloud.

Eight

Simon visited Tim every day. He even puffed on the odd cigarette, just to be sociable. They made him cough violently; Tim laughed.

'Seriously,' he said, 'don't start smoking just because I do it. Cigarettes are good currency in here. You're much better off trading with them. Besides –' Simon was about to light another: Tim snatched it from his lips '– do you know how much those things cost in here?'

There only appeared to be one other regular worker in the laundry room. He was in charge, and his name was Gorman – in his mid-thirties, permanently unshaven, his shirt always hanging out at the waist, its lower buttons undone. He never seemed to speak a word.

'I like it in here,' said Simon. 'I used to manage one of these places, on the outside.'

Tim's eyes widened. 'You should come and work here,' he said. 'We're short-handed. It's a real perk, working in the laundry, and Craigie hates handing out perks.'

'How did you get the job?' Simon asked.

Tim shrugged his shoulders – did Simon sense that same unease as before in his friend? – and lit up. 'Just lucky, I suppose,' he said.

'So how can I get a job here?'

'I'll have a word with Gorman,' said Tim. 'I know how to get around him.'

Simon started work in the laundry the next day. The duties he knew well – loading and unloading, stacking, pressing. He also knew a bit about maintaining the machines – where to give them a kick if they went wrong.

Simon and Tim chattered while they worked. Gorman was only occasionally present, and only for short periods of time. He never seemed to do any work.

'You won't see much of him,' said Tim. 'He just stays in the storeroom all day. I reckon he's a bit gone in the head.'

'How d'you mean?'

'You'll see,' said Tim, grinning.

Simon saw, that very afternoon. He approached the storeroom to get some more washing powder. The door was ajar.

Simon stopped. He could hear noises coming from inside. Muffled whimperings, and a quiet, sticky, squelching sound. He edged forward. In the little cupboard, he could see Gorman sitting on a low wooden box, his trousers and pants around his ankles, his cock sticking up through the bottom of his shirt. He was masturbating; he clutched at his tall, hard cock with both hands. His cock bubbled with foam: next to Gorman was an open bottle of liquid detergent.

He moaned and whimpered as he wanked. He pulled hard at his loose foreskin. One hand moved down to his low-swinging balls. He slapped them hard against the wooden box, letting out a quiet yelp. He slapped and yelped again.

Something seemed to disturb him; he turned his head, and saw Simon. 'Yeah?' he said, not breaking his cock-stroke.

'I . . . I just came for some more powder,' Simon stammered.

'Come on, then,' said Gorman, and slapped himself in the balls again.

Gingerly, Simon tried to work his way around the masturbating man, hugging the wall of the tiny closet.

Gorman began rocking backward and forward on his seat. The box creaked and groaned and wobbled under him. He was about to come. Simon grabbed for a box and, at the same time, Gorman lunged for his waist and pulled Simon backward, into his lap. He groaned as he came. Simon felt a warm wetness up the back of his shirt. Gorman clung to him, shaking.

At last, he relaxed his grip, and Simon fled.

Tim was outside, laughing. 'I told you he was gone in the head. He just spends all day in that cupboard, wanking. I should have warned you – if you're in there and he's coming, he tends to make a grab for you. He likes coming over people.'

'Yes,' Simon snapped, 'you should have warned me. I'm soaked.'

'Come here,' Tim said. 'Take your shirt off. I'll stick it in with one of our loads.'

Simon allowed Tim to peel the shirt from his back.

'Eww,' said Tim, grinning. 'Messy.' He slung it in a machine. 'Relax,' he said to Simon. 'It'll be a while.'

He scrambled to the top of the mountainous pile of bedlinen, almost to the ceiling, and lit a cigarette. Simon clambered up next to him.

'You're still smarting, aren't you?' said Tim.

Simon shrugged. It was odd, after all that had happened to him, that this little incident should make him so annoyed.

He felt a light pressure on his slim chest. A fingernail, tracing the underside of his pectoral, sitting at the bottom of his breast-bone, circling a nipple.

He shot a smile at Tim. Tim was looking steadily at him, grinning his summery grin. The pressure from his hand became harder. He pinched Simon's nipple between two fingers, pulling it out and letting it go.

'Your nipple's hard,' he said to Simon, and moved his hand across his chest to the other one. 'So's this one,' he said.

Tim spread his palm wide, and ran his fingers down Simon's chest. He pulled playfully at the tiny fringe of golden pubic hair which poked above Simon's belt.

Simon stretched out a tentative hand and began unbuttoning Tim's shirt. He pulled it back off his shoulders and down his arms. Tim shook himself free of the shirt. His chest was hairless and slim; his back, like his nose, was lightly belted with freckles.

Holding each other's eyes, they stroked and massaged each other, outspread hands gliding over chests and arms, down backs, across necks.

Simon placed a hand on Tim's cheek, gently pulling him forward. They kissed slowly, their lips barely grazing at first, then their tongues gradually emerging, the lightest of touches, tongue to tongue, then harder, lips sealing, tongues darting forward, waltzing wetly around each other.

Suddenly, they were clinging to one another, hugging one another as if their lives depended on it, bodies pressed together, lips in an unbroken seal. All the loveless days since he had been sent to this place had filled Simon with a hunger for real human warmth; now he gorged on it.

Tim relaxed his bear hug. Simon became aware of him sneaking at a button and tugging at his trousers. He let him remove them, and his pants. He looked down at his cock, erect and throbbing. Tim touched it lightly. It quivered. Tim giggled.

Simon began easing off Tim's trousers. Tim wore a pair of pale red pants, tight and stretched over his erection. Simon tucked his hand inside the elastic waist band and ran his fingers down the rigid shaft he found there. Tim wasn't large, but as hard as steel. Simon ran his fingers up the underside of his friend's cock, paused at the frenum, then traced the edge of his helmet in a full circle.

He was circumcised; Simon could tell just by feel. How many times had he done this to Mehmet? He swept Tim's pants down, and Tim kicked them off. He watched a droplet of pre-come ooze from the eye of Tim's prick, alert and quivering slightly.

Tim rolled over, pushing Simon on to his back on the collapsing linen mountain, straddling his hips, his buttocks on Simon's thighs, his bollocks resting on Simon's hard cock, coarse pubes rustling on coarse pubes.

In the background, Simon could here the faint whimper of Gorman starting up again.

Tim slid backward down Simon's body, and lowered his face to his chest. Simon felt the sharp tweak of Tim's teeth, biting on a nipple, testing, pulling. He gasped. Tim moved to the other nipple, biting hard, then moved down to Simon's bellybutton, extending his tongue, probing wetly. Simon flinched with ticklish pleasure.

Tim was on his cock now: Simon felt first the wet warmth of his tongue, peeling his foreskin back, licking at his cock-head like it was a lollipop. He nipped with his teeth at Simon's frenum, sending out a sharp, delicious spasm of pain. He nibbled his way down Simon's shaft, catching the taut skin between his teeth, pulling, relaxing, until he had the edge of Simon's ball sac between his teeth, then he nibbled his way up again, finally enveloping Simon's throbbing prick with his wet, sensuous mouth.

The feeling of delicious engulfment spread down Simon's prick as Tim's lips went lower and lower. He could feel his knob against the back of Tim's mouth. Tim pulled his head up; Simon's helmet scraped against Tim's palate, the soft barrier of his lips, then plunged again as Tim went down. He ran his fingers through Tim's lanky brown curls as Tim's head bobbed on his cock. Tim managed to catch his eye – even now, with his mouth full, he seemed to be smiling. His eyes smiled.

Things were moving too fast. Simon already felt close to coming. He pulled his cock out of Tim's mouth, and slid down the linen pile, grabbing Tim's head and crushing it to his in a frantic, passionate kiss.

'My turn,' he said, and began to crawl across the precarious slope.

There was a landslide. Spunk-soiled sheets and tear-stained pillows cascaded down around them. They fell, rolling among the acres of cloth, laughing, tumbling. Simon landed on top of Tim. They were both hopelessly tangled in bedding.

'Ugh,' exclaimed Tim, still laughing. A huge spunk stain coated the sheet which separated them. 'It's still wet,' said Tim.

They kissed, fumblingly, passionately. Tim wrestled with tangled cotton and freed Simon's cock. He wanked it vigorously.

Simon twisted around and dived under a sail of cloth, seeking Tim's naked body beneath. He burrowed through the layers of cotton like a mole, until he saw Tim's hard cock in the tunnel ahead. He gobbled it hungrily. Once again he felt Tim's lips curl around his prick. They lay there, each with the other's cock deep in his throat, sucking and pulling with wet lips stretched over teeth. Simon tasted Tim's salty juices.

The sheets were sliding again. They rolled now, over and over each other, clinging together, mouths clamped tight over cocks. Simon felt Tim's prick slewing and skidding around in his mouth as they rolled, battering his teeth and palate.

They were still again. Both sucked earnestly now, hearts thumping, breath short, pulling each other towards orgasm. Quite suddenly, Tim's thighs clamped themselves around Simon's head, tight and twitching. He groaned slightly, and shot his load deep into Simon's throat. Simon was coming, too: his cock slipped from Tim's mouth as he began to shoot, and danced about, hosing Tim's face in thick white semen.

They lay, breathless, for long minutes. Behind them, they heard Gorman whimpering as he came. They started to laugh, freely, uncontrollably, with a carefree ease Simon had thought lost for ever.

Nine

The days dragged for John in the hospital. He knew he should be grateful for his stay there – it was probably shielding him from the treatment he knew he was going to receive when he got out.

And yet a part of him was impatient to leave – to face whatever trials had to be faced. It wasn't just a matter of getting it over with. Part of him wanted the experience to happen.

In fact, he dwelt little on his future, and almost entirely in the past. Days he spent dozing and dreaming, while the nurses and, once in a blue moon, a doctor moved about the ward, tending to their charges. John was bruised, but that was all. No head injuries. He suspected he was being kept there for his own protection.

He had a visitor on his third day in the infirmary: the prison chaplain called to see him.

'How are you?' he asked in a tone of forced politeness which could not quite mask his contempt.

'Well, thank you,' John replied. 'Our Lord suffered worse.'

The chaplain's nose wrinkled. His lips tightened. 'I know all about you,' he said in a vicious whisper. 'As far as I am concerned, your presence in this prison – on this earth – is a form of

72

pollution. What happened to you out there is no more than you deserve.'

'A very Christian attitude,' said John.

'I even read one of your books, once. The sort of liberal rubbish that is bringing the church to its knees. And look at you now. You are a degenerate.' He leant in close over John's bed. 'This is a Christian prison,' he hissed. 'The governor is a man of strict moral standards – a former man of the cloth himself. He and I both strive, insofar as it is possible in a place like this, to provide a decent set of values for the men to aspire to. I know all about your ability to twist words, to argue that black is white, that sin has no place in God's plan, that evil does not really exist. I will not have you spreading your filth and lies and lusts in this prison.'

'Have you been on any of the wings recently?' John demanded, incredulous. 'Has the governor? Have you seen the way they interpret your decent set of values out there? Not just the prisoners – the guards, too, if you can ever find one.'

'They're going to have your guts for garters, nonce,' the chaplain spat. 'And I, for one, shall pray for them.'

Craigie and the chaplain were not the only visitors John received in his sickbed. On his final night, he became aware of scuffling feet and whispered voices. He tried to see who was there, but instantly found his bed surrounded by shadowy figures.

He tried to cry out. Immediately, a hand was clamped over his mouth. There were hasty, whispered words, and then a tearing sound. The hand was removed and a length of thick, sticky tape was plastered over his mouth. He tried to struggle; barely glimpsed hands held him down. Another piece of tape was stuck over his eyes. His arms and legs were pulled apart and taped to the bed-frame. He felt hands tugging and tearing at his pyjama-bottoms. The material gave way with a rending sound.

From what he could hear, he guessed there must be three or four of them. Their whispered conversations weren't enough; he couldn't recognise them from their hushed voices. He tried to relax – surrender to the inevitable. The road to Calvary.

'All right, Danny,' somebody whispered, 'your big moment.'

Danny: John knew him – a small, timid lad of about eighteen, with an odd sort of a squint. Quite cute, in a runty sort of way . . . and almost certainly a virgin.

'I dunno,' said Danny. 'I'm not sure.'

'Fucking get up there,' a voice hissed savagely.

John felt the pressure of someone climbing on to the bed, crawling between his splayed legs, panting with fear or excitement. He felt fingers inexpertly probing his buttocks, looking for his rectum. He felt a cock – smallish – butting uncertainly against the sphincter, then pushing, worming its way in.

He felt the unseen figure of Danny brace, then begin fucking him in a slow, uneven stroke. John was growing hard. This was almost touching. He felt his lengthening cock bobbing against Danny's belly, bending against it, then springing upward.

Danny's breathing was already becoming fast and irregular. He couldn't be coming already . . .

'Fuck –' it came out as a sort of choking sound '– I'm.' His little strokes were suddenly rapid, frenzied. He clutched at John's shoulders as he came.

There was a scuffle next to the bed.

'What the fuck do you call that?' a voice exclaimed.

John felt Danny's cock suddenly twisted from him. Unseen hands pulled the lad from on top of John, and John heard him tumble to the floor, swearing.

There was a hawking sound, and he felt the warm splat of saliva on his cheek – someone had spat in his face. Dry fingers – two or perhaps three – thrust themselves suddenly into his anus, causing him to flinch and buck. Someone climbed on to the bottom of the bed – and John felt his buttocks suddenly lifted from the bed.

A prick, hard and dry, was butting against his arse-cheeks, trying to force its way inside him, alongside the fingers. Slowly, he felt his sphincter stretching, yielding to the pressure, and the stranger's cock sank painfully into his hole.

His fingers, squashed inside John alongside his cock, twisted painfully as the stranger fucked.

John tried to struggle. The fingers were pulled from his arse, and he felt a hand around his throat, crushing, squeezing. The tape held him fast. He couldn't breathe.

The room started to swim. The pain from his sphincter was different now – more remote, somehow. Warmer, deeper.

His cock was hard again.

'He's fucking enjoying it – dirty bastard!' a voice next to the bed hissed. 'I've got a better idea. Get off him.'

'Fuck off,' the slightly strangled voice of John's unseen violator replied. 'I haven't come, yet.'

John felt him speeding up his stroke, gaining some sort of a rhythm. The stranger was leaning forward now, his face pressed against John's – he could feel stubble raking against his cheek. The stranger released John's throat and let out a series of short breaths – almost like the yelping of a dog – as he began to hit orgasm. John raked air into his lungs. He felt his shoulders gripped tightly. With a faint groaning sound, the stranger climaxed.

'Come on!' the voice beside the bed hissed again.

The stranger rolled off John. His cock left John's arse with a wrench.

'Look what I found,' the voice said. There was muffled laughter. 'Shall we?'

There was movement, and the voice whispered, close in his ear. 'Playtime's over . . .'

John felt a hand on his inner thigh, and something hard and cold against his buttocks. Something unfamiliar. He began to panic now, tugging against his bonds. He felt a sharp pain as the object was pushed inside his hole. It was glassy smooth, but it had a rough edge. A bottle – it was the neck of a bottle, he was sure. He winced as it pushed its way in, was dragged back, and plunged in again.

'Are you enjoying that, nonce?' a voice whispered. 'Is that what you used to do to your altar boys?'

John clenched his fists against the pain. His fingernails bit into his palms.

He had a sudden, overwhelming sense of panic – the bottle might break inside him.

In the darkness, someone climbed on to the bed. A foot was planted at either side of John's head. He heard a fly unzipping, then felt something warm and wet splashing on his face. He caught the acrid tang of urine. Someone was standing over him, pissing in his face. Piss soaked his hair. Piss flowed into his nostrils; it soaked the tape which covered his mouth and eyes.

Someone was turning and wiggling the bottle inside him. He squirmed in pain.

'Right, let's split,' a voice whispered. 'I think someone's coming.'

John felt the bottle go still inside him. The piss-stream dried up and the figure jumped from the bed. He heard the sound of running feet, and then silence.

He lay there, bound and helpless in the dark, gagged and blindfold, covered with piss, a bottle rudely jutting from his most private self.

Things seemed to get easier for Simon as the week progressed. Over the next few days the random beatings stopped. No one was friendly to him, but neither did they target him. He noticed they treated Tim in the same way – somewhere between respecting his space and completely ignoring him.

Simon had one lingering bit of trouble. It began with Gary, the huge Texan. Every time he saw Simon, Gary would blow an obscene kiss, or wiggle his tongue at Simon. On one occasion, he got his cock out and started stroking it hard, there in the corridor as Simon mopped the floor. Once, by unhappy chance, Simon came upon Gary in the showers. He stripped and walked in to find the Texan huddled over the pale form of one of the fraggles – a skinny guy called Tom, monkey-faced, with dark, ill-kempt hair. Tom had his back to the tiled wall and his shoulders crushed between the shower-heads. Water cascaded down him. He was balanced on one leg; the other was hooked around Gary's bare arse and thighs. Gary's cock was up Tom's arse; with short, hard thrusts, Gary rammed upward into him. The taps banged into Tom's back, the nozzles into his shoulders, as Gary thrust, grunting as his cock rutted Tom's arse.

Simon backed away, but felt a hand gripping his shoulder hard. A man was standing behind him – a black guy, as tall as Gary, heavily muscled. Simon started – it was the other guy they'd seen on video. He twisted in the man's grip, trying to free himself. The man's huge fingers cut into his shoulders.

'Where you think you're going?' the black guy said. Another American accent. 'Anybody'd think you didn' like ol' Louie. You do like ol' Louie, don't you, boy?'

Smiling a broad crocodile smile, he forced Simon on to his knees in front of him. His ebony cock was hard and huge, its purple head part-exposed beneath his foreskin.

'Do a good job,' the man said. 'Do a good job for Louie.'

Simon opened his mouth and closed his eyes. He wrapped his lips around the great pole and sucked it inside his mouth. His teeth grazed the rim of Louie's helmet.

'You watch with them teeth, boy,' Louie said, with quiet menace in his voice.

Terrified, Simon did his best to shield his teeth with his lips. Louie's cock was immense; Simon felt himself choking on it. He spluttered and coughed.

Louie hissed angrily, and grabbed Simon by the back of the head. He forced the boy to his knees, then bent his head until it was touching the floor of the shower. Water cascaded past Simon, filling his nose and mouth, stinging his eyes.

'Let's see if your arse is a better fuck than your mouth,' said Louie.

Simon tried to force his head round, to breathe. Out of the corner of his eye he saw Louie deftly tearing the wrapper off a condom with his teeth.

'Governor's orders,' he grinned malevolently, and expertly rolled it down his great prick.

He squatted behind Simon, still holding his head to the floor, and poked at Simon's buttocks with his hard-on, unsuccessfully seeking his hole. He swore. 'Guide me in, boy,' he snarled.

Simon reached behind him. His fumbling fingers caught the thick root of Louie's cock, groped their way up the shaft, found the bulbous head. Simon placed it between his own cheeks, nested it in the entrance to his hole, and braced himself.

Letting out a long sigh, Louie rocked forward. His cock bored into Simon, slowly, remorselessly. Simon felt Louie's cock would never stop going in – he felt he was being split in two. He tried to breathe slowly, to relax around the huge member, but he could scarcely breathe at all with his head in this torrent. Louie began to plunge his cock home; Simon's arse closed gladly around his every withdrawal, only to be forced apart again by the next plunge.

The tiles were slippery: slowly, Louie's thrusts were pushing Simon across the floor. Ahead of him, he could just make out Gary's tree-trunk legs, braced as he shoved his cock into Tom's arse.

Louie relaxed his grip on Simon's head. He was directly under Gary and Tom now, his head caught in the tangle of their legs. He twisted his head round – he could see Gary's big, hairy balls dripping with water, swinging as he plunged in and out of Tom. He could see Gary's great cock emerging from Tom's stretched hole, then disappearing into him again. He watched as Gary's stroke – and his grunts – became more frantic. His knees shook slightly as he rammed his orgasm home. Tom's feet left the ground as Gary drove up into him, bellowing his climax.

'Oh, shit . . . yeah . . . oh, yeah, man . . .' Louie was also coming. His huge, blunt fingers gripped Simon's shoulders painfully. His cock seemed to swell inside Simon. He hammered it in and out in a frenzy. Simon's arse burnt with the pain.

At last, Louie slowed and was still. He pulled out slowly. Simon's passage closed blissfully.

No one said anything. Simon waited, face down on the floor, until their footsteps had receded and the shower was quiet. Even

Tom was gone. Slowly, delicately, he picked himself up and began to wash.

The next day, Gary and Louie sought him out in his cell before breakfast. Simon tumbled from his bunk, naked, and cowered at the far end of the room. Paul watched impassively from his bunk.

Louie stepped forward, and Simon held up his arms to shield himself.

'Look,' Louie said, 'about yesterday: we didn't know, OK? We're sorry.'

Gary shuffled awkwardly alongside him. 'Yeah,' he said. 'Sorry. We didn't know.'

And, with that, they both turned and left.

Simon was flabbergasted. No one on the wing messed with those two; not even Spalding's gang.

He tried to question Tim about this new-found amnesty. Tim just shrugged. 'I guess they lose interest,' he said, and pitched into his work.

'But Gary and Louie . . .'

'They're brutal lovers,' said Tim quietly, 'and they won't ever take no for an answer – but they're not vicious. They don't hurt people, except by accident.'

'But they apologised to me.'

'Then you're lucky,' Tim replied. 'They like you.'

Ten

Paul had seen Gary and Louie's apology, and been impressed, though he'd tried not to show it.

'The way I heard it,' he said, 'they're ex-American marines. Hard as fuck. No one fucks with them. So what's up? Who're you going down on?' He was trying to sound cynical and contemptuous, like Spalding always did. 'You must be fucking the governor.'

He'd mentioned Gary and Louie's apology to Spalding, who had reacted with fury. 'I don't want to talk about that little ponce!' he'd ranted. 'We can't touch him! He's a fucking choirboy!'

Paul hadn't asked for clarification — there was an accepted vocabulary on the wing, and it was just assumed you understood it. It was bad manners not to. He drew his own conclusions. A choirboy. Singing for his supper.

Paul watched Simon carefully. Could Spalding be right? 'Spalding reckons you're a nark,' he said. 'You and your boyfriend.'

'What?'

'That bloke from the laundry room that you're so pally with.'

'A nark.'

'An informer,' said Paul impatiently.

'I know what a nark is,' Simon said pettishly. 'I'm not. Of course I'm not. What do I know? No one tells me anything in here.'

'You've got eyes, haven't you?' snapped Paul. 'Anyway, that's what Spalding told me. That's why people leave you alone.'

'If I'm a nark, why doesn't Spalding get me?' Simon asked.

Paul pondered the question. He couldn't come up with an answer.

Spalding, in truth, was much more preoccupied with Simon and Paul's neighbour – 'the nonce', as Spalding invariably called him. He was annoyed that someone had got to the nonce first. On the day of John's release from the infirmary, Spalding was in a grimly upbeat mood, as if preparing to attend the funeral of an old enemy. Paul saw him chatting to one of the guards, and the two of them laughing. He recognised the screw – Dave, the one who had searched him so diligently during his induction. Dave shot him a sensuous wink, and carried on with his conversation.

At four that afternoon, Jock appeared at the door of Paul's cell. 'He's coming,' Jock said to him.

Paul jumped down from his bunk and followed Jock into the next cell – the nonce's cell. Spalding was already in there, his albino eyes flashing with expectancy. Another of his cronies, a big, moronic skinhead called Ant, was also there. Paul and Jock joined them, and waited. There was an air of forced nonchalance as they stood about – no one seemed to know what to say.

They heard footsteps in the corridor, and the door swung open. The nonce was standing there, escorted by Dave the screw. When he saw them waiting in his cell, he turned in panic towards Dave. Dave smiled, and pushed him into the cell, closing the door on their private party.

'You're a disgrace!' the nonce shouted through the door to his gaoler.

Paul heard the key turn in the lock – they were locked in. The nonce turned to face them.

'Four against one, is it?' the nonce asked.

'Shut it, vicar,' Spalding spat. 'You're a disgrace to the church, you know that?'

'Young man, people better qualified than you to judge have already told me that. If you have nothing more interesting to tell me —' He doubled over as Spalding's fist pistoned into his stomach. Gasping for breath, he straightened up again. 'You'll have to do better than that,' he said, staring Spalding in the face.

Spalding stared around at his comrades. 'Well?' he shrieked. 'What the fuck are you waiting for?'

Ant was in first, shoulder-charging the nonce into the wall. John hit it with a sickening thud. Ant clubbed him to the floor with his fists, and then started kicking him. Jock joined in.

Spalding was watching Paul. Swallowing hard, Paul stepped forward and kicked out at the nonce's back. He kicked him in the kidneys, once, twice. He felt a fury welling up inside him. He saw the same fury in the faces of his comrades. His cock was half hard as he kicked and kicked, until the nonce was insensible on the floor of his cell.

The door opened and Dave beckoned.

'Don't cash all your chips in, now,' he said. 'Have some fun.'

'That's just the beginning, vicar,' Spalding hissed at the nonce and, beckoning to his troops, left the cell.

Paul and Jock ran back to Spalding's cell and threw themselves down on the settee. They were savage, breathless, laughing. Spalding didn't join them — he was pacing the corridor, his face like thunder.

'Ach, ignore him,' said Jock. 'He gets like this. He wanted the bloke to crawl to him, and he didn't — that's all.'

Paul felt exhilarated — incredibly alert, vibrant, his heart pounding. He still had a hard-on. So did Jock, he could see. The lanky Scot was surreptitiously playing with it through the thin material of his prison trousers.

'You horny?' asked Paul. Jock nodded.

'Me too.' Like Jock, he began squeezing his hard cock through his trousers. He lowered his buttocks on the seat, spreading his legs slightly. Next to him, Jock did the same. Paul undid his fly and put his hand inside. Again, Jock copied him. Paul gave his balls a squeeze, ran his fingers up the hard pole of his cock, peeled the foreskin back and felt the rough lick of his trouser cloth on his sensitised bell-end.

He looked across at Jock. Jock was staring into his own lap, his straggly once-highlighted hair hanging messily down his face and chest. He had pulled his long cock free of his trousers. He played the loose foreskin back and forth across the bulb beneath. Paul, too, freed his cock from his trousers and stroked it.

Jock glanced at Paul's hard cock, then caught his eye, grinning. He reached across and swatted Paul's hand from his cock. Paul felt the pressure of Jock's fingers close around his shaft and begin twisting it about like a gear stick. He reached across and gripped Jock's hard pole, and did the same.

Jock bent Paul's prick hard to the left.

'Ow!' Paul howled, and rolled on to his side. 'Right . . .' He gave Jock's prick a ferocious tug, bending it forward with all his strength.

Jock pivoted forward. 'You bastard!' he shouted. Paul tugged again, and Jock twisted to the floor.

'Right . . .' He still had hold of Paul's cock, and dragged him by it off the settee and on to the floor. Paul collapsed on top of Jock, laughing.

Each paused to catch his breath. Paul looked down at Jock's cock. He began stroking it properly now, with a long, smooth action that stretched Jock's ample foreskin out beyond his cock-head before letting it relax back, then drawing it down the Scot's pole to reveal the leaking purple bulb beneath.

Paul felt Jock's hand start to move up and down his cock. He watched his cock-head appearing and disappearing as his foreskin rolled back and forth in the Scots lad's firm grip. Neither was laughing now – each was concentrating on the other's prick.

'Christ . . .' Ant, the big-boned, stupid skinhead had just walked through the door. 'Fucking homo action!' He dropped into a squat in front of them and began undoing his own fly. 'Circle jerk,' he chuckled.

He had his cock out in a second – already half-hard. He began stroking it to its full length and thickness. Paul looked at it as it swelled – and went on swelling. Its length was impressive – so was its girth – but the thing which made Paul start was the size of Ant's cock-head.

Ant spat into his hand and started working directly on the head with his palm, smearing his saliva over its bevelled surface, gripping it with his fingers, kneading it almost like dough. He stuck his other hand inside his trousers, underneath his balls, between his legs, stroking his perineum. Paul thought Ant might be putting a finger up his arse.

'Last one to come's a homo,' grunted Ant.

'Right,' said Jock, 'you're on.'

He began stroking Paul's prick hard. With his other hand, he appeared to be copying what Ant was doing. Paul felt Jock's clumsy fingers poking their way into his flies, tweaking at his balls, roughly rubbing his perineum. He opened his legs to make it easier.

'I could use some work down there, too,' Jock said.

Paul reached for Jock's trousers with a little trepidation – Jock wasn't the cleanest bloke on the wing – and stuck his hand inside. His fingers ran through a coarse undergrowth of pubic hair, over his balls and down on to his perineum. He rubbed as Jock rubbed, and stroked as Jock stroked.

Ant sounded as if he was getting close. He breath was becoming short.

'Shit,' said Jock. He moved his hand back along Paul's perineum and extended a finger between his arse-cheeks. With his other hand, he kept a steady rhythm on Paul's hard prick. Paul twitched involuntarily as Jock rested a finger on his ring-piece and began vibrating it. He reached far back into Jock's trousers and found his hairy cheeks, his hairy hole. He too nested a finger there, and began to quickly wiggle it. Jock let out a long sigh of pleasure.

'Christ,' muttered Ant. His head was thrown back, his eyes tight shut. One hand was still busily at work inside his trousers, between his own legs, while the other maintained a quickening pace on his cock-head and upper shaft.

'Right,' said Jock. He pushed a finger hard and straight into Paul's arse. A sudden flush swept through Paul's body. His orgasm was suddenly and unexpectedly upon him. His orgasm was spinning out of control. He snatched his cock from Jock's fist as it started to spurt, and rubbed furiously, jetting spunk high into the air.

Ant came seconds later, pivoting forward, firing his hot load into Paul's face.

Finally, Jock came in a slow flood, spilling like lava, messily over Paul's hand.

'Well, look at this.' Spalding was standing in the doorway. He kicked a chair savagely. 'I'm surrounded by fucking homos,' he spat.

John lay on the floor of his cell a long time after the attack. It was painful when he moved. He thought he might have some cracked ribs. He ought to go back to the infirmary.

He smiled grimly to himself. No. Spalding would have to kill him before he'd be driven off the wing. Gingerly, he picked himself up, wincing with the pain.

The pain was almost pleasurable. It fuelled his sense of purpose. He thought of saying a prayer, then dismissed the notion. He knew how the flagellants of old felt, the hermits, the Stylites. There was no need for him to pray: right now, he felt hot-wired into the Almighty.

Eleven

Nobody expected to see John at breakfast the next day. The word had gone round that Spalding had passed sentence on him, and that the sentence would be carried out any day now.

The thought troubled Simon. He kept remembering that John had willingly shouldered the burden that ought to have been his.

He sat with Tim and another young lad called Martin, with whom Tim seemed to share some unspoken complicity. Martin worked as a general dogsbody in the governor's office. The rest of the company avoided him, like they did Tim and Simon. They ate practically alone at a table.

John's entrance was greeted by shocked, expectant silence. All eyes were upon him. He looked rough – he walked with a hunched, pained gait. His face was cut and swollen.

He picked up his plate and filled it from the serving hatch. He looked around the room.

Then he sat at Spalding's table.

Spalding rose slowly, an albino thundercloud. He looked at John through his malevolent red eyes for a long moment, during which his fury seemed to ignite an explosion in him. He leapt on to the long table and bore down on John in two huge strides, sending his comrades' half-eaten breakfasts flying into the air and into their laps. He was holding a knife.

He dived from the table on to John, sending his chair flying backward. They crashed to the floor. Spalding had his knife pressed against John's throat.

Simon made to rise to his feet, but Tim stopped him.

'I've got to try and do something,' Simon pleaded.

'Sit down,' said Tim quietly. 'Spalding won't kill him. Not here. He can't – there are two many witnesses. Screws.'

Two officers, as usual, stood with their backs to the wall, looking anywhere and everywhere except at the possible murder happening in front of them.

'Spalding's made a mistake,' said Tim. 'He'll have to back down.'

Everyone seemed frozen to their seats. Nobody seemed to be breathing, even. Not even Spalding's cronies. Their eyes told a story of uncertainty, confusion, conflict. They didn't know what to do. They remained as immobile as the rest of the company. Some had spilt food drying in their laps. They let it.

Paul sat among them. His reaction, his expression, was exactly like theirs. For the first time, Simon realised just how much Paul had adapted to their world.

'Beg for your life, vicar,' Spalding snarled. 'Tell me why I shouldn't just cut your throat.'

'Because you're too smart for that, Spalding,' John replied with unnerving calm. 'And because you're too much of a coward.'

Tables away, Simon heard Spalding's breathing becoming fast and harsh. He saw the albino's grip on his victim tighten, the knife blade press harder into John's neck. A bead of blood appeared at its tip.

'You're clever, Spalding, I know that. Everyone in here walks in fear of you – but any one of us, almost, could beat you in a fair fight. But you never let it come to that, do you? You hide behind your cronies, who're too stupid for the most part to think of anything better to do than run around hurting people on your say-so. And your reputation, of course, as a hard man. You fake these tempers – convince everyone you're a psycho. You're faking, now. Believe me, I spent enough of my life as a fake to know one when I see one.'

Spalding released the knife pressure on John's throat. He straightened up and took a step backward. John sat up, and wiped the dust and food from his shirt. He looked up at Spalding. 'People fear you because they don't perceive the trick,' he said. He shrugged his shoulders apologetically. 'I know the trick, so I don't fear you.'

Spalding's face creased with fury. He let our a sort of roar, and began laying into John with his boots, sobbing with fury as he kicked him.

John barely flinched – he looked as if he wasn't feeling the blows.

Spalding's cronies were on their feet, arguing.

'We've got to get him off him!' Blue, the Chinese guy, was arguing. 'He's going to kill him.'

Others wanted to steam in with Spalding.

Paul was still and tense, watching and listening, his eyes flashing between his debating comrades.

In the end, they did nothing. Spalding gave John a final savage kick, and stormed, choking with emotion, from the canteen.

The rest of the meal was taken in silence. Nobody knew what to say; this was something close to embarrassment. John picked himself up and sat down to eat what remained of his meal. He ate slowly, then rose with dignity, and walked back to his cell.

'Where were you fuckers?'

Spalding was in a cold fury. Paul stood at the end of a shuffling line – Jock, Vince and Blue (Paul was sure they were holding hands, behind their backs), Ant and others. They were crowded into Spalding's cell.

'We weren't sure,' Blue ventured.

'Don't think I didn't hear every fucking word you said,' Spalding spat. 'All of you.' He stood directly in front of Vince and Blue. 'Especially you two queers,' he spat.

'We'll get him tonight, Spalding,' Jock interjected. 'You an' me an' Vince an' Blue – we'll go into his cell and do him.'

'Maybe,' Spalding mused. 'There's something I've got to sort out first. Now get out!' Suddenly he seemed angry again. 'Go on, all of you. Fuck off! You all make me sick!'

The line shuffled sheepishly from the room.

'Paul,' Spalding said. He beckoned him back into the cell. When the rest of the gang had departed, he said. 'Sit down.'

Paul sat.

'I don't hold you as much to blame as the others for what happened this morning,' he said. 'You're still new here. You don't know the honour codes. You were just following them, not knowing any better. I understand that.'

Paul said nothing.

Spalding seemed lost in thought. 'I mean – the others, they all get a damn good life on this wing because of me. They know that. Now Jock – he's loyal enough, I suppose. Blue and Vince, though, they trouble me. They're fucking queers, I swear. Now, God knows, you've got to have a woman in here – everybody knows that. You'd go mad without one. But those two –' He screwed up his nose and hawked a great gob into the sink. 'Their days are numbered with the firm, I think.'

He sprang to his feet. 'Come with me,' he said. 'See a bit of the prison. It's time you started learning the ropes properly. I can teach you. Who better?' He walked from the cell, Paul trailing in his wake. 'You'll do all right with me,' he said. 'Anything you want for your cell, anything you want to know – just ask me.'

'What's a choirboy?' asked Paul.

He followed Spalding down through the recreation area and into a far corridor that Paul had never been down before. Nobody much, apart from the cleaners, ever used it. It led to the offices, and then off the wing.

A screw sat in a glass booth at the corridor's end. Next to the booth was a sliding metal door. The door was shut. As they stood before it, there was a hydraulic hiss, and another slid closed behind them.

'The airlock,' Spalding said. 'Metal detectors and the like. Camera.' He pointed to a lens set in the roof.

They waited a few minutes, and then the door ahead of them opened.

They were in a wide, carpeted expanse with oak doors leading off two walls. Rubber plants stood in pots. Quiet classical music played. A guard sat at a desk.

'Tell Craigie I want to see him,' Spalding said to the guard.

'Senior Officer Craigie's busy,' said the guard. 'What business do you have out here?'

'That's for Craigie to find out,' Spalding hissed. 'Tell him I'm here!'

'It's all right, Officer Drake.' Paul spun around to see the hawklike face of Craigie standing at his shoulder. 'Travis, isn't it?' Craigie said. 'Paul Travis.'

'Yeah,' said Paul.

'I've heard things about you, Travis,' Craigie said. 'Good things, mostly. I've heard you can handle yourself.'

Paul saw Spalding scowl. 'I do my best,' he said gruffly.

'Good,' said Craigie. 'Now, why don't the pair of you come into my office?'

'I think this had better be just between you and me,' Spalding cut in. 'You wait here,' he said to Paul.

Craigie raised an eyebrow. 'As you wish, my little kapo,' he said. 'Just you and me, then.' He ushered Spalding into his office. Paul took a seat next to the door, and did his best to listen to the conversation inside.

'I expected to see you, Spalding,' Craigie said. 'Sit down.'

'I'll stand,' Spalding said. He was edgy, Paul could tell. 'I want your permission for an execution,' he said.

'Yes, I imagine you do,' Craigie replied smoothly. 'Your priest friend. I heard about the incident in the canteen this morning. I heard he faced you off in front of the whole wing.'

'I'd have killed him,' Spalding spat. 'I swear to God! I've done it before –'

'And that's why you're in here,' Craigie interrupted. 'A nasty, messy murder, for which you were picked up the same day.' His voice neared the door – he was pacing. Paul immediately picked up an old magazine and pretended to read it. 'I give you virtually a free hand down there,' Craigie growled. 'And, in return, I expect you to keep order. I expect you to use your brains, Spalding, and not indulge in bad melodramatics every time someone clever-dicks you. Executions – as you call them – draw attention. We'd have every politician, every bleating liberal down on our backs. Enquiries . . .'

Craigie's voice receded from the door, and took on a conciliatory tone. 'Don't worry about your priest,' he said. 'Wear him down. Let the stigma of being a nonce take its toll. Let the world forget about him. Then let some moron from the basic life skills class beat his head in, in the showers.' Paul heard the creak of a chair, and a drawer opening. Papers shuffling. 'Now go,' Craigie said. 'Keep order.'

John lay in his bed in pain. The moment he had pushed his cell door to, his composure had abandoned him. Pain had washed over him – the cracked ribs of yesterday now screamed at him. He felt dizzy. He staggered to the metal toilet at the far end of the cell and collapsed on top of it, vomiting a great gout of blood into the bowl.

He knew he couldn't take too much more of this.

He also knew how easy it would be for Spalding and his mates to catch him in some quiet corner where there were no officers and no witnesses, and kill him in a second. He thought perhaps he would fight back – he still believed he could beat Spalding in a fair fight.

No, Spalding was far too clever to be drawn. And besides, this was the work of the Lord. Swords into ploughshares, and all that.

All he could do was wait. God was with him.

His musings were interrupted about an hour before lock-up.

There was a tapping at his door. He tensed – then forced himself to relax. His enemies would hardly knock.

The lad from the next cell – Simon – entered the room. John could tell from Simon's face that he was in a state.

'Have you had yourself seen to?' Simon asked.

John shook his head. It was painful to speak.

'You should.' Simon lightly touched a bloodstain on his shirt. 'Here,' he said. 'Let me help you. Get you into bed.'

John allowed the lad to unbutton his shirt and remove it. It was a painful and difficult business. In places, where Spalding's boots had broken the skin, the shirt was stuck to the skin with dried blood.

The shirt was removed. Simon knelt down and carefully took first one then the other of John's shoes off. He took John's socks off, then began to unbutton his trousers. John lifted his buttocks to allow their removal. He grimaced with the pain.

When he was down to the older man's underpants, Simon covered him with a blanket, and knelt quietly by the side of the bed. 'That was a brave thing you did for me,' he said.

'I acted according to my vocation,' John replied, 'and my conscience.'

'All the same,' said Simon. He lightly fingered a bruise on John's shoulder. John winced slightly. 'It must hurt like hell,' Simon whispered.

John smiled weakly.

'I hate pain,' said Simon. 'I hate violence, aggression. I hate this place.' He leant forward and gently kissed the bruise.

There was a slight twinge of pain, accompanied by a pleasing coolness about the touch of his lips.

He kissed a bruise on John's chest, his lips wet and soothing, then he kissed another. He kissed the edge of a cluster of bruises which disappeared beneath John's blanket. John watched as Simon lowered the blanket, his lips tracing the mass of purple which ran down John's body.

His cock was hard. The memory of gentleness – Toby's

gentleness – suffused him. He wondered where this lad would stop.

Simon pushed the blanket down further. The angular bulge in John's underpants poked up from the blanket's fringe. Simon twitched the blanket to the floor. Gently kissing John's flat stomach, he let his hand close over the white cotton ridge. He squeezed. John gasped slightly. Simon began rubbing John's cock through the material, loosely at first, and then more firmly. John felt a frisson of pleasure; a droplet of pre-come seeped through the stretched cotton at the point where his cock-head pressed against it. Simon extended a thumb and rubbed the juice into the cotton, on to the head beneath.

Slowly he eased the elastic waistband over the swollen member and pulled the pants down. John winced again; even his hips were bruised. Simon began to gently masturbate him, drawing John's foreskin slowly back to its fullest extent, so that his cock-head was wholly exposed, then slowly forward again, over the swollen orb. John bucked his hips a little, then let out a moan of pain.

In spite of his discomfort, the gentleness of Simon's lovemaking soothed him like a balm.

Simon was looking up at him, staring into his eyes. John wasn't sure what he could see in his eyes – compassion, certainly; fear; and longing. Above all, a desperate longing. It wasn't for him, John was sure, but he hoped that he was at least bringing something to Simon of whatever was the object of his longings – whatever it was he'd lost.

Simon released his hold on John's cock and instead cupped his balls in his hand. He lowered his head over the shaft, then, with a final, parting glance at John, sank his delicate mouth around it. He drew John deep into his throat, and held him there. John's cock pulsed, cool and wet. After a long pause, Simon drew John's cock back out of his mouth, nipping the ridge of his helmet ever so slightly with his teeth.

He caught John's eye again briefly, then plunged again, sucking in John's cock, dragging it into the sea-cave of his mouth with the slightest lapping sound.

John was drowning in the sensation. He no longer felt the pain of his bruises. He no longer half heard Spalding's footstep outside the door every minute. He focused on the feeling in his cock – the delicious, wet pressure of Simon's throat, the slap of his lips, the tickle of his tongue along the sides of the shaft, the occasional nip of teeth.

Simon's movements became faster. John's cock was buffeted now as Simon rose and fell, his teeth grazing, his ridged palate rubbing on the fat cock-head. John tensed. He placed a hand on Simon's golden head, clutched at his hair. He felt a distant orgasm building. He clenched his fists and toes.

He remained on the brink. Simon's head thundered up and down his cock, slurping wetly, greedily. John's mouth was open. He was drawing in breath in rapid, staccato gasps. His eyes were shut tight.

There was a rushing in his ears. He began to tremble – arms, legs, torso.

He came. His entire body spasmed, sending darts of pain through every cut and bruise. His cock jerked from Simon's mouth and danced like a fire-hose, dousing Simon's face and his chest with sticky white globules of spunk.

He relaxed, breathless and panting. He was still holding Simon by the hair. He stroked it now, watching it fall in great fronds through his fingers.

Quite unexpectedly, he began to cry. There was no bitterness in his tears – just the by-now-familiar, gentle longing which haunted the cells and corridors of this place, riding always just out of sight, behind the anger.

'Thank you,' he said quietly to Simon. 'You can't possibly know what that meant to me.'

Twelve

Simon saw little of John over the following days. He barely seemed to leave his priest's cell. He seemed to have stopped eating. Once Simon went in to see him, but found him on his knees, staring into a corner, an ecstatic, frozen look on his face. Taking him to be at prayer, Simon left quietly. He wondered whether John were preparing himself for death. The thought scared him, and he suppressed it.

Work in the laundry was far from arduous, even though Gorman did nothing but wank in the storeroom all day. Everybody was entitled to clean bedding once a fortnight; most people didn't bother.

A few were more than fastidious. Spalding sent a young Indian lad called Sanjay in for clean bedding on a practically daily basis.

'Spalding has to get his little tribute out of everybody,' said Tim. 'Even the laundry.'

Sanjay proved to be good company. He was always so cowed around Spalding, gazing at the ground like a servant, waiting to receive his orders, most of the time being ignored. Away from the albino's thrall, he proved to be cheerful and even shyly witty, with a brilliantly white, toothy grin.

In a quiet moment, Simon asked Sanjay why he trailed after

Spalding all day. Sanjay stared into his lap and shook his head, his thick, long curtain of hair quite covering his face, and wouldn't say. He spoke little of his master, but Simon could always tell as soon as he came into the laundry what sort of mood Spalding was in. He could read it in the bruises on Sanjay's face. They got worse in the days after Spalding's stand-off with John.

One day, he could barely talk.

'Why does he do it to you?' Simon asked, more out of despairing pity than anything else.

Sanjay tried to smile. 'I'm his punch-bag and his laundry-bag,' he mumbled. Simon could hear the tremor in his voice.

He tended to see Paul only at the beginnings and ends of days now, and then they barely communicated. Sloughing off the strutting arrogance of his days, Paul seemed subdued, tired, by the time he came to bed.

Simon became aware of Paul looking at him with a curious, queasy expression – a sort of revolted sympathy, Simon began to think. Whenever he became aware of Paul's lingering eyes, Paul would immediately turn his attention elsewhere.

Simon challenged him about it.

Paul was cryptic. 'Just trying to imagine . . . that's all,' he said, turning over and going to sleep.

Simon spent most of his waking hours with Tim, either in the laundry, or after work in his cell. He was already (though he hadn't dared voice the thought) starting to think of Tim as a sort of boyfriend – not that that would ever do in here, of course. They talked inconsequential love-talk most of the day: there was never much news in prison, and their sweet nothings helped conjure the illusion they were somewhere else. Simon thought of telling Tim about his night-time encounter with John, but decided against it. It still felt a little strange to him. In an odd way, it had been for Simon a sort of pilgrimage. Tim wouldn't understand. Simon barely understood, himself.

Tim had a cell to himself – and a bigger one that Simon shared with Paul. Simon was impressed. 'How d'you manage this?' he asked, flopping down on the bed.

Tim turned away from him. 'You ask a lot of questions,' he said.

'Only because I want to get to know you better,' said Simon. 'I want to know all about you.'

'I'm in jail, OK?' said Tim tetchily. 'I'm a prisoner, just like you, trying to get along as best I can.'

'What's a choirboy?'

There was a long pause. 'Where did you hear that?' Tim asked quietly.

'It's a word I've heard floating round. I've heard it used about me.'

'Well, you needn't worry about it,' said Tim, 'because you're not one.'

'Everybody seems to think I am.'

'And so you get treated with a bit of respect. So no one beats you up any more. Be grateful.' Quite suddenly, he dropped on to the bed next to Simon and kissed him on the lips. He was smiling, the upturn of his nose wrinkling with pleasure. 'Be happy,' he said. 'We've got each other.'

He threw his arms around Simon in a bear hug. Simon hugged him back. Their lips slapped and locked together. Tim drove forward with his tongue; Simon's tongue darted around it like a fish. They mouth-sparred for several minutes, laughing as their tongues jousted.

Tim rose to his feet. Simon followed, kissing still, their lips barely separated. Like two drunken men, they waltzed and stumbled about the cell, kissing throughout. Simon felt Tim blindly grappling for his belt. He managed to release it, and opened the button on Simon's trousers. He pulled down the zip, and the loose garments fell to the floor. He stepped out of them, and the dance continued.

His cock was hard, pushing against the tightness of his pants. He fumbled with Tim's trousers, clumsily undoing fly buttons, not undoing enough, dragging the trousers down half-opened, so that they caught on Tim's erect cock and he toppled to one side, laughing.

Simon caught him and pulled him close. Their cocks, restrained by prison underwear, bumped and squashed together. Tim reached down and caught hold of both pairs of pants, and pulled. Twin cocks sprang out – Simon's tall, slim, stately member and Tim's smaller, circumcised, bolt-hard prick – bouncing and bobbing into one another.

Simon hugged Tim tight to him; Tim hugged back. He started rocking with his hips, grinding his cock up and down Simon's belly. Simon began moving his pelvis in sympathy. Their cocks rubbed together, planing roughly up and down in the tight press of their bodies.

Simon pushed Tim backward, and lowered him on to the bed. For the first time, his lips left Tim's. He kissed him gently on the neck, on the chest, he ran his tongue around Tim's nipples, enjoying the salty taste of his sweat, drying from the laundry room.

He kissed harder, sucking flesh up into his mouth. He sank his teeth into Tim's neck –

Tim flinched, and sat upright. 'No lovebites,' he said tersely.

Simon was startled. 'All right,' he said.

Tim was smiling again. He turned Simon on to his back on the bed, and rolled on top of him. They kissed again, with urgent passion now. Tim was grinding his hard cock into Simon's groin, his balls, the side of his prick. Simon watched Tim's cheeks rippling and flowing as Tim stimulated his cock.

Tim paused, and reached under the mattress. He produced a condom, which he deftly unwrapped. 'Are you ready for this, darling?' he asked.

Simon nodded, and kissed him again. He plucked the condom from Tim's hand and placed it on his circumcised knob, rolling it down with two fingers. Then he lay back, raised his hips from the bed and opened his legs.

Tim spat into his hand and smeared it over Simon's arsehole, working it in with one delicious, slippery finger. He sank the finger in deeper, and Simon wriggled with delight. He withdrew the finger, and placed the head of his cock in Simon's crack. Simon hooked his legs over Tim's shoulders. Tim pushed forward, working his cock into Simon's hungry hole. Simon felt his muscles relax around Tim's cock, letting it slide in deeper. Smiling, Tim reached forward and gripped Simon's throbbing hard-on. As he began to undulate his hips, working Simon's arsehole with his prick, so he began to wank Simon with long, sensuous strokes. Simon gazed blissfully at Tim's pretty, freckled face, screwed up with concentration and desire, his eyes shut and mouth open.

Tim ran a tantalising fingernail down the underside of Simon's cock, pausing at the frenum, and again where his ball sac began. He cupped Simon's balls, testing their weight. He tugged sharply at them, making Simon clench his buttocks tight around Tim's cock. 'Mm. Nice,' whispered Tim.

He tugged at Simon's balls again. Simon clenched again around Tim's pistoning prick. He moved his own hand to his cock and started wanking himself as Tim rubbed his perineum and played with his balls.

Tim shifted his balance to the balls of his feet, raising Simon's buttocks. Simon clung tightly to Tim's neck and shoulders with his legs. Tim was fucking him faster now. Simon began wanking himself faster, keeping pace with Tim. Suddenly, Tim rose to his feet, lifting Simon's legs and buttocks into the air. He leant forward, bearing down on Simon, using him as a prop while thrusting his cock down into him. Simon's head was buried in the pillow, his neck bent, his shoulders braced.

Tim began to fuck frantically, his mouth open, his breath ragged. He sighed slightly as his sheathed cock exploded inside Simon, as his body bucked and bucked again.

Simon's orgasm was not long in coming, sending a great, shivering fountain of spunk over his own chest and face.

Tim collapsed to one side, laughing breathlessly. 'That was fucking great,' he declared.

'I know,' said Simon. 'I was there.'

They lay close together, hugging, petting, dreading the inevitable moment of their parting, until lock-up, when an impatient screw sent Simon scurrying back to his own loveless cell. Paul was asleep, or pretending to be asleep. Simon lay awake deep into the night, serene – almost – watching the stars through the little barred window.

Thirteen

———————

Spalding was like a time bomb. Since his meeting with Craigie, Paul had seen him beat up Sanjay because his head got in the way of the television screen, throw a chair through the same screen a day later, and banish Vince and Blue from his cell. Paul was with him most of the time, now; the rest of the gang, Spalding had little patience with. He talked about the nonce all the time.

'Craigie knows I've got to do this. He understands.'

Paul had nodded in sympathy. He'd already heard this a dozen times.

'But the boys,' Spalding had lamented bitterly. 'Can I trust the boys?'

'Course you can, boss,' Paul assured him. 'They're right behind you. We're all behind you.'

'You don't know them, Paul – without me to hold them together, they'd be like the fraggles.'

'We'll do him,' Paul had said, coaxingly. 'You, me, the boys – we'll do him together. I tell you what, I'll go round and have a word with them. Gee them all up.'

Spalding had looked ready to hug him, for a moment.

★

'Spalding's losing it.'

Ant peered at Paul from beneath heavy brows.

'I'm telling you because I respect you, Ant, but Spalding's losing it big time. You saw what that fucking nonce did to him. Faced him off, in front of the whole wing.'

Ant nodded uncertainly.

'And you saw what he did to his TV. I tell you, he's losing it, Ant. I don't trust his judgement any more.'

Paul watched Vince and Blue closely. They seemed to snatch every moment they could to be alone together. Paul suspected Spalding was right about them. One evening, after the canteen had shut down, he followed them into the big kitchens, keeping out of sight.

They thought they were alone. They kissed, hurriedly, furtively, passionately. Their hands clutched at each other's clothes. They tore one another's shirts open, sending buttons flying; they tugged at one another's trousers, pulling them down to their ankles, and kicked them off. Their cocks strained at the taut cotton of their pants.

Each grabbed the other's cock through the material, kneading it urgently. Blue dropped to his knees and nuzzled the stretched fabric around Vince's cock. He folded his lips over the cotton-covered cock-head and sucked his rockabilly friend through the cloth. Vince clutched at the Chinese lad's long, tied-back black hair and moaned slightly. The cotton was wet from Blue's saliva and Vince's leaking cock-juices. Blue caught the damp cotton between his teeth and pulled, stretching Vince's pants away from his long, stiff, circumcised prick and pulling them down. His mouth returned to Vince's exposed prick and closed hungrily around it, gobbling him quickly while he caressed his inner thighs and tickled his balls.

Vince stripped off his shirt and stepped out of his pants. Blue, too, tore his shirt off, never breaking mouth-stroke on Vince's prick. He peeled off his pants to reveal his upright prick, thick and squat with its upward curve. Both lads were now naked – one standing, one squatting – except for their boots and socks.

Blue removed his mouth from Vince's cock and twisted around. Vince opened his legs, and Blue slipped his head between them, arching his neck back, licking and biting at the underside of Vince's heavy balls, at his taut perineum, at his arse-crack.

Vince bent forward and pulled his buttocks apart with his hands. Blue's tongue descended on his dark hole. His lips formed a seal around it. Gradually, still rimming him, Blue drew Vince down on to his hands and knees. He broke the seal and rummaged in his trouser pocket. A condom. He rolled it over his prick and mounted Vince, guiding his prick towards his friend's arsehole with his fingers. He slowly inserted himself, leaning forward over Vince's arched back, sinking his teeth into his shoulder and pushing forward with his hips. Vince gasped slightly as Blue's cock sank deep into him.

Paul, watching from cover, smiled as Blue's cock began its rhythmic drilling of Vince's arse.

The Chinese lad reached around the rockabilly's waist and grabbed his cock, wanking in time to his own sweet rhythm. Their heavy boots squeaked against the kitchen's stone floor.

Paul himself was hard. He stroked himself idly through his trousers as he watched his friends fucking doggy style, enjoying the rough feel of the material as much as the floor show.

Blue fucked Vince frantically now; he was rushing headlong towards orgasm. He tugged fast at Vince's cock. Vince gave a little cry; his cock twitched in Blue's hand and began pumping spurt after spurt of come over the stone flags. Blue came quickly after him, his arms clasped tight around Vince's waist, his lips clamped to his neck, his cock thrust deep inside him.

Slowly they separated. Blue kissed Vince lightly on the lips. 'I love you,' he whispered

Paul stepped from the shadows. 'It's all right,' he said. 'I won't tell Spalding.'

★

Paul spoke to many in the gang as the days passed. Conversations born of concern for their overlord, of course. Intimate conversations – not to be spoken of with anyone else.

As he intended, the wing was soon awash with gossip and speculation. The only inmate seemingly unaware of it was Spalding himself. He was busy planning the destruction of his nemesis. He would stand at the far end of the corridor and stare at John's cell for hours, a look of pure malice on his face.

'It's not an execution, as such,' he said to Paul. 'Loads of people survive it.'

Finally, Spalding could stand no more. He summoned the gang, one evening. 'Craigie's given me the go-ahead,' he told them. 'The nonce gets it tomorrow morning.' He talked for another half-hour without stopping. He was badly stoned, and babbling.

Paul left the cell with a headache. He followed Jock to the recreation room. 'Game?' he said, indicating the pool table.

They knocked the balls around for about ten minutes. Paul was concentrating much more on Jock than on the game. Jock was the most loyal of Spalding's lieutenants, and the most intelligent. If Paul got this wrong, he was in trouble.

'Spalding was lying,' he said with studied casualness.

'What?' Jock queried.

'Craigie didn't give him permission to knock off that nonce. I was there – I was outside Craigie's office. He told Spalding to fuck off.'

Jock was motionless for a long time, puffing out his cheeks thoughtfully. 'Nah,' he said at last. 'Spalding wouldn't be that stupid.'

'I tell you, I was there!' Paul persisted. 'You've seen what he's been like recently.'

'So, what are you saying?' Jock asked cautiously.

Paul let out a heavy breath. 'Spalding's a mate,' he said. 'But I'm worried about him.'

When Paul wasn't plotting his coup, he was helping Spalding plan the nonce's demise.

'I'm gonna fucking jug him,' Spalding declared. 'That's what I'm gonna do.'

That was the plan. John would be corralled into the recreation area – there were rarely screws in there – and a jug of boiling hot water laced with sugar would be thrown in his face. The water would stick, and would take his skin off.

'Sometimes they survive,' said Spalding, over and over again.

And then, one day: 'No – we're all going to jug him.'

The word went out the next morning, and the gang assembled. Vince and Blue, Jock, Ant, Rob, Newt, Ginge . . .

'Newt,' said Spalding to a short, ratty-looking bloke with a scar across his mouth, 'you and Ginge get the boilers going. And those big metal jugs.' Newt worked in the kitchens. 'Jock and Ant – you find the nonce. Get him to the rec room. The rest of you, wait in there. Cover the entrances – I don't want him or anybody else leaving. And keep an eye out for screws.'

They moved into their positions. The rec room was at its most crowded at this time of day – the lull just before dinner, when stomachs were at their emptiest and minds at their most bored, and tensions were always running high.

As the gang descended, the atmosphere in the room thickened immediately. The action on the pool table stopped. Conversation ceased and eyes were turned from the telly. Just for a moment. Then everybody went back to what they were doing with a forced enthusiasm and concentration which was oppressive.

One or two people tried to slip out. A flick of the fingers from Spalding and one or other gang member moved to block their way. Invariably, they returned to what they had been doing.

Everybody was waiting.

John staggered into the room, shoved from one of the corridors, and fell to the floor. His hands were strapped behind his back with his own belt. Jock and Ant, wielding brooms like spears, prodded him viciously.

Gamely, the nonce staggered to his feet. His eyes blazed.

Spalding stood in front of him. 'Hello, nonce,' he said, sweet as a razor.

Newt and Ginge were dragging the steaming jugs into the room.

'Well?' demanded Spalding, his red eyes flashing around the gang. 'You know what to do.'

Paul could sense the unease of his comrades. Many flashed him uneasy glances – Rob, Blue, even Jock.

It was Jock who strode over and picked up one of the heavy vessels. One by one, the rest of the gang followed suit. Paul too picked one up. It pitched slightly. The lethal, sticky liquid sloshed up the sides.

Everybody else in the room was frozen, silent, watching.

Spalding was the last to arm himself.

'Well, here we are,' he simpered at John. 'Isn't this nice?'

'What's the matter with you, Spalding?' John demanded. 'Why are you acting like this? Like a cheap playground bully. Why haven't you grown out of that? Didn't you get enough love as a child?'

A thrill passed round the room. The nonce was insane.

Spalding's eyes were wide, his mouth frozen in a snarl. 'Oh, nonce,' he whispered. 'Are we going to have some fun with your corpse.'

'Or did your father used to creep into your room at nights and fuck your white little arse? Is that it?'

The gang was motionless. Spalding's eyes raked the room. 'Well?' he demanded again. 'What are you waiting for?'

No one moved. Spalding's eyes darted from one to another. They were all looking at Paul. Waiting for his lead.

Slowly, he put the boiling jug down.

Slowly, one by one, the rest of the gang followed: Vince and Blue, looking relieved; Ant, his clouded brow puzzled and troubled.

Only Jock remained motionless.

'Jock,' Spalding said levelly.

'Sorry, Spalding,' Jock whispered, and put down his jug.

Spalding glared at Paul. 'I'll get you for this, Travis,' he said. 'But first I'm going to deal with this fucking nonce!'

Several things happened at once. Spalding raised the jug to swing it full into John's face. John straightened up, tensed for the pain. Two guards appeared from a side corridor and charged towards them.

And Paul, almost before he knew what he was doing, launched himself across the floor of the rec room and cannoned into Spalding in a sort of half-rugby tackle. Spalding crumpled to one side. The jug flew from his hands and past John's head, and crashed against the far wall.

Spalding was on his feet before Paul. He launched a savage kick at his head. Paul rolled, and the kick barely connected. Spalding was off-balance: Paul grabbed his leg and pivoted to one side. Spalding crashed into an old armchair and sent it crashing on to its front. He tumbled over it, and Paul followed him, leaping over the chair and kicking the crawling Spalding hard in the chest. He went over again, and Paul kicked him again.

With a hiss of malevolence, Spalding staggered to his feet and ran from the room.

Paul looked around. The guards were beating up the nonce. One caught him by his bound wrists and began dragging him from the room.

'Brawling, eh?' the guard said. 'Right, you're on a charge.'

Nobody spoke for a long time in the rec room. Slow and erect, Paul turned and walked out. At once he could hear the dull rumble of voices behind him.

He returned to his cell and picked up his towel, then made for the shower room. His heart was pumping, his skin itched and tingled. His mind was sparking – he felt kind of charlied . . .

A shower, to calm him down.

Was that all? Didn't he feel just a little soiled by all this?

He shook the thought from his head and stripped out of his shoes, his grey shirt and trousers, and plunged into the hot torrents.

The steaming water brought to mind the lethal sugar water in the jugs. For the first time, it occurred to him – he'd almost taken part in the killing of a man today.

He'd stopped it, of course. But hadn't he also encouraged Spalding to do it?

For the first time, it occurred to him he'd played a game with this bloke's life.

There was a noise behind him. Naked, he spun, tensed for danger. It was Vince and Blue. Naked, they stepped into the jets. They were smiling – laughing.

'Boy, oh, boy,' said Vince, 'did you see the look on Spalding's face?'

Each wore an open, untroubled expression which Paul had never seen before. Blue came up close to Paul. 'Thanks,' he said. 'I ain't no murderer.' He kissed Paul gently on the cheek.

'Nor me, neither,' said Vince, and punched Paul playfully on the shoulder.

Suddenly Paul grinned, laughed out loud. He felt . . . happy. Playfully, he punched Vince back. Then he punched Blue. Laughing, they began jabbing and pushing one another about the big shower, naked, soaked, water bouncing off them. Blue's long black hair, untied, was plastered to his neck and shoulders. Vince's rockabilly quiff now sprawled comically over his forehead

Paul could see Blue's neat cock becoming hard. Vince's cock lolled and slapped, half-hard and heavy, against his thighs. Paul's own cock was loosening, swelling, hardening as he charged and skidded about the wet tiled floor.

Blue's feet went from under him. His legs skidded; he grabbed Paul's cock to steady himself. Righting himself, he didn't let go, but squeezed slightly.

Blue and Vince were standing close together. They moved in closer, so that their cocks were almost touching – Vince's tall, straight, circumcised pole and Blue's smaller, dark prick, with its upward curve. Clenching and unclenching, they bobbed their cocks against one another, heads bumping and buffeting, shafts clashing, jousting and laughing. Blue pulled Paul forward by the cock, then released him so that he could join in the tournament.

He clenched, and his long, thick cock bounced off Vince's. Blue's slapped against his. Vince took hold of his own cock, brandished it like a sword, and swung it hard against Paul's balls. Paul grabbed his weapon and retaliated. The three of them cock-fenced, swiping and jabbing, their cocks clashing and bouncing off each other as the warm water showered down over their naked bodies.

Gradually, their cockfight subsided. Blue was actively wanking his cock now; Vince and Paul followed suit, each of them stroking his cock in silence. Blue released his hold on his own shaft and took hold of Paul's. Paul relinquished his grip and allowed Blue to draw his foreskin deliberately back and forth over his swollen cock-head. Vince had taken hold of Blue's hard, curving prick and was wanking it vigorously. Paul himself reached across and took hold of Vince's hard, straight, pole. His fingers squeezed tightly and played back and forth across the ridge of Vince's circumcised helmet.

This reminded Paul of his earliest sexual encounters – hiding out in the boiler room in the basement of the flats with his little friends, daring each other to show their cocks. Paul had instantly become hard – the others had laughed at him, although their cocks were swelling fast. There, among the throbbing boilers, they'd wanked each other off: furtively, mischievously, always risking detection.

Paul had thought he'd left all this far behind. Now, naked in the shower with Vince and Blue, he felt he was rediscovering a long-lost innocence. A glad shudder ran through him as Blue's unfamiliar hand stroked him.

He felt fingers probing at his buttocks – Vince's free hand, seeking his arsehole. Vince pushed a finger inside him, wiggling it, stretching his tunnel. Paul clenched with pleasure. He extended his left hand around Blue's back, running it over his tight, round buttocks, tracing along his arse-crack, settling in the entrance to his tight hole, drilling inward. He felt Blue's sphincter tighten around his finger. He could see Blue's hand reaching for Vince's hole.

Fingers up one another's arses, hands on one another's cocks, the smiles and giggles subsided as each of them neared his climax. Vince came first, his seed spilling warmly out over Paul's hand, his finger jabbing hard into Paul's arsehole. The sensation was enough to push Paul over the top – he felt a sudden rush and his cock erupted in Blue's hand. Blue was coming, too, shooting his seed high into the water jets.

Paul began to laugh. He didn't know why. The other lads began to laugh too. Huddled close, arms around one another, the three of them slumped together, naked, laughing, their softening cocks still dribbling the last of their love-juices.

Paul dried off and returned to the cell. Simon was lying on his bunk, silent and staring.

'What are you staring at, choirboy?' Paul said.

'You,' Simon said blandly. 'Spalding wants to meet you in the rec room tomorrow at six. The whole wing's talking about it.'

Paul jumped up on to his bunk. He should have thought ahead more. He'd have to finish Spalding now. He reckoned he could do it. John had been right – for all Spalding's studied nastiness, Paul reckoned he was a wimp at heart. He was wiry, but not muscular. A pretty-boy in wolf's clothing. He reckoned he could do it. He had to.

The door swung open, and Dave the screw walked in. 'Travis,' he said. 'Travis. Quite the little general, aren't you, Travis?'

Paul didn't reply.

'The SO wants to see you,' Dave said.

'The what?'

'Senior Officer Craigie.' Dave leant in close, his voice low. 'You've been summoned. Come with me.'

Paul followed Dave through the wing, all the time aware of the surreptitious stares of his fellow inmates. One or two smiled quickly at him. Some he could see in fast, whispered conversation, their eyes constantly darting to him, then away again. They passed through the security door – the airlock, as Spalding had called it – and into the plush lobby beyond.

'Go straight in,' said Dave.

Paul cautiously pushed open the door, and walked up to Craigie's desk. Craigie was writing, and didn't look up.

'I heard what happened in the rec room today,' he said at last.

Paul didn't reply.

'I heard you stepped way out of line with Spalding.'

'He was going to kill that bloke,' said Paul. 'The nonce.'

'Don't misunderstand me,' said Craigie, 'Spalding has been unreliable for some time. I'd been hoping a . . . challenger would arise.' He put down his pen and looked at Paul for the first time. His black eyes were cold. 'Nevertheless,' he said, 'the fact remains that you have created a vacuum: you must now fill it.'

He slid open a drawer in his desk, took something out and put it on the table. It was a battery. A big, square PP9, about the size of a man's fist, but much more lethal.

'The guards will be instructed not to interfere,' said Craigie. 'You must finish what you've started.'

Fourteen

Paul lay awake most of that night. Before he went to bed, he took a rugby sock and dropped the battery into it. He tested its weight, swung it a few times. Then he lay down with his weapon clutched in his fist, and tried to go to sleep.

What little sleep he did manage to snatch was restless and fitful and plagued by dreams – disjointed, disturbing dreams which fled on waking, leaving only a vague sense of unease and menace. He woke often and lay motionless, sweating and listening to the slumbering silence, waiting for the never-coming dawn.

When at last the light crept through the little window, he rose. He dressed and went in to breakfast. Hoping he looked more relaxed than he felt, he collected his food and walked slowly and deliberately to the head of Spalding's table, where he sat in the leader's seat.

A murmur went around the hall. The rest of the gang looked tense, nervous, as they sat in rows on either side of him. They ate in silence for once, and left quickly.

They were scared, he realised. Uncertain. They would follow the leader, whether that be he or Spalding, but at the moment they didn't know which way the wind was blowing, and that scared them.

He went around each of them, quietly and privately, as the day ticked away. He said the same thing to each of them.

'I don't expect you to steam in with me,' he said. 'This has to be between me and Spalding. I just want to know you'll stay out of it.'

Their relief was palpable – all of them.

Of Spalding, Paul saw no sign. He made a point of seeming as relaxed as possible – confident, treating this day like any other. He played pool, watched television, chatted amiably about anything except the main business of the day.

By six o'clock, Paul couldn't remember a single conversation he'd had, nor a single programme he'd watched.

At five to six, he left the rec room and returned to his cell. He pulled his weapon from under Simon's mattress, swung it a few times and retraced his steps.

The rec room was full and silent. Everyone was crowded about the walls. The middle of the room was empty – a perfect oval, a little arena. The crowd parted as Paul walked into the room. He stood at its empty centre and surveyed the expectant crowd. Practically everyone was here – the gang, of course; Gary, the huge Texan poof and his big black buddy; even the weird old bloke from the laundry room was there. Even the fraggles had crept out of their holes to watch.

At dead on six, Spalding came. He was carrying the handle of a snooker cue. Paul knew he'd also have his knife on him somewhere and, judging by the glazed, wild-eyed look on his face, he was prepared to use it.

They circled one another slowly, Spalding smiling throughout.

'You're a very stupid man, Travis,' he whispered. 'I thought you were smart, knew which side your bread was buttered on. I'm disappointed in –'

Paul struck. He snapped his arm upward, flicking the sock out at Spalding. It whipped into Spalding's face, the heavy battery catching him sharply on the chin. Not a good shot.

Spalding staggered back slightly, and let out a low gasp of

breath. Paul swung his arm hard now, the battery careering around his head, and brought it crashing down into Spalding's cheek. Spalding fell to one side and let out a cry of pain. Blood spurted out beneath his pale red eye.

Paul closed for the kill – one more blow should put him out of action for weeks. He swung the sock in a wide, fast arc and sent the battery flying at Spalding again. Spalding twisted, and raised the snooker cue. The sock hit it; the battery wrapped itself around the wooden pole. Spalding jerked back on the cue, and the sock was snatched from Paul's grasp. It unwound itself and clattered to the floor.

Spalding grinned unevenly. His cheek was misshapen and swollen, and bright with blood, stark against his white skin.

He lashed out with the cue – he was bloody fast. Paul threw up an arm to defend himself; the cue crashed down on it.

For a moment, Paul's whole body contracted with the pain. He barely saw Spalding bring the bottom of the cue up, fast, into his gut. He doubled over. Spalding brought the cue crashing down on Paul's neck. He sank to the floor. Spalding hit him again and again – head, neck, back. Paul crouched in a ball, covering his head with his hands. His vision was flashing on and off like a light bulb.

The cue bounced from Spalding's hands under the impact of a blow. He began kicking Paul, a huddled ball, viciously in the ribs. Paul rolled over. Spalding kicked him again.

'Well?' Spalding suddenly shouted. He was casting his malevolent red gaze about the room. One by one, the gang stepped forward – Jock first, Blue and Vince bringing up the rear.

They crowded in around Paul, and began kicking him. Some of the kicks were half-hearted – some weren't. None of the gang would meet his suffering eyes.

'All right,' Spalding said at last. 'I'm not going to kill him. Get him up on the snooker table.'

Paul felt himself being lifted, and dumped hard, face down on the torn green baize.

'I'm not going to kill you, Travis,' Spalding said. 'I'm going to make you into my own personal fraggle. My bitch – understand, Travis?' He turned to his loyal lieutenants. 'Hold him down,' he said. 'And get his trousers off.'

Strong hands – Ant's and Rob's – pinned Paul to the table. Other hands – he couldn't see whose – tore at his belt, yanked his trousers and pants from him, pulling them over his shoes.

'Grab his legs,' Spalding ordered. 'Drag him back a bit.'

Paul felt himself being pulled backward along the table, until he felt his balls lodge tight under the top cushion. His legs were held fast, and open.

He looked around the room. It was still packed. Everyone was watching the show.

'Welcome to Fraggle Rock,' hissed Spalding, and pushed between his open thighs. Paul could hear the clink of his belt and the rasp of his zip. He winced and clenched as Spalding thrust three fingers unceremoniously into his arsehole.

'You're tight,' said Spalding. 'Could you possibly be a virgin?' His dry, callused fingers rammed in and out of Paul's burning ring. 'It's been a while since I had a virgin,' he said. 'I'm going to enjoy this.'

He snapped his fingers, and Paul saw one of the gang pass him something. The snooker cue – he felt it butting, hard and cold, against his cheeks, forcing them apart, pile-driving its way into his hole. It hurt like fuck.

Through unfocussed eyes Paul could see the audience watching; he could hear them catcalling. Some had taken their cocks out and were wanking openly at the spectacle of his humiliation. Spalding pushed the snooker cue deeper and deeper into him, twisting it as he pushed. Paul no longer felt the pain of his bruises – all he could feel was his burning arsehole.

His cock was hard – he could see – but he felt nothing down there. They say fear can make you hard . . .

Spalding withdrew the cue and mounted the snooker table, running his long, slim cock along Paul's crack, towards his battered arsehole.

'There,' said Spalding, his cock nestling inside Paul's ring-piece. 'That's loosened you up nicely.'

He jabbed his prick viciously into Paul, withdrew it slowly, jabbed hard again. Faster and faster the stabs came. The hands that gripped Paul's legs pulled hard, jamming his balls against the table's top cushion. Other hands pushed his face into the torn green baize.

Spalding's cock hammered into him. The spectators whooped and wanked.

Paul's own hard cock was rubbed and crushed on the baize in time to Spalding's thrusts.

'Turn his head,' Spalding ordered. 'I want his mouth.'

Paul's head was forcibly twisted. Fingers prised his lips and teeth apart. Spalding was wielding the snooker cue again. It clunked against Paul's cheek, and sank between his lips, into his mouth.

'Taste your shit, fraggle,' gasped Spalding, fucking Paul breathlessly. He jammed the cue into the back of Paul's throat.

Paul felt like choking. The strong taste filled his mouth. His prick was raw and sensitised against the cloth-covered table.

Spalding let out a low groan and lost control of his cock. It began spasming inside Paul as Spalding came, long and fervent.

He leant forward, and spat in Paul's face.

'You're mine whenever I want you, fraggle,' Spalding said. 'Remember that.'

'Will you stop fucking staring at me?' It was driving Paul mad.

Simon lowered his eyes. 'What will you do?' he asked quietly.

'Shut it!' Paul spat.

He didn't know what to do. He'd taken on Spalding and lost. He'd never get the gang behind him, now. He was finished. He was lower than Simon. Lower than John. Spalding was mad, Paul was sure. He could do what he liked to him. Sooner or later, he'd probably kill him.

Every doorway, every corner, became a threat to Paul. Every movement in the corner of his eye, every sudden footfall, seemed to presage a sudden and brutal attack. He took to creeping and skulking. People instinctively avoided him. The actuality of what had happened – he'd been taken, debased in front of the whole wing; he'd been marked – was something he thought little of. The memory was fuzzy. Every time his mind threw it up, his head would start to throb and flash with images – random images and memories. Anything to blot it out.

He became obsessed with the minutiae of moving about the wing in safety – the shadows and footfalls, the voices and the clang of doors.

It did no good. Spalding caught him the next day in a dead-end corridor, lined with the open doors of cells. While Ant and Rob, the two skinheads, held him against the wall, Ant's fist jammed into his mouth, Spalding ripped the seat of his trousers out with his knife and thrust his cock unceremoniously into him. It hurt – Paul clenched in pain around the dry, fast fucking.

'Mm,' Spalding moaned. 'You know how to please me, fraggle.'

Rob reached in and grabbed Paul's bollocks, hard. Paul winced at the sharp, deep pain.

He could taste the sweat on Ant's knuckles. His balls throbbed. Spalding, grunting slightly, stabbed him frantically with his hard, long prick, murder in his red eyes. Paul could sense the listeners behind the open cell doors, all of them knowing exactly what was happening to him.

Spalding came quickly, pulling out at the last minute, firing his load over Paul's buttocks, his perineum; Rob's hand was still pulling at his balls. As Spalding stepped back, Rob tugged hard. Sick with the sudden pain, Paul groaned and sank to the floor. Spalding immediately kicked him, and strode off.

The next day, the same three plus Jock dragged him into the showers, all fully clothed, and played a vicious game of handball – with him as the ball. His feet were kicked out from under him and he was tossed like a sack from one to another of his tormentors while the water soaked them all. Spalding caught Paul and ripped his wet shirt from his back. He tossed him to Jock, who snatched at his trousers. Numbly, knowing he'd come off worse for it, Paul fought back. The others closed in on him, bore him to the tiled floor and tore shoes, trousers and pants from him as he squirmed and twisted and lashed out with his feet.

Spalding was standing over him, coiling and uncoiling a length of plastic-covered wire – a net-curtain rod. Paul closed his eyes and covered his face as Spalding raised his arm and lashed him, again and again – arms, legs, back. He felt the wire bite into his buttock-cheeks. He could already see long, thin red weals rising on his thighs. The hot water stung the wounds.

'This is for the sock,' said Spalding. He gave Paul a final, brutal lick, and tossed the wire to one side. 'Get him up on his knees,' ordered Spalding.

Paul's head was spinning; his whole body ached and stung, and his head throbbed. He was hauled from the floor by Ant and Rob, and made to kneel in front of Spalding. He felt Jock gripping a great handful of hair on the back of his head. He could see Spalding unzipping his soaking wet trousers and pulling out his hard cock. Spalding slapped Paul across the mouth with it several times, then angled it downward, and waited.

'Well?' he said.

Jock tightened his grip on Paul's hair and pushed his head forward on to Spalding's cock. Paul tried to twist, turn his head away, but Jock held him fast. He clamped his mouth tight shut; Spalding's cock-head bumped against his taut lips.

'Make him open, please, Jock,' said Spalding calmly.

'I'll fucking bite it off, I swear!' Paul snarled.

'Then you know I'll kill you,' said Spalding sweetly. 'Jock?'

Jock suddenly clamped a hand over Paul's face, and another over his jaw. Two sets of callused, dirty fingers dug into Paul's lips and forced their way between his teeth. Slowly, Jock prised Paul's jaws apart.

'Gently, now,' said Spalding, and he stepped forward and pushed his cock between Jock's fingers, into Paul's mouth.

Paul struggled in vain against the strong arms which held him on his knees, held his mouth open. He thought his jaw would break beneath Jock's grip. He thought he would choke as Spalding's cock sank deep into this mouth, butting the back of his throat, making him retch. Again and again Spalding plunged Paul's mouth with his swollen prick. Hot water ran in between his lips – between Jock's vicelike fingers – swirling around Spalding's cock, threatening to drown him.

Spalding gripped his hair as his climax approached. His hip thrusts became urgent. With a whispered oath, he shot his load, filling Paul's mouth with spurt after spurt of hot, salty come. He pulled out, breathless, and let the last few drops shoot over Paul's face.

'Hold him,' said Spalding. 'I haven't finished yet.' His cock was softening. With a slight twitch, it began to disgorge again – not spunk, this time, but dark yellow piss. Spalding fired the golden jet into Paul's eyes, into his hair. Piss bounced off Paul's cheeks and chin and neck. Finally he aimed the jet directly into Paul's mouth – still clamped open by Jock. The hot, bitter, salty liquid filled Paul's mouth. It burnt his throat. He retched, and found himself swallowing.

'There now,' said Spalding, shaking the last drops of piss from his cock, and putting it away.

They left him there, naked on the floor of the shower, his mouth awash with piss and come, his body covered in vicious welts, his clothes ripped to pieces.

He was aware of footsteps, and someone standing over him. Two screws. One of them was Craigie.

'False alarm,' said Craigie. 'Just some fraggle.'

And the pair turned and walked away.

Paul crept back to the cell, bent almost double, holding his ripped clothes bunched against his nakedness. His shame.

Simon was there. He regarded Paul in awesome silence. Then, at last, he said, 'Did they hurt you?'

Paul didn't reply. The pity in Simon's voice angered him. He felt tears of rage welling up.

'They trashed my clothes,' he whispered. 'I've got no clothes.'

Dumbly he climbed on to his bunk and shrunk beneath the

covers. His clothes. They'd even denied him clothes. He no longer felt wholly human.

Simon rose and left the cell. Paul closed his eyes. He desperately didn't want to be alone now. He sensed fully how lonely it was possible to be in a place where you were never actually alone. Even Simon couldn't bear the sight of him. Who could blame him? Paul felt the same way about himself.

He tried to sleep, but couldn't. He heard footsteps approaching the cell, and cowered beneath his blanket, dreading the approach of his persecutors.

It was Simon. 'Here,' he said gently, laying something out on the foot of Paul's bunk. A new pair of trousers, pants, shirt, socks. 'One of the perks of working in the laundry,' said Simon.

Paul couldn't reply. He watched Simon lay back down on his bunk, and the two remained silent until lights out.

He listened to Simon turning in the bed below him, to his slow, measured breathing. Right now, he desperately wanted to hold someone. He slipped from his bunk to the floor and slid under the thin prison blanket, next to his cell-mate. Both of them were naked, and Paul gasped slightly as he felt the warmth of Simon's smooth body rubbing lightly against his. Simon lay on his back; Paul cuddled up to him, his face on Simon's shoulder, resting in the crook of his neck.

Simon turned slightly, and slipped an arm around him. Paul felt the nudge of Simon's cock against his leg. He was hard.

Paul was half hard himself. The scent and smooth texture of Simon's skin, the accidental nudge of his cock against him, soon had him fully erect. He turned slightly; his cock brushed against Simon's. Simon pulled him tighter, so that their bodies were pressed together, cocks now jammed hard against one another.

Simon kissed him gently on his bruised head and face. His warm, wet, balmy lips traced the line of cuts and bruises down Paul's dark chest and stomach. The touch of his lips both stung and soothed Paul. He felt Simon's head nestling in his thick pubes, his teeth running lightly up his hard cock, biting gently at his foreskin, teasing it away from his cock-head.

Simon ran his tongue around the rim of Paul's helmet and then took him into his mouth. His lips sank down into Paul's pubes; his tongue played around Paul's stiff pole. Simon began to blow Paul, slowly and soothingly, his hands running lightly over Paul's beaten body, fingers lingering in his bellybutton and around his nipples.

Paul lay back and lost himself in the feel of Simon's caresses – pleasure lanced with occasional shafts of pain from his bruises – and the sensation of his mouth, rising and falling wetly around his hard cock. He clutched Simon's bobbing head tightly, bunching the other man's fronds of straight golden hair between his fingers.

Paul felt the bed begin to creak rhythmically. Through the darkness, he could see Simon's naked buttocks rising and falling as he ground his cock into the mattress beneath him. Simon's body writhed like a snake as both head and cock worked in smooth rhythm. Simon's fingers wandered to Paul's bollocks. He ran his nails teasingly over them, backward and forward, playing them between his fingers, tugging gently at their loose, hairy sac.

Simon's head began to work its way faster and faster up and down Paul's throbbing shaft. His buttocks rose and fell frantically as he pumped the mattress with his cock. They came almost simultaneously; Paul trembled as he shot his seed into Simon's mouth, and Simon crushed himself into the mattress as his come burst from his cock.

Simon crawled back up the bed and kissed Paul on the mouth. He could taste his own come.

They held each other close, saying nothing, until Paul sensed Simon had drifted off to sleep. The memory of the day still haunted him. He felt ashamed – unworthy. He disentangled himself from Simon's arms and returned quietly to his own bunk, where he eventually fell asleep, hugging his pillow tight to his chest.

Fifteen

No one on the wing spoke to Paul any more, at least not publicly. Everyone – even Simon, he was sure – was nervous of being seen with him.

The solitude suited him, and he didn't seek out company. Where he was forced to interact with the other inmates, their reaction was usually one of mixed fear, revulsion and embarrassment. They treated him like a dead man who hadn't had the decency to accept his fate. Spalding had put his mark on him.

Every day for more than a week, the gang attacked him, often in public, and Spalding penetrated him. Paul was growing numb to it. The tears of impotent rage he cried afterward were becoming less. He came to expect it; he even become nervous if no attack happened. He almost found himself looking forward to it. Everybody had to find their niche in this place, and any niche – almost – was better than none. He came to accept – almost to be grateful for – his position.

He had to fight that shit, he knew, but just now he felt he'd had all the fight fucked out of him. After that first week, the assaults became sporadic. Much of the time, Spalding seemed to forget he was there. Paul sensed he was growing bored – looking for new outlets for his wrath. The violations continued, but they grew less savage as they grew less frequent. Paul began to hope for an end to his ordeal.

His hopes were quickly dashed. They took him on a narrow stone staircase – Spalding, Vince and Blue. He was pushed, face down, on to the cold stone steps.

'Hold him, then!' Spalding shouted.

Paul felt Vince and Blue's hands holding his shoulders. They weren't holding him tight. Paul could sense their lack of enthusiasm. He could probably have broken free, but he didn't struggle. There was no point. If they failed to take him now, they'd take him soon enough.

He felt his trousers, already torn from previous attacks, yanked down. His pants . . . He felt the now-familiar sensation of Spalding's long cock butting its way between his cheeks, banging at his hole, forcing its way in, the familiar slap of Spalding's belly and balls against his buttocks as he began to fuck him.

'You two,' Spalding suddenly called to Vince and Blue, 'fuck him in the mouth.'

There was a slight hesitation.

Spalding ceased in his dry, hard stroke for a moment. 'Do it!' he spat.

Paul was hauled by the shoulders from the stone steps. He crouched on all fours, dog fashion. Below him on the steps, Spalding began again to fuck his arse.

Paul was aware of Blue's thick, curved prick hovering by his lips. Defeated, he allowed Blue to push it into his mouth without resistance. Paul tasted his musky sweat as the Chinese guy's cock began to mouth-fuck him.

'You, too!' Spalding commanded.

Vince's cock bounced against Paul's lips, trying to find its way into Paul's mouth alongside Blue's thick prick. Paul's mouth was already stretched painfully. Now Vince's big shaft forced its way between his lips, grinding up the side of Blue's hard cock. The twin helmets jostled against one another inside Paul's mouth, fucking him irregularly, sometimes burying themselves in the hollows of his cheeks, sometimes butting at the back of his throat. Their pre-come oozed and mingled in Paul's mouth.

'You like that, fraggle?' Spalding hissed at him. 'You like the present your daddy's given you? You like that, cock-sucker?'

He was coming. 'Cock-sucker,' he repeated breathlessly. 'Cock –' His hands clutched at Paul's bruised shoulders as he climaxed.

Paul felt one of the cocks in his mouth swell, and heard a little moan from Blue as his semen cascaded from his cock-head. Vince was only seconds behind him. Both cocks pumped and spasmed and filled Paul's mouth with hot seed until it dribbled from his lips and down his chin. He swallowed the burning, tangy fluids.

Spalding pulled out of him.

'I'm going,' he said. 'You two can fuck him, if you like.'

Shamefaced, Vince and Blue put their cocks back inside their trousers. Their eyes mirrored Paul's suffering. They scuttled away after their master.

Paul had scarcely felt the blows and the penetrations. He sensed the situation had changed – perhaps become worse. He was no longer Spalding's alone – he was anybody's. A communal fuck-hole for anyone on the wing who wanted him.

He found himself thinking of John. The nonce. How he'd somehow, even in the face of defeat and humiliation, managed to make Spalding, the victor, look small. Look like the lesser man. Why hadn't Paul been able to do that?

He had to say this for John – nonce or not, he was a brave bastard. When Spalding had stood in front of him with a jug of boiling sugar water, he hadn't flinched. Fuck – he'd even taken the piss out of him!

John was in the solitary. Apparently, from the rec room, he'd been dragged in front of Craigie, who'd slung him straight in the can.

Paul found himself thinking of John a lot. He wanted to see him – wanted to talk to him. He smiled to himself. It was the first time in his life he'd ever thought that of a vicar. John was in solitary: no visitors. Paul began to consider how he might get in there.

Solitary was guarded through the day. He wondered if he could bribe one of the screws. He laughed bitterly. Bribe them with what? He had no money – he'd disdained work in here for a lousy six quid a week – and Spalding had walked into the cell and confiscated his stash days ago.

He took to watching the solitary block, watching the guards coming on and off duty. He memorised their rotation. He had a plan. Not one he was happy with, but one which should do the trick.

When the time was right, he went to the far end of the wing, to the narrow door that led to the solitary block. One screw was due to come off duty; another to go on. He heard the heavy footsteps of Dave, the guard who had searched him when he first entered the wing. His bulky frame and big, sandy head appeared round the corner.

Dave had frequently let his eyes linger on Paul in the intervening weeks, smirking as he stared. He'd never tried anything on with Paul – none of the guards had – but Paul reckoned he might be up for it.

He had nothing else to trade.

Paul stepped back into the shadows. Dave banged on the door to the block. The guard on duty emerged and locked the door behind him. He handed the key and a clipboard to Dave.

'He's quiet today,' the guard said.

'Good,' said Dave. 'I'll be able to get my head down.'

Dave watched his colleague walk away, then unlocked the door. Paul stepped forward.

'All right,' he said.

'What are you doing here, Travis?' Dave demanded.

Paul stood directly in front of him. 'I came to see you,' he said. 'I need a favour.'

Dave smirked. 'I hear you're Spalding's bitch, now,' he said. 'What do you want from me?'

'I want to get into the solitary block,' said Paul. 'I want to talk to John.'

'The nonce,' Dave sneered. 'Why? Want to get some tips on how to pleasure Spalding?'

'I just want to talk to him,' said Paul. 'Through the cell door – it doesn't have to be face to face.'

'And why should I –' Dave never finished the sentence. Paul had reached forward and cupped his hand over the bulge in Dave's uniform trousers.

'I see,' said Dave. He looked hastily about him. 'Not here,' he said. 'Come with me.'

Dave grabbed Paul by the wrist and dragged him quickly along the corridor. At one end of it was one of the stock cupboards that were dotted about the wing. Dave took a key from his belt and opened the door. He pushed Paul through it and followed him, fumbling for the light switch. He slammed the door behind them, and locked it.

They were standing, chests almost pressed together in the cramped space, shelves of buckets and mops, detergents and toilet paper on either side of them.

Dave's cock was large and hardening beneath his uniform. His mind a blank, Paul dropped to his knees and undid Dave's belt and trousers. As he lowered the zip, a heavy cock sprang forward, bent out of shape by the screw's patterned boxers. Paul pulled them down and hooked them under Dave's big balls. His cock was thick and long, lolling to the left in a slow curve. An unruly mass of sandy pubes sprawled around the thick root of his prick and up his belly, clung and curled over his balls and back towards the darkness of his arsehole.

Paul peeled the screw's pale foreskin slowly back, watching the dark bulb beneath slipping into view.

Dave grabbed his head impatiently. 'We haven't got all fucking day,' he said. Unceremoniously, he pulled Paul's head towards him and down on to the swollen bulb.

Paul spluttered and tried to take it in, slowing his breathing, feeling Dave's fat cock-head rubbing against his teeth and palate, relaxing his throat before its advance. Christ, he thought – he was actually getting good at this.

Dave had Paul's head clamped between his two massive hands. He began driving his cock forward into Paul's throat – pulling back – driving again. His balls shook and swung and smacked; the keys on his belt – halfway down his thighs – jangled as he bored into Paul's mouth.

He muttered and gasped to himself as he thrust – 'Good . . . good boy . . . good boy . . .' – only just audibly. Paul could taste Dave's juices leaking out on to his tongue.

Dave's thrusts became wilder. His arse banged against the shelf behind him. A box of detergent fell to the floor and burst. Paul himself was jammed up against a metal bucket.

He suddenly remembered the day of his hearing – ducking into a toilet cubicle with Jill. Then, she'd been the one on her knees. He'd never have dreamt of . . . But he was the woman now. That was what Spalding had done to him.

Dave's cock, thick and rough and veiny, slimy with Paul's saliva, drove and drove again into Paul's face.

'Play with yourself,' Dave commanded in a hoarse whisper. 'Go on. Let me see you play with yourself.'

Kneeling on the floor of the stock cupboard, still sucking on Dave's cock, Paul fumbled for his own. It was semi-erect as he pulled it from his trousers, and he stroked it swiftly to hardness, enjoying the familiar sensation.

'Oh, yeah,' Dave gasped. 'Wank that cock.'

Shit, thought Paul: a man who's watched too much American porn. Dutifully, he drew his foreskin back over the globe beneath, forward and back, getting faster, squeezing harder.

Dave was leaning forward now, bracing himself against the wall behind Paul, leaning over to watch him wank, still plunging into Paul's stretched mouth with a savage rhythm. He was close to coming.

'Shit . . . Oh, Jesus . . .' His cock spasmed inside Paul's mouth. He pressed Paul's head to him as his prick began to spurt, filling Paul's throat so that he gagged.

Dave slumped, still holding Paul's head to his groin. Paul felt Dave's prick twitch its last inside his mouth, then begin to shrink. Dave released his hold on Paul's head, and let his cock flop, still dripping slightly, from his mouth.

'Put yourself away!' he hissed at Paul, and hastily did his own trousers up. He bundled Paul from the tiny room and back to the solitary block. He unlocked the door.

'You've got five minutes,' he said. 'I'll stay out here and watch – I could get in deep shit for this. If I bang on the door, you come straight out, all right?'

'Fine,' said Paul, and Dave opened the door and pushed him into the unlit cave.

Before Dave closed the door on him, he managed to make out the row of grey metal doors lining one wall. All but one were open.

What he hadn't managed to see was the light switch. He groped his way to the locked cell door and stood before it in the total darkness.

'Hello,' he said.

There was a faint noise of movement beyond the door.

'John,' he said. 'It's me – Paul Travis.'

'Paul,' a quiet voice behind the door said. 'I owe you my thanks.'

'What?'

'For what you did in the rec room. That was very brave of you.'

'No, I . . .' He hadn't expected this. He'd come here . . . why? To confess? 'You don't understand – I wasn't trying to save you. Not really. I was trying to topple Spalding.' His voice fell. 'I failed.'

'You probably saved my life. Don't forget that. You may have acted for most of the wrong reasons, but I looked into your eyes when you put the jug down. And I knew you weren't going to let him hurt me. Our motives are rarely simple, Paul.'

'Spalding's top dog again,' said Paul. 'I'm the lowest of the low. He makes me . . . He . . .' His voice trembled and failed.

'They whipped and spat at Jesus on his way to Calvary,' said John. 'Yet, even in defeat, he was victorious.'

'They fucking crucified him,' said Paul, fighting back tears. 'Is that what you want? Is that why you let Spalding do all that to you? Well, not me. I came down here – I don't know – I came down here to ask you about your . . . bottle. Your bravery. Your strength, up against Spalding. I understand now. You're just a nutter.'

'You weren't listening to me,' said the voice. 'You have the strength. I saw it in your face. You're not like Spalding – and you're stronger than him. He can't hurt you.'

There was a frantic knocking at the blockhouse door. 'Get the fuck out here!' came Dave's earnest, hoarse stage whisper.

Paul began to grope his way to the door.

The voice in the cell came again, urgently. 'Remember! Remember what I said!'

John Williamson knew little of what happened after he was dragged from the room. He was beaten up some more, then a door was unlocked and he was dragged down a steep, narrow flight of stairs into a long, quiet corridor, painted grey. Six metal doors lined one wall.

Craigie was waiting for him there.

'You're a disruptive influence, Reverend,' he said. 'A trouble-maker. A hundred days in solitary.'

One of the metal doors was opened, and he was thrust inside. The door was slammed shut, and he heard the sound of receding footsteps. It was dark, except for the thin crack of light around the door, and within a moment even that was extinguished. He sat in the darkness and silence, thinking about what had happened.

He had seen the boy, Paul, launch himself at Spalding, seen the lethal jug fly past his head. He had braced himself for the impact of water . . .

Now he sat and contemplated the silence. It felt unbelievably refreshing – like a cold stream. He wondered whether Craigie wasn't helping him, in a way, putting him down here. At least he was safe here. For a hundred days.

The lad's brief visit troubled him. Why had he come? What was he looking for? What had John said to him? Somewhat bitterly, he reflected on the ease with which, as a priest, he'd handed out such platitudes. Assuring people, in the grand old tradition of the Anglican church, that everything would be fine if they just stood firm at the wicket with a straight bat and a keen eye.

Bullshit. What gave him – a vicar, of all people – the right to hand out such advice? Frankly, he didn't know what he was talking about. He never had. People had faith in him, but he had merely become skilled in the art of seduction.

What assurances had he given Toby, when luring him into his bed? How had he convinced him that everything was going to be fine, as long as this remained their secret? What lies and platitudes had he told him?

That's why he was in here. For the lies and hypocrisies he'd peddled over the years – to Toby, to his wife, to his parishioners, even to himself.

He had already half forgotten Paul's visit. The total darkness was like a mirror. We see through a glass darkly. From the darkness, he stared back at himself.

Sixteen

The weather was warming up outside. Simon spent long hours thinking about the countryside of his youth. The way you noticed the return of the birds, the trees budding, the first appearance of the crocuses and daffodils. In here, all the onset of sunny days meant was that the laundry turned into a sweat box. Their shirts, his and Tim's, became plastered to their bodies as they worked, heaving loads in and out of the machines, washing, drying, operating the huge, steam pressing table.

They worked steadily through the heat.

'It's like a sauna in here,' said Tim, on one morning of increasing heat. He stripped off his shirt to reveal his skinny, sweat-shiny torso. Grinning, Simon followed suit, peeling the wet shirt slowly from his skin. He could see Tim watching as his slender body emerged from its covering.

'Let's just get this lot finished,' said Tim. 'Then we can take a break.'

For nearly an hour, they hefted bundles of sheets and clothes into and out of the machines.

'Gorman's still at it,' said Simon, emerging from the storeroom with a new box of washing powder. 'You'd think in this heat –'

Suddenly he felt something hot and wet splattering against his bare back, stinging slightly. A pair of underpants, still wet from the wash, slipped to the floor. Before he could react, another pair hit him square in the face. Tim was standing next to a full machine, grinning from ear to ear.

'Hey —'

A T-shirt flew across the room. He ducked to avoid it. 'You swine,' he laughed.

Simon dragged the wet contents of the machine out on to the floor, and began grabbing for more ammunition. He charged. He connected with Tim and pushed him back against one of the huge washing machines. Laughing, they kissed, their lips jammed roughly, hastily together. Simon plastered Tim's face and neck with kisses. He licked and slurped, enjoying the salty taste of Tim's sweat. He let his lips trail down Tim's thin, hairless chest to his nipples, where he sucked vigorously, caught the teats between his teeth, nipped and tugged.

He lodged his tongue in Tim's salty bellybutton and fumblingly unbuckled his belt, unzipped his trousers and let them fall. He gripped Tim's hard shaft through the white cotton of his briefs, rubbing gently, letting his fingers play around the cloth-softened, circumcised cock-head, squeezing the head tight in his fist. His wet tongue trailed back up Tim's pale, sweat-slick stomach.

Tim was unbuttoning Simon's trousers. He felt them dropping below his knees. He kicked his shoes off and stepped out of them. Tim's hand was inside his pants, cupping and scratching at his balls, scratching the long, hard underside of his cock, pinching his frenum. They kissed again, mouths passionately locked. Each of them pulled the other's pants down. Simon drew Tim to him, and felt him hugging back. Their sweaty cocks smashed together as they hugged. Simon bent Tim's head and let his lips get lost in his lover's loose brown curls. He sniffed deeply, relishing the smell of his hair.

Tim twisted round so that he was facing the tall humming machine. He reached above his head, feeling for something on the machine's top. Simon hooked his hands under Tim's arms and planted his lips hard against Tim's lightly freckled back, kissing his shoulders and the back of his neck. He pressed himself close to Tim, letting his hard cock slip into the crease between Tim's pale buttocks. He began bucking, running his cock wetly up and down the sweaty, slippery crack, play-fucking his friend. He reached around and ran a hand down Tim's stomach, into the little forest of his pubes, than gripped Tim's small, hard prick and began stroking and pulling.

Wet undergarments twisted and tangled around their feet. The washing machine kept pace with them, clicking into spin cycle. Tim groaned with pleasure. Simon could feel the tantalising vibrations through Tim's body. He pressed Tim tight against the machine. He let go of Tim's cock and pushed it hard against the machine's warm, throbbing, metal casing. Faster and faster he ploughed up and down Tim's wet arse-crack with his painfully throbbing cock. He began to tremble. He heard Tim moan and felt a warm, generous splash of semen against his hand, still trapped between man and machine.

He was coming, too. He clutched Tim to him and gasped as his orgasm shuddered through him, sending jet after jet of semen guttering up Tim's buttock-crease, splashing his back.

They slumped to the floor where they stood, and sprawled in the pile of warm, wet washing. Tim picked up a pair of purple pants from the pile and wiped his belly with it. 'That was amazing,' he said. 'I mean, just the vibration of the machine . . . Christ, you make me so horny.'

They lay back on the wet pile and kissed, lazily and generously. For ten, maybe twenty minutes, their mouths were loosely locked together, tongues playing hide and seek.

Tim unclenched his fist to reveal what he'd picked up from the top of the washing machine – a condom. He got to his feet, pulling Simon after him. They were both erect again. They shed what little remained of their clothing and Tim led Simon across to the big steam press. It was open and still warm. Tim pushed Simon's buttocks back against the edge of the press and ripped open the condom packet. Smiling, he placed the rubber over the tip of Simon's tall, slim cock and rolled it slowly down the shaft.

Simon was a little startled. He was used to being passive. He had fucked only rarely in his life.

'It's time you learnt,' whispered Tim gently, and hoisted his buttocks on to the padded bottom board of the press. He scampered back across the board and lay on his back, grinning at Simon, his legs in the air, his tight brown arsehole exposed.

'I want you inside me, baby,' he whispered to Simon.

Simon climbed on to the board on top of Tim. He lay between Tim's splayed legs and rubbed his latex covered cock against his pubes and the side of his hard little cock. Tim hitched his buttocks into the air and wrapped his hands around their pale cheeks, pulling them apart, pulling his hole slightly open. Simon spat on to his hand, and ran his fingers slowly up and down Tim's crack. Saliva mingled with sweat. Simon extended a cautious finger, and slipped it inside Tim, working in the slippery liquid. Tim let out a small, glad moan. Simon probed gently with his finger, exploring Tim's soft inner walls while Tim himself squirmed and giggled with pleasure.

Simon extracted his finger and lined his cock up with Tim's rosebud hole. He pushed forward, and watched the latex shaft disappearing inside Tim. He shuddered slightly at the feel of Tim's arse muscles opening before his probing cock-head, then closing tight around his shaft. Tim wrapped his legs around Simon's waist. Simon arched his back and, in a sort of snaking motion, pulled his cock back out of the delicious hole, then plunged it in again. Tim gripped the sides of the steam press; with his legs, he held on tight to Simon. Simon rocked his hips and watched as his cock appeared and then disappeared, back inside Tim, again and again.

Faster, now. Tim's arse-walls hugged and stimulated his cock, rolling up and down the shaft in a wave of little contractions. Simon's balls, low-slung in the heat, slapped against Tim's buttock-cheeks. Tim's legs held him tight.

With one hand, Tim still clung to the press; he was running the other over his own body, tugging at the little pubic bush around his cock, probing his own bellybutton, gliding across his stomach and chest, massaging and pulling at his own nipples. He released his grip on the press and began to wank himself in short, fast strokes which concentrated on the circumcised head of his cock.

'I love you,' he whispered.

Soon his hips began to buck slightly, and his arse muscles began to spasm deliciously around Simon's cock. He was coming, his mouth drawn back in a wide, open-mouthed smile, his cock shooting its second load up his already sticky belly.

Simon was coming, too. He gripped Tim's buttocks as his cock burst deep inside Tim, filling the condom with his seed.

They collapsed – slowly, like the mountain of laundry – into a sticky heap on the steam press, and lay there, breathless, bodies close, enjoying the feel of one another's sweat and come, mingling beneath their pressed-together chests.

Sexual activity punctuated their day. It became as much a part of life in the laundry as the work itself.

'What did you expect,' Sanjay quipped, 'with Gorman in charge?'

Gorman obviously knew what was going on. They made no effort to hide their lovemaking from him. If Simon was still naked when something was needed from the stockroom, he just walked in, maybe still half-hard and dripping, past Gorman, forever with his hard cock in his hand, and took what he needed. If nothing else it meant that, should Gorman catch him when he was coming, it wasn't going to stain Simon's clothes. This happened two or three times: Gorman going into overdrive, grabbing Simon and dragging him, butt-naked, into his lap, shooting his seed up his back and along his arse-crack. Simon didn't mind too much. There was plenty in the laundry to wipe it off with.

Sanjay, too, was no stranger to what was going on. As the only regular visitor to the laundry, for most of the day, it was probably inevitable. Twice he caught them at it: the first time, they were fucking behind the dryers. They froze, and he carried on as if nothing was out of the ordinary, dumping Spalding's heavy laundry bag and emptying the contents into one of the big machines.

'Don't you two mind me,' he said casually, not looking at them. 'Carry on. I know how to operate the machine. It'll help cover the noise.'

The second time, Simon was fucking Tim up against the wall, his bare buttocks rising and falling rapidly. Naughtily, grinning from ear to ear, Sanjay stuck a sudden and unexpected finger into Simon's arsehole, stabbing for his G-spot, sending him to sudden, unexpected and overwhelming orgasm.

'Sorry about that,' he grinned. 'I couldn't resist it.'

One day, when Simon was in the little stockroom negotiating his way around Gorman, he noticed Sanjay entering the laundry room and looking furtively around. He beckoned, and another lad followed him through the door. Simon had seen him around. His name was Ben. He was slight and black, about twenty, a close-cropped head of tight curls and a handsome face. Tim was out on an errand; the laundry was quiet.

'It's OK,' said Sanjay. 'We're alone.'

Ben spun around and the pair hugged one another in a frantic, tight embrace, their lips kissing greedily.

Simon slowly stepped from the stockroom and edged behind the row of dryers. He watched as Sanjay and Ben snatched at each other's clothes – shirts hastily unbuttoned, belts loosened, shoes kicked off. Naked to the waist, their trousers and pants sagging around their buttocks, they strained together.

They were a good-looking pair: Sanjay, with his pretty brown face, his black hair falling in a torrent almost to his waist, his tight, hairy buttocks poking out from his sagging trousers; Ben, with his lean, toned body, his skin as smooth and dark as ebony.

Sanjay lowered Ben on to the mountain of dirty sheets where Simon and Tim had first discovered each other's bodies. He removed Ben's trousers and pants. His cock stood up, black and huge, its purple head half-unsheathed at its tip. He was quite hairless, apart from the thick black patch around his cock, which spread thinly over his balls. Ben pulled at Sanjay's trousers, and they too came away. Both lads lay and rolled among the sheets, kissing and biting and hugging and laughing. Sanjay was a lot hairier than Ben: his coffee-brown chest was sprinkled with dark fuzz, dense around the nipples, thinning out as it descended to join the great black jungle of hair which sprawled around his thick, long cock and trailed itself luxuriantly over his balls and back along his perineum to his arse-crack.

Simon watched as Sanjay took Ben's huge cock in his mouth, swallowing slowly as the great trunk buried itself in him. Sanjay continued to swallow until Ben's balls were resting on his chin. Simon was impressed.

Crablike, Ben edged himself round, never letting his cock leave its warm, wet nest, until his head was level with Sanjay's groin. He buried his face in the Indian lad's thick pubic mat, sniffing and chewing at the coarse black hair, pulling it with his teeth, working his way down Sanjay's belly, around his cock, grazing on his balls, breathing deeply in as his face pressed against Sanjay's hairy perineum, licking the taut belt of muscle with his tongue.

At the same time, he began to pump his cock into Sanjay's wide-open mouth in long, deep strokes. Sanjay's breathing was deep and slow and measured. His lips hugged Ben's black shaft as it worked its way in and out of him.

Ben was working his teeth back up Sanjay's balls, biting at the root of his shaft, nipping and nibbling his way up the fat cock to the sensitive frenum. There, at the base of his swollen orb, he bit hard. Sanjay's buttocks clenched suddenly. Ben bit again; Sanjay's arse puckered, on cue.

At last, Ben sank his full lips around Sanjay's expectant cock-head and swallowed deeply. Both lads, their cocks sunk deep in each other's throats, mouth-fucked in rhythm; slowly at first, then gaining in speed.

Ben was the first to come – a mighty eruption which filled Sanjay's mouth and flooded out of his leaking lips and across his face. Sanjay barely seemed to notice; he was coming himself, his arse clenching and puckering, his thighs like a vice around Ben's head.

Simon remained motionless. The lovers lay for a while, their soft cocks lolling in each other's faces, then Ben reached into his discarded trousers and pulled out a condom. He stroked himself back to hardness and turned himself round. He rolled Sanjay fully on to his back, and kissed him on the mouth.

'You ready for this?' he whispered. He eased himself on top of the Indian lad and lined his huge cock up with his tight, dark hole.

Sanjay gasped as Ben pushed into him, stretching his sphincter wide. Simon could see Sanjay's toes clenching and unclenching as his arsehole strained to accommodate Ben's great pole. 'No,' Sanjay gasped. 'Too big.'

'I'll take it slow, baby,' Ben whispered. He pushed another inch into Sanjay.

Sanjay gasped again.

'Easy, baby,' Ben said. 'You can take it.'

Simon watched, spellbound. He felt a sudden warm pressure on his neck, and nearly jumped out of his skin. Tim was standing behind him, kissing him on the neck. He reached around him and started unbuttoning his shirt. Simon stretched like a cat and allowed Tim to remove shirt, trousers, pants. He was hard, of course. He heard a slight tearing sound; Tim was rolling a condom over Simon's cock.

He turned to see Tim removing his own clothes, hopping slightly as he stepped out of his trousers and pants. He pushed Simon gently towards the huge laundry pile, and lay down next to Sanjay. He opened his legs wide – his knee rested against Sanjay's.

The Indian lad was still straining, fighting the pain.

'Just a little bit more,' whispered Ben, pushing forward slowly. 'Nearly there.'

Simon climbed on top of Tim and probed for his arsehole with his cock. He found the tight entrance, and penetrated it in a single long, slow stroke. Tim smiled as his arse swallowed Simon's cock, right up to the hilt. Ben was now fully buried in Sanjay. He flashed Simon a quick grin as he began to fuck Sanjay with slow, short strokes.

Sanjay's eyes were tight shut, his brow creased and troubled. He groped for Tim's hand and clutched it tight. Simon too began pushing his cock into Tim's arsehole and pulling it out again, enjoying the enveloping sensation of Tim's soft, moist inner walls on his swollen prick.

Ben's stroke was harder now, gaining in confidence as Sanjay's arse gradually relaxed around him. Simon kept time with Ben. The two of them grinned at one another as they fucked their lovers. Ben raised his open hand, and Simon clasped it in a high five. Beneath them, Sanjay and Tim lay, legs split, hand in hand, gazing at each other and smiling. At the same moment – as if with one mind – each of them started wanking himself: twin upstanding cocks, twitching and straining as they rubbed them towards orgasm.

It was Ben who came first, biting down on his lower lip as he shot his load into Sanjay. Sanjay began bucking and jerking as Ben shot into him, and fired his own fat load into the air, over his hairy chest and belly, where it hung in tiny streamers.

Simon and Tim were not far behind them, coming together, Simon into the latex dam which lined Tim's arsehole, Tim high into the air so that his come bounced off Simon's face.

Tim giggled. Simon, too, began to chortle. Sanjay and Ben joined in; uncontrollably, ecstatically, the four lads lay in the laundry pile and laughed.

There was one surprise visitor to the laundry, a few weeks after Simon had begun work there. The governor, accompanied by Craigie, was doing a grand tour. Craigie gesticulated at the washing machines and quoted theoretical (and highly inaccurate) turnover statistics.

Governor Keating was an imposing figure. He could only have been about forty – taller than Craigie, with pale skin and black hair, greying slightly. Strong, honest features: a square jaw and a burning blue gaze.

He was nodding and trying to look interested in what Craigie was saying. Finally, he interrupted him.

'Hello, Tim,' the governor said. 'How are you?'

'Very well, sir,' Tim replied.

'And who's your friend?' the governor asked.

'His name's Simon Muir, sir.'

The governor looked Simon over with a cool, discerning eye. 'Yes,' he said. He seemed to snap to a decision. 'Thank you, Mister Craigie,' he said. 'Where next?' He turned towards the door. 'Choir practice, next week,' he said to Tim. 'You can bring your friend along, if you like.'

He walked out, followed by Craigie. Tim immediately returned to the pile of washing he was unloading.

'Tim,' Simon asked with mounting anxiety, 'what did he mean?'

Tim wouldn't answer him.

Seventeen

Tim barely spoke to Simon for the rest of that day. He barely looked at him. Simon returned to his cell, deeply troubled. Paul was already lying on his bunk, staring in silence at the ceiling, as he did most evenings nowadays.

Simon sat on the bunk beneath him. 'Paul,' he said, 'will you tell me what a choirboy is?'

Paul had remained silent for a moment, then let out a sort of quick snort. 'You trying to tell me you don't know?' he sneered.

'No,' said Simon. 'I don't. Tim won't tell me.'

'Really?'

Simon didn't bother to reply. There was no point.

After a moment, Paul started to speak. 'The way I heard it,' said Paul, 'the governor likes his boys. Every so often, he has a sort of gathering, him and some mates, I suppose, where he gets his pretty-boys together and . . . well . . .'

'What?' Simon demanded.

'Weird games, the way I heard it. Sex games. Pretty heavy stuff, I suppose. Only the governor's choosy. He likes them clean – that's how come this place is drowning in condoms – and he doesn't like any blemishes or marks, other than the ones he makes. That's why no one touches them. That's why no one gives your boyfriend any trouble. Governor's pet. Apparently, Spalding comes down like a ton of bricks on anyone who messes with the choir. Everyone reckons you're one.'

'Well, I'm not,' said Simon. 'At least, not yet.'

He tried to talk to Tim about it, the following day.

Tim seemed defeated. 'So you know, then,' he said.

'I was bound to find out, sooner or later,' Simon replied gently. 'I'd rather have heard it from you.'

'Do you hate me?' said Tim quietly.

'Do I . . . Christ, no!' Simon exclaimed. 'Why would I hate you?'

'For doing that – with the governor, with screws.'

'In case you hadn't noticed,' said Simon, 'everything's up for sale in here. Sex is just another form of barter.'

'But the stuff he makes us do . . .'

Simon placed a finger on Tim's lips. He could see his lover was becoming upset. 'Don't think about it,' he said.

But he himself couldn't stop thinking about it. Choir practice, next week. What would they do to Tim? And was the governor's casual invitation to him in fact a summons?

As the following week approached, Tim became noticeably more tense and depressed. Still, he never mentioned the festivities to come.

At last, one evening, he said, 'It's tonight. And I'm to bring you.'

When the long shift at the laundry ended, Tim led Paul in silence to the showers. 'He likes us washed,' he said quietly.

Simon watched as Tim soaped himself down, working the lather quickly around his chest and arms, his cock, small against his body, his back and buttocks and legs, never lifting his gaze from the floor. Simon half-heartedly washed himself.

At last, Tim raised his head. Their eyes locked and they flew into each other's arms. They hugged one another tight beneath the hot, clean water jets. Tim caught hold of Simon's limp cock and squeezed it gently.

'I want to come with you,' he said. 'Here. Now. It won't be the same, afterward.'

He pressed his groin into Simon's. His prick was already stiffening against Simon's belly. Simon felt his own cock slacken and grow in Tim's hand. He closed his own fist around Tim's circumcised cock and squeezed and rubbed. Gently, slowly, holding each other close beneath the shower's spray, they masturbated each other. Neither moved, neither spoke. Only the slow rhythm of their hands, working each other's cocks, disturbed their statuesque stillness. Like two Greek godlings, entwined in stone, they stood. Tim's curly head and sweet, freckle-dappered face rested in the crook of Simon's neck. Simon kissed him gently on the head.

They worked their cocks in tender silence, until Simon felt Tim tense. His grip on Simon's body tightened and he let out a little choking sound, and his cock spat its load in several gobs, up on to his stomach and Simon's. The water carried it instantly away.

Simon, too, felt himself coming. He kissed Tim urgently on the mouth and felt his seed shooting from him, into the wall of his friend's belly.

'I love you,' Simon whispered. 'Whatever happens, I love you.'

'I love you, too,' Tim whispered back.

After the shower, Tim led Simon out of the wing. It was amazing – security doors slid open for them and they swept through them, like VIPs.

'Is it just us?' Simon asked Tim.

'No, there are others,' said Tim. 'From other wings. We're the only ones from D wing. There was another, but . . .' His voice tailed off.

Simon felt his panic rising, and fought to control it. Panicking did no good in here. There was nowhere to run to.

He followed Tim out of the wing, and along a winding, windowless corridor. They descended several flights of steps. A screw at the bottom opened a door for them and they entered a small lobby.

'Just do what I do,' whispered Tim.

Simon nodded, then blinked in surprise. Tim was removing his clothes. The door opened and another lad entered – small, in his late teens, with a head of tight golden curls.

'Martin,' said Tim, in curt greeting.

The lad nodded briefly at Tim and began removing his shirt.

Tim was down to his underpants. As Simon watched, he dropped them to the floor and stepped out of them. Tim's cock was small.

Self-consciously, Simon began unbuttoning his shirt.

'We're not allowed clothes in here,' whispered Tim. 'Clothes are for human beings.'

The other lad, Martin, was pulling his pants down. He was slim and hairless, save for a small golden patch around his soft cock. He and Tim stood, naked, next to each other. Martin started squeezing his cock. It began to grow in his hand. Simon looked at Tim. He was wanking, too, stroking himself to hardness as Simon watched.

Feeling as if he'd entered some bizarre dream world, Simon removed the rest of his clothes. Tim tweaked Simon's soft cock with his fingers.

'You'll have to get that hard,' he said. 'They take offence if they think you're not enjoying it all as much as them.'

Simon watched Tim, still idly playing with his own hard prick, and Martin, still working his pale, tall pole. Simon began to play with himself. He squeezed, he stroked, but it didn't seem to be doing any good. It remained soft and small.

'I can't,' he said.

'Here,' said Tim, and dropped to his knees in front of Simon. He took Simon's soft cock between his moist lips and sucked it into his mouth. Simon shuddered at the warm, soft, delicious sensation. His cock began to grow at once.

When it was fully hard, Tim stood up. 'We don't want to be caught doing that here,' he said. 'They hate faggots.'

Martin opened a door in the far wall and walked through it.

'Ready?' whispered Tim.

Simon nodded. Tim squeezed his hand and led him through the door.

They were in a somewhat larger room, plushly carpeted in crimson, with dozens of large cushions scattered about the floor, along with a clutter of furniture – low-slung armchairs, settees, pouffes. At the far end of the room was a broad window. Simon could make out vague movements through the glass, but Venetian blinds on the other side prevented him making out any details.

Inside the room, five other boys in addition to he, Tim and Martin stood about: all young, all small and slender and pretty, all naked, and all hard.

His eyes scanned the naked bodies surrounding him. One black guy, small and smooth with a proud cock, the purple head of which was peeping from its ebony-dark hood . . . a bloke who looked Chinese to Simon, his dark hair shaved almost to the skull, his cock small and alert and cheekily curving . . . a pale-skinned little guy with a brown pudding-basin haircut, who was still idly playing with his hard prick, teasing the tight foreskin back and forth over the bulb beneath . . . and twins. Dirty blond hair – a darker blond even than Simon's – worn slightly too long and scruffy, a leather thong ending in a painted stone around each of their necks. They looked like a couple of young surf-bums; they were even tanned. Each held the other's balls, tickling them slightly, giggling quietly as their twin hard-ons bounced together.

Strangely, Simon was reminded of his first day in this place – men standing around, the endless wait in that room, not knowing what was going to come through the door. He'd been petrified, then. He could cope, now – he reckoned he'd cried all the tears he could ever cry since being locked up – but, in a way, this was worse. Because it was so surreal. Perhaps because they were all naked. Defenceless. Perhaps because they were underground – there was something hideously secret about all this.

What came through the door was Craigie.

'Welcome, lads,' he said genially. 'You privileged few . . . Once again our illustrious Governor Keating has dreamt up a wonderful, magical entertainment for you, and I, through my hard work and dedication, have brought his vision to life!' He rubbed his hands together gleefully. 'Oh, you lucky lads,' he chortled.

Another screw came through the door. Craigie nodded to him, and he began passing among the naked boys handing out . . . handing out . . .

'Blindfolds,' whispered Tim. 'Just a little parlour game to soften us up before the hard stuff starts.'

'You know what to do – put them on,' commanded Craigie.

Simon watched Tim don his blindfold, then did the same. He felt a shudder of dread as everything went dark. He groped for Tim's hand, and squeezed it in the darkness. Tim squeezed back, then let go.

'We've got to move,' he whispered. 'The governor calls this his "rats in a box" game.'

'What do I do?' pleaded Simon under his breath.

'Go with the flow,' Tim whispered back. 'Get into it. Put on a good show and try to make someone come – but don't come yourself. The first one who comes . . . well . . .'

Simon took an uncertain step forward in the darkness, then another. He felt a naked body bumping against him. A cushion became tangled up with his feet. He tried to side-step, but collided with some piece of furniture or other and fell forward to the carpeted floor. Someone fell on top of him. He felt a hand blindly groping his thigh, fumbling for his buttocks. A finger probed his arsehole, pushing through his tight sphincter. He felt the painful nick of a fingernail against his soft inner flesh, and another hand fumbling for his bollocks, squeezing them tightly, pulling and pinching. A third hand massaged his chest and tugged at his nipples.

'Get into it,' Tim's voice whispered into his ear. 'Don't be too passive – but, whatever you do, don't come.'

Simon groped in the darkness with an uncertain hand. He touched what felt like a leg, a thigh. He ran his hand down to the knee, then up again, against the grain of sparse, short hairs. The hair thickened at the top, and Simon felt a pair of tight, hairy balls, and the hard root of an erect cock.

146

He felt something else: a head. A face, wrapped around the cock, slurping wetly up and down the shaft. He ran his fingers around the small carpet of hair which surrounded the base of the shaft, feeling the regular kiss of a pair of lips on the back of his hand, then traced back down to the stranger's balls and along their underside along the hard perineum which led to two tight buttock-cheeks. His fingers wormed their way between the taut buns, touching the pucker of flesh they found there, making it contract and loosen.

Simon sensed movement. The hands which fondled and pinched his chest now seemed to be trying to roll him on to his back. He lost contact with the puckered arsehole and felt fingers clumsily feeling their way across his face. He felt a pair of cheeks descend and plant themselves over his nose and mouth. He took in a frantic, startled breath, and smelt a sharp, sweaty tang. Cautiously, curiously, he extended his tongue, feeling the tight rosette of an arsehole, tasting its moist richness.

He raised his buttocks from the carpeted floor. The finger which probed his arsehole so tantalisingly slid out, instantly to be replaced by a pair of fingers, which nicked their way past his sphincter and along this passage, bending and flexing against his tube as they pushed their way inside.

His cock was hard, of course. He remembered what Tim had said about not coming, and was relieved that no one was trying to bring him off. He feared it wouldn't take much to bring him off – in spite of the fear and uncertainty, he was starting to get off on the weird sensation. His tongue pushed against the unseen, bitter-tasting hole, slipping into its ring of muscle.

Inside his own arsehole, he felt a sudden pressure as two more fingers were roughly inserted. The four fingers danced inside him, stretching and pulling on his passage.

Barely able to breathe, he felt the buttocks lifting from his face. He gulped for air.

The blindfold was dislodged slightly; one eye could now see the tangle of naked, blind bodies around him – groping hands, exploring tongues, swollen, hard cocks. The Chinese lad was climbing off his face. Tim was next to him. Blindfold, the Chinese guy groped his way down Tim's body, feeling for his cock with his hands, sinking his mouth down over its circumcised head, right down to Tim's brown pubic mat.

Between his legs, he could see Martin and the black guy. Each had a hand reaching up into his arsehole; each had two fingers inside Simon. With their free hands, they wanked each other vigorously. Martin pumped hard on the other guy's ebony pole, its bulbous head a dark, dark purple in his pale fist. The black guy reciprocated, squeezing Martin's pale, tall cock, its head barely darker than the shaft on which it strained, pulling his foreskin back, his black hand resting for a moment in Martin's small, white-blond bush, then drawing the foreskin back up.

Nearby, one of the twins lay spread-eagled. His brother crouched on top of him. Each sucked greedily at the other's cock, dirty, scruffy blond curls bouncing off each other's taut, practically hairless bellies; each drove his heavy cock into the other's face. The pale, slim lad with the brown pudding-basin haircut was on all fours, scampering around the twins like a little dog. His small, tapering cock was hard. His tongue was out and he lapped one twin's buttocks, burying his face between the muscular cheeks, sniffing and licking at his arsehole. After a few moments, he moved around to the other twin and did the same, licking and biting his perineum as the twin raised his butt from the floor to afford the lad's tongue access to his hole.

Through the window, Simon could see a huddle of indistinct figures watching. Their audience. They were putting on a show.

Simon watched the Chinese guy's lush, shapely lips running up and down Tim's hard little pole. The guy's curving prick was hovering not far from his face. He reached forward and grabbed it with his fist, fondling the balls which hung below it and roughly kneading the foreskin back and forth over the head beneath. Simon pulled on the Chinese guy's cock and arched his neck. He placed the pole in his mouth and teased its underside with his tongue, before taking it to the back of his throat. He could taste the steady leak of cock juices.

It was Tim – Tim, of all people – who was the instrument of Simon's undoing. Blindly he groped about him, and found Simon's belly, bucking slightly in response to the twin pair of fingers, Martin's and the black guy's, which continued to rifle his hole. Tim's hand closed around the base of Simon's hard prick and ran up its full length. He squeezed Simon's bulb hard, before drawing the foreskin tightly back and forward in a quick motion which concentrated on the distended head.

Tim was too good at this. Simon instantly felt an orgasm starting to build inside him. From the corner of his eye, he could still see the twins, their mouths wrapped around each other's bulky cocks, gobbling with abandon, and their pale lapdog, still burying his face first in one, then in another, swabbing out their arseholes with his tongue. As Simon watched, one of the twins grabbed the lad's hair and dragged him forward. The twin raised his mouth from his brother's cock and turned round, pulling his own cock free as he did so. Groping blindly, he pressed his hard cock against his brother's identical hard-on, wrapping a fist around both of them. Still holding the pale lad's hair, he guided his head down on to the twin pressed pricks. The lad opened his mouth wide and gagged slightly as he swallowed the two bulbs. Pulled by his hair, the lad was raised from the pressed-together cocks, only to be pushed down on them once again – up, down, up, down, as he struggled to contain them in his delicate mouth. The other twin reached beneath the pale guy's head and gripped his little pole, shunting his hand up and down it, occasionally stopping to slap and tweak the guy's balls.

Simon could see Tim, his head arched back, revelling in the sensation of the Chinese guy's lips playing about his cock, swallowing it, ejecting it, swallowing it again, while Tim himself, one hand idly extended, stimulated Simon's own cock with his brisk, tight strokes. The taste of the Chinese guy's cock, and the musky smell of his balls and pubes, filled Simon's nose and mouth. Inside his arsehole, blond Martin and the black guy still worked their fingers, pumping them together roughly in and out of him. Each still wanked violently at the other's hard prick.

Heads bobbed and hands rubbed; cocks sprang from mouths and bumped against chins and cheeks, before being recaptured. The group wanked and sucked in a straggling, irregular daisy chain of sweating skin.

Simon was coming. He suppressed a groan as his seed erupted from him, splattering his belly and Tim's hand, showering his fuck-buddies.

Tim froze for a moment. The look on his face was one of concern. He removed his hand and wiped it on the carpet.

Between Simon's legs, the black guy was coming. 'Fuck, no,' he choked as his cock spat rudely. Simon felt the warm, sticky juices hit his inner thighs and buttocks.

He remembered the audience behind the glass, and resumed wanking the Chinese guy's pert cock. He scanned the writhing mass of bodies. The twins were coming together, their seed filling the pale lad's mouth and dribbling out of his lips. He began to come at the same time, his small, steely cock twitching as it pumped into the hand of the twin who was wanking him.

Martin was next. His pale cock was swollen to bursting in the black guy's pumping fist; he let out a long, ragged breath and a long fountain of spunk spurted from its twitching head.

Only the Chinese guy and Tim were left to come. Simon remembered Tim's warning about not coming too soon. If Simon could spare him some unnamed trial, later on . . . He went to work in earnest on the Chinese guy's cock, wanking it hard and fast. He reached across with his other hand and squeezed and tickled his balls; he rubbed the Chinese guy's perineum, then finally inserted a pair of fingers between his arse-cheeks and up into his puckered hole.

He saw Tim's face crease and his mouth open. Tim gripped the Chinese guy's ponytailed head with both hands and drove up into his mouth, shuddering as he came between his lips. At the same time, Simon felt the Chinese guy's buttocks clench as his own jet of semen flopped out over Simon's hand and ran down the curved shaft and into the trim mat of his pubes.

At length, all were still and breathless on the carpeted floor. One by one, the blindfolds were removed.

Tim leant across to Simon, a look of deep concern on his face. 'I'm sorry,' he whispered.

'What?' Simon queried.

'It was you, wasn't it? I made you come. I'd recognise you coming anywhere. I couldn't see you . . .'

'It's all right,' Simon tried to assure him.

'No, it isn't,' said Tim, anguished. 'I'm so sorry.'

The door opened and Craigie walked in, followed by two fellow screws. 'Enjoyed yourselves?' he sneered. 'You dirty little shits. On your feet.'

The eight lads did as they were told.

'Through here,' Craigie ordered. 'Move!'

Naked and drained, their limp cocks dripping and drooling down their legs, the boys shuffled through the door.

Beyond was a huge open area, stone-walled and low-ceilinged, lit by long rows of chain-mounted lights. A cellar of some kind – vast and cold.

Part-way along one wall was a raised area containing several rows of banked seats, like a university lecture hall. Huge red-and-gold banners hung behind the bank of seats, topped with eagles.

SPQR.

Simon was puzzled.

About a dozen men, Governor Keating among them, were standing about the room, sipping wine or beer. Some were screws; others looked merely anonymous in expensive suits. As the lads entered, the men took their seats.

The governor stood and surveyed the little huddle. 'Well,' he said. 'My beloved boys, together again.' He gesticulated about the room. '*Morturi te salutant*,' he said. 'We who are about to die salute you – that's what the gladiators in the Roman arena would say to their emperor before the slaughter commenced. You know, I was watching an old film the other week – *Spartacus*, with Kirk Douglas. It gave me an idea for today's festivities.'

Three of Craigie's guards were dragging a number of large wooden teachests into the room.

'Now,' the governor continued, 'to review your performance so far – you!' He pointed at Simon, and Simon was pushed forward by a guard, on to the low dais. 'You know what the Bible says about spilling your seed on the ground?' asked the governor.

Simon was silent, unsure whether or not to answer.

'And yet you spent your seed in indecent haste,' the governor continued. 'Added to which, you were the slowest in producing an orgasm in one of your companions. Performance: poor. You will have to fight longest and hardest to obtain absolution. Over there.'

Simon was pulled from the stage and over to the wooden crates. He shook his head in disbelief. A guard handed him a little round wooden shield and a short sword.

He'd always hated these games as a child.

The governor was addressing the black lad. 'You were the second to spend your seed,' he said.

The black guy was also led to the boxes, and handed a sword and shield.

'You two will be first,' said the governor. 'Now, fight.'

The black guy moved out into the centre of the underground arena, testing his arms, a tense grin on his face. Simon ran his finger along the edge of the sword, then snatched it away. A hairline of blood remained on his fingertip. These swords were real.

Simon understood now. He knew exactly what he read in the black guy's face. Already, tumbling together in the outer room, they'd been working to bring one another off as fast as they could manage, each trying to spare himself this. Sex as a game of Russian roulette. Their blood was up. The guy now facing Simon would fight for his life.

He swung his sword. Simon raised his shield awkwardly. The blade clanged off it, sending a sharp pain juddering up Simon's arm. The black guy swung again. Again, his sword crashed off

Simon's shield. His own sword hung limp in his hand – an alien object, totally unfamiliar. He was backing away with every blow. The audience started to boo.

He glimpsed the other lads being equipped to fight, filing out into the arena. The twins stood back to back, one fighting blond Martin, the other Tim. The two smallest of their number – the Chinese guy and the pale little chap with the pudding-basin haircut – fought one another. Their cocks were already half-hard, flapping and swinging as they wove about one another, swords jabbing.

The men in the little crowd were cheering and shouting. Simon reckoned bets were being taken.

He was practically in a corner. The black guy's face wore a savage grin. His cock was hard, its purple bulb standing proud of his drawn-back foreskin. Simon ducked his head and raised his shield, and charged. He crashed into his opponent, sending him reeling. A cheer went up. He ran into the centre of the arena and turned. Beside him, the twins fought hard, their backs pressed together, buttock-cheeks rubbing and smacking off one another. They both wore angry, dancing hard-ons.

Simon threw a frantic glance at Tim. He was fighting with spirit, battling hard against his much bigger opponent, who fended off his blows with confidence. Tim's cock was growing . . .

With a growl, the black guy threw himself on top of Simon, sending him reeling backward, crashing to the floor. The black guy threw his shield to the ground and raised his sword in both hands. He turned to the dais, to the governor. Keating's arm was extended, his fist closed, his thumb jutting out horizontally.

Thumbs up or thumbs down. Would Simon be spared, or . . .

Panic overwhelmed him. He closed his eyes and thrust upward with his sword. He heard a small cry, and then felt something warm trickling across his hand.

He'd caught the black guy in the ribs. Blood flowed down his sword. The black guy stumbled backward, a look of horror on his face. Simon dropped his sword in dismay. There was a commotion from the crowd and two officers ran forward. They grabbed the black guy. One of them pressed a cloth to his wound and they walked him from the arena.

Simon's heart was pounding. Weapons clashed around him.

Suddenly, the governor clapped his hands. The fighting ceased.

'One among us,' the governor intoned, 'has brought dishonour on to this gathering. He struck an opponent who was appealing to me. The tournament is over!'

The governor strode from the dais. Tim immediately squatted alongside Simon.

'Are you all right?' he asked.

Simon managed an unsteady nod. 'What will they do to me?' he asked.

'I don't know,' said Tim. 'Things are different every time. The governor's mad. He already had it in for you –'

'What about him, the guy I –?' Simon couldn't express what he'd done.

'He looked all right to me,' said Tim. 'He's out of the choir, though. Scarred. No use. He was luckier than some.'

'On your feet!' a screw bellowed. 'Put these on.' He tossed each lad a long white smock – a choirboy's surplice. Silently, the choirboys robed themselves.

They filed through a door. The room beyond was dimly lit, and it was a moment before Simon could make sense of the decor. Against the far wall seemed to be an altar. Nothing out of the ordinary – a simple cross, a table covered with a white cloth, one of those cup things . . . He remembered it all from Sunday school. Next to the altar was a pulpit. Again, a simple wooden thing with a big Bible at the top.

Then things got strange. There was a black altar-rail running the width of the room, but standing against it were things Simon had never seen before. They looked a bit like saddles – or those four-legged vaulting-horses Simon had so dreaded at school. There were about ten of them in a row, level in height with the altar-rail, jutting out from the rail into the room.

The men crowded in behind them. Some began to undress.

There was a wooden creak as someone mounted the altar steps.

It was the governor. He was robed like a vicar, in a long white cassock and an ornate woven mantle. Simon had heard tell that he used to be a vicar.

'Welcome, boys,' he said quietly. 'Once again we are gathered here in the sight of God to crave forgiveness for our sins. For the wages of sin, as we know, is death.' He stared about the congregation. 'I want each of you to look into your hearts,' he said, an angry inflection in his voice now, 'and reflect on what you find there.' He was beginning to shout. 'Reflect on your lusts, reflect on your sins of onanism and fornication, of practising abominable and unnatural acts that offend the very eyes of God!'

He hammered down with his fist on the wooden pulpit. It shook.

'Step forward,' he said darkly.

From out of the darkness, two officers emerged and pushed them towards the altar-rail. Simon watched as Tim was pushed to his knees and bent forward over the length of one of the saddles. Other boys followed suit spontaneously – Martin next to Tim, then the twins, then the Chinese guy, then the lad with the pudding-basin haircut. Each hitched up his cassock so that his bare buttocks were exposed. Numbly, Simon moved to take his place next to him.

'Not him,' the governor barked. 'Keep him there. He's my altar boy, today.'

A guard grabbed Simon roughly by the shoulder and pushed him against the wall. He gazed past the pulpit to the altar. For the first time, he saw the straps on each of its lily-white corners.

One by one, the officers were strapping the other lads' arms and legs to the feet of their saddles. Simon watched as the screws reached in between each boy's legs. He sensed several of the lads tensing in pain. The screws seemed to be strapping their genitals.

On an unseen command, a guard suddenly propelled Simon around the altar-rail and stood him under the cross.

'Lie down,' the guard said, removing the silver cup and a plate from the table. 'On your front.'

Nervously, Simon did as he was told.

The guard hitched up Simon's long white garb, then made a quick circuit of the table, strapping his arms and legs tightly. Simon felt the guard reach between his splayed legs and grab his cock and balls savagely. He felt the roughness of a leather strap being buckled around them, tight and painfully, anchoring them to the end of the table.

The governor was standing over him. The governor curtseyed to the cross, then, singing very quietly under his breath, placed the silver plate beneath Simon's face and the silver goblet between his legs, hard and cold against his perineum.

The governor returned to the pulpit and began to speak.

'And Satan answered the Lord, and said, Skin for skin, yea, all that a man hath he will give for his life. But put forth thine hand now, and touch his bone and his flesh, and he will curse thee to thy face . . .'

The screws and the other men were all now in a state of semi-nakedness. Jackets were removed, trousers loosened, hard cocks exposed. They closed around the saddles. Some took the lads from the front, some behind. As Simon watched, a burly officer and a tall, sallow-faced man in a suit took Tim. The screw plunged his fat cock into Tim's open mouth, while the suit sought his arsehole with his long prick.

Others in the line were also being taken. A pair of screws stood in front of the twins, their cocks still soft, laughing and conspiring together. One by one, they began to piss, showering hot jets of dark yellow liquid into the twins' faces, into their scruffy blond hair, their eyes, their mouths. The little guy with the pudding-basin haircut was struggling to take two hard cocks in his mouth, while one of the men in suits fell to his knees behind him and thrust his tongue hungrily into the boy's exposed arsehole. One of the screws was riding Martin like a cowboy, lashing at his buttocks with a thick leather thong.

One figure stood alone at the back of the room, watching, smiling slightly. Craigie – the orchestrator of the horrors – made no move to join in.

The governor closed the Bible and stepped down from the

pulpit. He was carrying a thin bamboo cane, which he flexed in his hands.

'Miserable sinner,' he whispered. 'I do this for you. For your immortal soul.'

He raised it high in the air, and brought it flashing down across Simon's buttocks. It stung hotly. The governor thrashed him repeatedly, until his cheeks blazed. Then he threw down the cane and hitched up the front of his vestments: he was naked and hard underneath. He began wanking his cock and, whimpering slightly, dropped to his knees, out of sight, between Simon's legs.

Simon felt the governor's frantic fingers clutching at his buttock-cheeks, frenziedly probing his hole. He felt the governor's hot face against his crack, the wet tongue licking the weals which crisscrossed Simon's buttocks like brands, probing his ring.

'I'm sorry,' the governor whimpered as he sucked at Simon's arsehole. 'I'm so sorry.'

He clambered over Simon's back and bit down on his neck. Simon could feel the governor's hands guiding that hard cock into his arsehole. He fucked Simon quickly and breathlessly, whimpering as he drove his cock into Simon.

The governor spent himself quickly.

'Take,' he whispered. 'Eat: this is my body which is given for you.'

That was the signal. Guards and guests swarmed about the altar, fighting and jostling like dogs to get at Simon. One tried to thrust his hard cock in Simon's mouth, only to be pushed away by a rival cock. The two clashed together in Simon's face, both trying to force entry into his face. He felt a sudden weight on his back, and an urgent cock thrust itself between his buttocks. One screw took a handful of Simon's hair, yanking his head to one side, and wrapped it around the head of his fat cock, clamping it in his fist. He wanked himself hurriedly with Simon's hair and came almost immediately against Simon's head in a great stream.

The two cocks succeeded in forcing themselves into his mouth at the same time. Simon gagged. His jaw felt about to break. They pummelled the back of his throat.

Choking, he started to panic. He felt stubby fingers forcing their way into his arsehole, crowding in around the cock that was already pumping him. He felt something else: a second cock, forcing its way in alongside the first. He tried to scream, but couldn't.

Two cocks fucked his mouth, another two stretched his arsehole almost beyond endurance.

He was hard . . .

In spite of everything, he felt close to coming.

He could just about make out Tim and the other choirboys watching him.

Bizarrely, some music started up. There was a small organ to one side of the room, and Craigie was now sitting at it, thumping out chords. Uncertainly, the choir, still strapped to their saddles, bare buttocks still exposed, began to sing.

'All things bright and beautiful . . .'

One of the screws fucking Simon's face let out a sudden grunt and shot a great gob of spunk down his throat. The other continued to pump him. The first didn't remove his cock, but let it relax and soften slightly. Simon felt a sudden, warm sensation, far to the back of his mouth. His mouth was suddenly filled with an overpowering, acrid, salty tang. His cock still embedded in Simon's mouth, his tormentor was pissing. His partner suddenly shot his load – heavy spunk mingling with an ocean of piss, raging around Simon's mouth.

The two men at his rear were coming, too, their cocks twitching and spasming.

The choir continued to sing.

All the guards took him that night, and all the governor's smart guests. When they had all taken their fill, they dressed and stood around, chatting and drinking wine, as if nothing had happened. The choir remained strapped in their places in silence until the last guest had left. Then the few remaining screws untied them, let them dress and escorted them back to their cells.

Simon couldn't meet Tim's eye.

Eighteen

Paul decided he had to get off the wing: if not permanently – which he reckoned was impossible – at least for as much time as he could manage. It was the only way to keep Spalding off his back. He decided to get a job. Something that would take him off the wing for most of the day. The screws were looking for volunteers to work outside the prison on rural renovation schemes: some government deal or other. Trusted inmates only, of course. He doubted he'd qualify.

He went to Dave again. He found him in a quiet corridor, far from the cells. 'I hear they're looking for people to work outside,' Paul said.

'And you reckon they'd take you?' came the sneering reply. 'You're a little yob, Travis. You're trouble.'

'I used to be,' said Paul quietly.

'Oh, yeah,' Dave smirked. 'Spalding sorted you out, didn't he? Turned you into his bitch. I was forgetting – you're a fraggle, now.'

Paul didn't need this. Swallowing hard, he cut to the chase and put his hand on Dave's cock. It was already hard beneath his uniform.

ROBERT BLACK

'You think you can bend me round your little finger like that?' said Dave. 'Do you?' He slapped Paul hard across the head. Paul ignored the blow and began slowly massaging Dave's pole through his trousers. Dave made no attempt to move away.

Slowly, Paul sank to his knees, unbuttoning Dave's flies as he did so, releasing his thick, tall, side-curving cock and his huge balls. He parted his lips and wrapped them carefully around his teeth, then placed them around the swollen head of Dave's cock and drew the swollen bulb up into his mouth. It smelt musky, and tasted unwashed.

'Is that what you think, eh?' said Dave breathlessly. 'Is that what you think?' He was practically shouting.

Paul sensed he was becoming angry. Earnestly, Paul ran his lips up and down the length of Dave's shaft, burying his face in the sandy tangle of his pubes.

'You need teaching a lesson, boy,' Dave gasped.

Quite suddenly, he struck Paul a blow to the head that sent him reeling to the floor. Then he sprang on Paul and pinned him on his stomach. 'That's what you need.'

Paul felt the big screw ripping at his trousers, dragging them down. There was a shuffling and rustling behind him, and he felt Dave's prick stabbing his buttocks, searching roughly for his arsehole, pushing its way hastily in.

'You need to know who's in charge, here,' snarled Dave. He began thrusting into Paul's arse, grunting and drooling over Paul's neck. Pinned to the hard corridor floor, Paul could only close his eyes and try to ignore the rough, dry, frantic stabs which seemed to gouge their way into him, high into his tunnel. His stretched, battered sphincter muscles burnt with the stretching.

'You need to – Ah –'

Dave's cock-strokes became fast and irregular. He clamped his lips around Paul's neck and bit into his skin as he came. Breathless for a moment, Dave picked himself up in silence, buttoned his flies and walked away.

*

160

The next day, while Paul was lying on his bunk, a screw handed him a memo telling him he was appointed forthwith to the external work detail.

There was a farm not far from the jail. Part of the farm's land had fallen into disuse – a small lake had become a stagnant rubbish dump, and trees and weeds had grown up thickly. It all had to be cleared. A dozen men were sent out there. Paul was relieved to see that none of them was from D wing. He made himself known to a couple of the blokes on the first day – happily, his name meant nothing to them. His lowly status hadn't got beyond the wing.

The men were quiet, for the most part, and well behaved. Most of them were near to having served their time, and were looking forward to getting out for good. Their guards were few, and more interested in catching the sun than preventing escapes. The work party was trusted with shovels, saws and axes.

There were a couple of more lively inmates: Mick – whose real name was Miguel – a swarthy Spanish guy of about Paul's age; and Kev, a thick-set and muscular guy in his mid-twenties, with coarse red hair and a face and back plastered in bright freckles. They messed about continually, and never seemed to get much work done – but, for the most part, the group worked quietly and diligently.

Paul was paired off with a tall Finn of about twenty-five, called Tomi; the Finn was pale skinned, with rangy muscular limbs and blond-going-on-brown hair. They were put to work at either end of a two-man saw, cutting the thickest and most obstinate trees. It was hard, hot work. They toiled bare-chested, their muscles bulging against the weight of the saw and the resistance of the wood. They didn't speak much – Tomi spoke little English – but nevertheless struck up an unspoken rapport, grinning as their saw-strokes fell into a pleasing rhythm against the grain.

Mick talked constantly. He talked about his girlfriend back in Madrid, and continually hatched wild escape plans involving axe battles with the screws. Dopey, wide-eyed Kev swallowed every word of it, and constantly sought Mick's promise that, when he went, he'd take him along. They were both full of shit.

After the party had been working out there for several days, a whisper began to go around. The farmer, whose sturdy old house sat at the edge of the tangled forest, had a daughter, and apparently . . .

Paul saw for himself, later that week. He heard excited shouts, and saw many from the work party down tools and start running towards the clearing where the house stood. He threw Tomi a glance, registered his uncomprehending smile, let go of his end of the saw and joined the flow of people. He reached the treeline and stopped.

'Told you,' said Mick. 'There she is.'

In one of the bedroom windows, facing the wood, stood the farmer's daughter. She was fit, Paul had to concede – slim, curvy in the hips, good tits, nice hair . . . And she was naked. She stood in the full-length window, looking out at the work party, swaying and wiggling, running her hands over her breasts and down her stomach, into her dark-brown, V-shaped muff and between her legs.

Mick already had his cock out, masturbating. So did Kev. Others of the crew also stood about, watching and masturbating.

Tomi lumbered up, curious. He saw the girl in the window and the men with their cocks out, and blushed furiously, grinning and lowering his eyes. He and Paul were the only ones not masturbating.

Paul was troubled by the sight. He'd almost stopped thinking about Jill – about women – at all. When he thought of sex, now, he thought of men. Of hasty and brutal sex in corridors and cupboards. He thought overwhelmingly of Spalding's brutal rapes. Could he be turning queer? Was that possible?

Paul didn't notice the front door of the farmhouse opening. None of them did. There was an angry shout, and a fat, red-faced man emerged, carrying a shotgun and shouting. He pointed the gun at the line of men and pulled the trigger.

Like frightened rabbits, they ran back into the trees, stuffing their cocks away as they ran.

The girl was there again the next day – and the day after. So were the men. And so, on cue, was the farmer with his gun. It became a game to them – a game which the farmer's daughter evidently enjoyed as much as the men.

After one of their mad flights for the cover of the wood, Paul found himself sheltering behind a muddy bank with Kev and Mick, breathless and laughing. His companions still had their cocks, half-hard, in their hands.

'Fuck, she really does it for me, that woman,' said Mick. He was still squeezing and stroking his prick, which grew again to full hardness as Paul watched. 'Such a long fucking time . . .'

Kev, the redhead, was wanking, too.

Mick cuffed Paul on the arm. 'You never do, do you,' he said. 'What's wrong with you? Don't you fancy her? You queer or something?'

Paul smiled to himself. In this strange, inverted world, he wasn't sure what he was. He settled back against the bank, enjoying the sun, undid his flies and pulled his cock out. He grew hard quickly. He looked across at his two fellow inmates lying next to him, cocks craning towards the sunlight. Mick wanked his long, dark cock vigorously. It leaked a constant stream of pre-come, which he rubbed around his cock-head and foreskin with his thumb. Next to him, Kev, thick-set and pale and freckled, tugged at his thick-set, pale and freckled cock, pulling the foreskin hard back over a pink bulb which looked curiously small and dainty on top of his thick shaft. Paul started to wank along with them, lazily, soaking in the sun. He felt secure here, male-bonding with some decent, ordinary blokes, far from the sexual tyranny of D wing. Quite unexpectedly, he started to hit orgasm. His hips jerked and his cock started to fountain into his trousered lap.

Mick laughed breathlessly. 'Dirty bastard,' he gasped. 'Oh . . .' And his own dark cock started to spurt.

There was a rustling in the undergrowth, and Tomi kicked his way clumsily into their little hollow. He stopped, startled, staring down at them. At that moment, Kev came with a shudder and an oath. His spunk shot wildly, missing him and peppering the thin grass of the bank.

'We were just . . .' Paul was embarrassed, for some reason, in front of Tomi. He hurriedly put his cock away.

The tall, shy Finn just looked at the ground, blushing.

The games at the farmhouse continued, day after day. Paul rarely went, and Tomi never. Paul liked the shy, silent Finnish giant. He sensed they both liked the calm which suddenly infused the wood when Mick's Spanish jabbering receded in the direction of the farmhouse, signalling the start of play. Usually the silence lasted a good ten minutes – sometimes twenty – before the farmer's gun shattered it.

One day, Paul couldn't help but notice Tomi had a hard-on which simply didn't go away. It stayed with him all morning as he worked, bare-chested and tanning in the hot early summer sunshine. Watching it all morning, Paul found himself both amused and a little aroused. When the time came for the crew to go to the farmhouse, Paul was struck by a notion.

'Shall we?' he said to Tomi.

Tomi raised his eyebrows in puzzlement.

Paul took his arm and tugged him in the direction of the farm. Realising what Paul meant, Tomi pulled back in alarm.

'Suit yourself,' said Paul. 'I just thought, with that thing in your trousers for the last four hours . . . I thought you could use a little relief, that's all. It's harmless.'

Tomi turned and trotted to a little thicket. He kicked his way into the middle of it and dropped to his haunches. He beckoned to Paul. Puzzled, Paul kicked his way over to Tomi. Only when he was beside him did he see that Tomi had his cock out. Hunched down, his knees bent, his legs shielded him from being seen from the path. He pulled Paul down next to him.

'All right, all right,' grinned Paul, dropping into a squat. 'You're a dark horse, aren't you?'

Tomi's cock was as big as the rest of him. He pumped at it eagerly with a huge fist. Paul pulled his own prick out and began wanking alongside him. Tomi stared down at Paul's prick in enthralment. He craned his neck to get a better look.

'What's wrong?' Paul asked. 'You never seen another prick before?'

Tomi stared, unblinking.

'No,' mused Paul. 'I reckon you haven't, have you? Not this close. What the fuck d'you do on B wing? All right.' He unbuttoned his trousers properly, and pulled them down below his buttocks. His cock sprang free of his pants, and quivered slightly. He lay back against the bracken and spread his legs. 'Take a good look,' he said.

He masturbated slowly and deliberately, both touched and turned on by the big Scandinavian's evident fascination with his prick. Tomi extended a shovel hand and clumsily touched Paul's balls with his big, blunt fingertips. He ran them under Paul's bollocks and along his perineum, then back again.

'You want a go?' Paul asked. He lay back even further and placed his hands behind his head. 'Feel free,' he said.

Tomi wrapped a finger and thumb around Paul's thick brown shaft and ran them slowly up to the tip. He pulled Paul's foreskin back as far as it would go, far back from his knob. With his index finger, he traced the ridge of his helmet in a full circle. Then he closed his great fist tight around Paul's rod and began pumping hard.

'Whoa!' cried Paul. 'Ease off. You'll burst it.'

Tomi seemed to get the message; he loosened his grip a little, and slowed his stroke.

'Mm,' said Paul. 'That's good.'

He looked across at Tomi's big, pale, untidy prick, still poking out through the grey flannel of his prison trousers. The Finn was trying to wank both of them at the same time, but couldn't seem to coordinate the movement. Every time he worked his own ragged foreskin up and down over the big pink bulb beneath, his rhythm on Paul's prick stalled for a moment.

165

'Here,' said Paul, and reached into Tomi's lap, batting the Finn's hand away from his prick. He grasped the thick, uneven shaft, and smiled. Tomi had a raw, unfinished look about him – his bones, Paul guessed. Except that it extended to his prick. It was as rude and raw as any he'd come across, leftward curving, its veins pronounced and rambling, the foreskin loose and flapping. Paul began running his hand up its rough-hewn length. It must have been ten, eleven inches. He hooded the bloated pink bulb completely, pinching the neck of Tomi's foreskin together, then pulled the skin out from the end of Tomi's cock, before letting it fall back, and allowing the bulb to poke through again.

He heard the farmer's shot. So did Tomi, who looked around in panic and tried hastily to put himself away.

'Relax,' said Paul. 'We'll be OK, if we're quick.'

They began hastily rubbing up and down each other's pricks now, furtive and fast, aware of shouts and running footsteps in the distance, getting nearer. They crouched close together, heads touching, faces staring down on to their exposed boners, hands flying fast, each concentrating on working the other's cock to a swift climax.

Paul heard footsteps, close behind them, then silence.

In the silence, he could hear the tiny squidging of the pre-come which had leaked from his cock-head, as Tomi worked it into the skin of the shaft, and the minute, rapid slap of his own hand, reeling in Tomi's loose foreskin.

'Where are Paul and Tomi?' Kev's voice, right above them, asked.

Tomi was coming. He opened his mouth, and a small choking noise emerged – almost a cry. His cock spat a single, fat glob of spunk into the air. It splattered back into his lap as his cock seeped a slow river of its pearly white fluid. Paul too felt his orgasm shoot through him and his cock explode its contents over their bracken screen.

'Mick?'

They heard Kev's footsteps receding. Tomi started to guffaw deeply. Paul began to laugh, too. Sitting there, with a decent bloke he barely knew, in the woods in the sunshine with their cocks in their laps, Paul suddenly, momentarily, felt free – free of the walls and doors and endless lock-ups, free of pimps and predators. He suddenly wished Tomi was on D wing.

D wing.

The moment was lost. The sun went behind a cloud. Shades of the prison house seemed to close about him.

'Better get back to work,' he said flatly.

Nineteen

Simon could hardly face Tim in the laundry the next day. His arms and legs ached; his cock and balls were raw from the strap. Most of all, though, he felt a burning sense of shame. This wasn't like the rapes and abuses of D wing – last night, he felt that somehow he'd been a willing contributor in the games. In his own humiliation.

'I wish you'd told me,' he said at last, breaking the morning's silence.

'I couldn't,' said Tim. 'I was ashamed, I suppose. You've seen the way everybody on the wing looks at me. I didn't want you to feel that way about me.'

'I'd never . . .' Simon began, then stopped. He could understand Tim's fears. They fitted the way he felt about himself, after last night.

'How did you . . . get into the choir?' Simon asked.

'It was Craigie,' he said quietly. 'He's got this surveillance gear. Cameras and stuff. He has a camera in my cell. He does it sometimes – to boys he thinks the governor will like. Then he persuaded Gary and Louie to come in and make me have sex with them. The governor saw the tape . . . and liked what he saw.'

The memory returned to Simon: that first day. Their induction. The video they had been shown. The boy on the bed, being taken by the two Americans.

'That was you,' he said.

'What?'

'Nothing.' Not for the first time, Simon felt like some kind of lab rat in a maze; experimented on, manipulated, and all the time watched. 'I won't do it again,' he said. 'No matter what.'

'You've got to,' said Tim. 'You've got no choice. If you quit, you're just a fraggle again. You've seen how they resent us on the wing – how they fear us. Once we lose the governor's protection, we'll be at their mercy.'

'I don't care,' said Simon. 'It couldn't be worse than last night. Someone could have been killed.'

'I know,' said Tim quietly.

'You mentioned another bloke from the wing, who used to be in the choir.'

Tim swallowed hard.

'What happened to him?'

Tim took a long time to answer.

'One of the governor's games,' he said. 'They had us dressed up like we were in a concentration camp. They had these metal tables, these surgical instruments . . .' His voice, barely a whisper, died away to nothing.

'They killed him?'

Tim nodded.

'But – didn't anybody say anything? His family?'

He didn't have any family to speak of. None of us in the choir do. I grew up in an orphanage –'

'I didn't,' interrupted Simon. 'I've got family.'

'And when was the last time you saw them?' asked Tim.

Simon lowered his gaze. 'When I came out to them,' he said. 'They practically disowned me on the spot.'

After the governor spotted you in here with me, that day, Craigie'll have been through your visiting records.'

'I never have visitors.'

'That's the point,' said Tim. 'Nor do I. Nor do any of us. Face it: who'd miss us?'

Simon thought of Mehmet. Stuck in a squalid shanty, halfway around the world. Would Mehmet miss him? Simon dismissed the thought. He was probably dead to Mehmet, anyway. He'd pretty much resigned himself to the fact that he'd almost certainly never see his Palestinian lover again.

He felt suddenly helpless, fragile and so very alone. He felt tears welling. He clutched Tim to his chest and buried his face in his neck and cried bitter tears.

After that, neither spoke of the choir again, though Simon thought about it constantly, and dreaded the next summons. He turned Tim's words over and over in his mind. *You've seen how they resent us on the wing . . . Once we lose the governor's protection, we'll be at their mercy.*

There had to be a way out of this. He began racking his brains for an answer. He thought of what Paul had said to him. *You've got to find a role for yourself. Something people can use – that way, you'll get protection.* It seemed so long ago, now.

A week passed before an idea began to take shape in his mind. It was Sanjay who triggered it; one morning, he ran into the laundry in a state of panic.

'You've got to help me,' the Indian boy pleaded. 'I'm in trouble.' He was carrying a two-thirds-full bottle of whisky. 'I pinched this from Spalding,' he said.

'You what?' Simon was both delighted and horrified.

'I was pissed off with him,' said Sanjay.

'About fucking time,' Tim cut in.

'He thinks it was me,' Sanjay continued. 'He wants it back.'

'What are you going to do?' Simon asked.

'Well, I can't give it back to him,' said Sanjay. 'Then he'll know it was me.'

'You could just leave it somewhere,' Simon mused. 'In a corridor.'

'Are you mad?' Sanjay exclaimed. 'That's Johnny Walker Black

170

Label! D'you know how much that stuff costs? No, Spalding can fuck himself. I'm having this.'

'But if he finds it on you, he'll kill you.'

'I know,' said Sanjay. 'Can't you hide it somewhere?'

'Don't be daft, Sanjay,' Tim said. 'You know what Spalding's like. He'll rip the wing apart to get this.'

Tim was right, of course. It started later that day, with the cells. Between them, Spalding and his gang went into just about every cell, pulled bed-frames and mattresses around, opened cabinets, threw their contents on the floor. From the laundry, they could hear the sounds of protest and the kickings which generally followed. As usual, the guards did nothing.

It was only a matter of time before they reached the laundry. They could hear Spalding, Ant and Jock in the next corridor. Sanjay was approaching a state of panic.

Simon was getting an idea. He went to the storeroom, reached over Gorman's hunched, transported form and removed a small key from a shelf. Crossing to the row of giant washing machines, he dropped into a squat and began rubbing the dust and grime off the bottom panel of the end machine.

'What are you doing?' Tim asked.

'There's a slot here, somewhere,' said Simon. He found it. He inserted the key and turned it. The panel fell away from the machine with a dull clang. 'In there,' he said. 'In the machine. There's plenty of room between the drum and the floor. Look.' He grabbed the bottle from Sanjay and stood it in the space. 'Give me a hand with this panel,' he said.

Tim sprang forward and helped him heave the heavy panel back into place. Simon turned the key and slipped it into his pocket as Spalding, Jock and Ant entered the room.

'Sanjay, you Paki piece of shit,' Spalding spat. 'Where's my fucking whisky?'

'I don't know nothing about it, Spalding, I swear to God,' Sanjay pleaded.

At a nod from Spalding, Ant and Jock began tearing through

the laundry, throwing clean and soiled linen about the room, emptying the big tubs of detergent, peering deep into the drums of the machines. In the drums, but not in the guts: none of them suspected the existence of the removable panel.

Ant lumbered into the stockroom while Jock crawled between the banks of machines. He emerged, filthy.

Spalding grabbed Sanjay by the throat and pinned him against the wall. 'When I find that bottle, you're fucking dead,' he said.

'It wasn't me, Spalding – honest!' Sanjay implored.

There was a cry from the stockroom, and Ant tumbled out. 'Dirty fucker!' he spat. A wet, sticky stain ran up the side of his trousers.

Simon, Tim and Sanjay had to suppress their laughter.

'You fucking retard!' Spalding snarled at Ant. 'You piss yourself or something?' He kicked a machine – the very machine which hid the booze. It echoed dully. 'Fuck it,' he said. 'It's not here. Let's go.' And with a final, evil glance at Sanjay he left, his lieutenants in tow.

The three friends were tense, listening for a long while after the gang's footsteps had receded down the passage. Then Sanjay collapsed backward on to the disordered mountain of dirty linen and began to laugh. The others joined in with abandon.

'We got him,' Tim sang. 'We actually put one over on Spalding.'

'This deserves a drink,' said Sanjay. 'Simon . . .'

While Tim propped a chair under the doorhandle, Simon opened the panel once again and removed the bottle.

They lay in clover and soiled bedding all afternoon, passing the bottle back and forth, chatting idly and laughing quietly. Simon hadn't drunk that much on the outside, and nothing since coming in here. The whisky went straight to his head. The others seemed equally out of it. He could see Tim, his head lolling, smiling at him. Sanjay, on the other side of him, seemed to have sunk into sleep, his warm, toothy grin filling his face.

Turning on to his side, Tim reached across and ran his hands through Simon's layers of golden hair. Simon turned as well, and shuffled closer to Tim across the uneven linen, and they kissed, slowly and lazily, their lips gently playing across each other, their tongues occasionally peeping out and nudging and nuzzling each other. Tim sneaked open Simon's belt and his fly. Simon wriggled slightly, working the trousers down his buttocks. He opened Tim's trousers and tugged them gently away from his hard cock, which stretched the red cotton of his pants. Simon's cock, too, strained hard against his white underwear. Tim began to tickle his balls through the cotton, slowly and gently. Simon did the same, running his fingernails back and forth along Tim's tight bollocks.

They lay like that for an age: lips and tongues, fingers and bollocks. Slowly, they came together in a passionate hug. Tim clutched at Simon's balls and kneaded his throbbing shaft hard through his pants. Simon did the same, running his palm forcefully up and down the underside of Tim's pole, squeezing at the circumcised head with his fingers. A droplet of juice seeped through the scarlet cloth.

Simon buried his face in Tim's neck, closing his eyes and breathing deeply, savouring the light musk of his lover's skin. He kissed him and nipped gently at his flesh with his teeth. Tim moaned slightly.

Simon's eyes opened for a moment, and fell on Sanjay. He was watching them; his hand in his pocket, slowly squeezing a towering hard-on. As Simon's gaze swept him, he instantly shut his eyes – then opened them again with a sheepish grin. Tim turned his head to see the distraction.

Simon and Tim shared a quick, enquiring glance, and a smile. Together, they beckoned Sanjay to them. Grinning his sunny grin, he slithered across the floor, his hand already lowering his trousers. His cock pushed at the front of his black boxer shorts, which stood like a tent. He pulled the front of them down, hooking the elastic under his balls, and his hard brown prick, thick and meaty and uncircumcised, sprang forward. It was surrounded by a thick eruption of coarse black pubic hair which extended up his belly and disappeared under his shirt.

Tim grasped a handful of Sanjay's belly hair and pulled it

playfully, drawing Sanjay closer to them. With his other hand, Tim unhooked Simon's tall, straight cock from his pants, again hooking the elastic under his balls. He grasped both cocks, Simon's and Sanjay's, one in each hand, and began slowly wanking them. Looking to Simon for permission, Sanjay released Tim's circumcised pole and grasped it in his fist, pulling at it, joyfully crushing it so that Tim gasped. Sanjay silenced his gasp with a long, deep kiss. He then turned to Simon, and plunged his tongue into his mouth. Lips locked and clashed; tongues jousted.

Tim began pulling harder and faster on Simon's and Sanjay's twin erections. Sanjay, too, increased the speed of his stroke on Tim's cock. Three mouths came together in a clumsy kiss – tongues extended to the full, clashing and diving. Free hands grabbed at clothes, pulling shirt buttons open. Simon ran his outstretched hand across the field of black hair which stretched between Sanjay's dark nipples and down to his bellybutton.

Sanjay wriggled down the laundry pile and cupped Simon's balls in his hand. He ran his tongue all the way around the ridge of Simon's helmet, and delicately rolled back Simon's foreskin with his teeth. He licked and nibbled his way down Simon's shaft and nipped tantalisingly around his balls; then, lightly kissing Simon's exposed helmet, wrapped his lips around it and plunged. Simon let out a long, cool breath of pleasure as he felt the full, warm wet lips descend around his shaft, and the moist cave of Sanjay's mouth engulf him. The Indian lad's head rose and fell slowly and warmly on his cock, sending little shivers of pleasure through his cock and balls.

His hand was inside Tim's pants now, roughly kneading his hard cock with an open palm. After a moment, he raised his head and switched cocks.

'Mm, nice,' he said as he lifted his face from Simon's cock. He licked Tim's head all over, trailing spit around its swollen surface and down the sides of his pole, before going down on it with relish.

Simon watched as Sanjay expertly gobbled Tim's cock, his luxuriant, silky mane flowing from his shoulders and cascading over Tim's belly and thighs. He noticed the Indian's cock was unattended and reached out a hand to take hold of it. It was chunky; it filled Simon's hand. He drew the foreskin back across the bulbous head, and forward again, with increasing speed.

He felt Tim twisting around, trying to reach Simon's cock with his mouth. He turned to let him engulf it in his pretty lips, enjoying the wetness of his lover's mouth. He himself turned – his cock rotating deliciously in Tim's mouth – and licked the head of Sanjay's prick. Stretching his mouth wide to take in the great girth, he went down on the Indian lad and felt Sanjay fill his mouth.

Lying half-undressed in a ragged circle on the laundry floor, the three friends sucked and slurped at one another's throbbing cocks. Sanjay arched his back, pushing his hips forward, his cock-head seeking the back of Simon's throat. Simon slowed his breathing, and took him in. He could just about make out Tim, enthusiastically fucking Sanjay's mouth with quick, shallow thrusts.

He felt the lick of Tim's dancing tongue around his bulb as his lover's head moved up and down his cock. He felt Tim's hand playing with his balls, rubbing his perineum, tweaking his arse-hole. He reached forward and did the same to Sanjay, marvelling at the luxuriant thickness of the hair on his balls and perineum, and the hair surrounding the tight rosette of his hole.

The three began to gather speed, actively fucking each other in the mouth now. Simon plunged lovingly in and out of Tim's mouth, while Sanjay's thick pole drilled in and out of him. They came almost together: Tim first, swearing under his breath as his orgasm ripped through him, then Simon and Sanjay, practically together. Simon felt his mouth drenched in hot, salty spunk while, at the same time, his own cock exploded. Tim lost it for a moment, and Simon's cock bounced out, wildly disgorging itself in Tim's face.

The three juddered to a standstill and lay back, content. Tim licked his sticky lips. They sprawled and passed the whisky bottle back and forth. Absently, Simon took the bottle from Tim. He nipped at it, then looked at the big washing machine, at his hiding place. And then the idea struck him.

'Oh, yes,' he said quietly. 'Oh, yes.'

'What?' asked Tim.

'I know how we can do it,' Simon said.

'What?' asked Tim again.

'Get ourselves a trade. Get protection. Get out of the choir,' Simon said. 'And stick it to Spalding.'

Simon's plan seemed almost too simple.

'Brewing,' he said.

'What?' Tim replied. 'Are you pissed?'

'Yes, a bit,' said Simon, 'but.' He was pissed, sure – but his mind was buzzing. 'Didn't you ever brew hooch when you lived out in the country?' he asked.

Tim shook his head.

'I did,' said Simon. 'Or at least, I knew lads who did. I watched them. It's simple – all you need is a little bag of yeast, some sugar, water and fruit. Or fruit juice, for preference. It's simple – you put them in a bottle and let the stuff do its thing. A week or so later, you've got a drinkable hooch.'

'You're mad,' said Tim.

'No, listen,' said Simon excitedly. 'We can get all the ingredients from the kitchen – that's easy. The bottles, too. The clever part is how to do it without being detected: where to put the stuff to brew.' He nodded at the row of huge washing machines, and took the little key from his pocket. 'We've got eight machines,' he said. 'That's a lot of hooch.'

Getting the ingredients was as simple as Simon predicted. Everything was up for sale in here; it was just a matter of meeting the price. By pooling resources, he, Tim and Sanjay paid off old Ernie, a life-long lag who worked in the kitchens, smoked about eighty cigarettes a day (people used to complain there was more fag ash than food on their plates), and constantly needed money or goods to sustain his craving. They bottled the ingredients, hid them beneath the machine, and waited.

The stuff turned out surprisingly well.

'For orange-flavoured beer, anyway,' teased Tim, starting on his second bottle.

'Go carefully with it,' said Simon. 'It's lethal.'

'It just might save our lives,' said Tim.

They drank the whole of the first batch to themselves, Simon, Tim and Sanjay, and they paid for it, the following day.

The second batch was larger, and tasted better. Simon carefully judged and juggled the ingredients.

'We're not drinking this lot,' he said. 'This lot's for sale.'

Simon had mapped it all out in his head. They'd let the cat out of the bag gently – let the rumours start with no apparent source; let people gradually find them. They'd start with some of the old lags – the lifers and long-termers who were getting on a bit and just wanted to serve out their time in peace. Hard, quiet men, mostly. They were avoided and treated with respect, even by the likes of Spalding. They had little interaction with the younger, fierier inmates, and the petty politics and power struggles on the wing left them largely untouched.

Simon had no intention of trying to deal with the toe-rags on the wing: at least, not yet.

He approached Ernie first, the chain-smoking kitchen worker. 'Half an ounce of snout for a bottle,' he said. 'Or a phone card. Come to the laundry and taste some.'

He was selling the stuff cheap, he knew. Most people in here, if they had anything to sell, would charge extortionately for it. Ripping off their fellow inmates was second nature to them. Simon had a different view. He wasn't interested in making easy money – his vision, still vague and unformed, was more long term.

He went next to Raymond, a guy in his sixties who'd been in here for ever, and who scrubbed and swept the passages around the solitary block. Then he went to three or four others, all with the same offer.

They all came, and they all liked what they tasted. Simon, Tim and Sanjay sold the lot inside a day, and set to making more.

Within a week, they had twenty-odd people calling on them for hooch, and the bases of all the washing machines were full.

Twenty

————————

The weather got hotter, and the work party's labour, clearing the farmer's land, got harder. They didn't seem to be making any headway, and the guards were getting tetchy. As the weeks passed, Paul noticed a change in Mick. The talkative Spaniard's voice was heard less and less through the thin screen of trees. He was staking out the farmhouse more or less full time.

Paul found him there one day, crouched behind a low wall, watching.

'There she is!' Mick hissed, beckoning him over. 'Look!'

Dropping into a stoop, Paul dived under cover of the wall, and looked. The farmer's daughter was crossing from the house to one of the outbuildings.

'She keeps a horse in there,' said Mick. 'She's always back and forth. It's doing my head in.'

Paul could see why. Long-legged and big-breasted, she wore tight blue jeans and an equally tight white T-shirt. Her long brown hair hung freely down her back.

She disappeared into the stable.

'Yeah, very nice,' said Paul. 'You'd better get back to work. The screws are really on the rag today.'

'Fuck the screws,' said Mick. 'Look.'

The stable door opened and the girl emerged on horseback. She cantered towards the house, then turned the beast and, with a wink towards Mick and Paul, spurred it into life and galloped out across an open field.

'Did you see that?' Mick spluttered. 'She winked at us.'

'She's been flashing her cunt at us for weeks,' said Paul. 'I shouldn't read too much into a wink.'

Paul returned to work and gave the incident no more thought. He and Tomi, the big Finn, sawed and hacked at trees, dredged the lake for old bicycles, and, every so often, lay in some thicket in the sun and masturbated one another.

The next day, Mick came looking for Paul. 'You've got to come with me,' he said. He was in a state.

'What is it?' demanded Paul, a little irritably. The day was hot and the work was slow. He wasn't in the mood for Mick's fucking about.

'Just come,' said Mick, and set off at a run towards the farmhouse.

Swearing and wiping the sweat from his forehead, Paul followed him. They stopped at the low wall.

'What the fuck's this all about?' Paul demanded.

'Her!' cried Mick excitedly. 'The girl – we're in!'

'What? Nah.' Mick was off on one, Paul thought. Again. He didn't have time for this. He wasn't interested in the girl, he realised. He could see exactly what Mick was going on about, but could barely raise a flicker of interest. Had he changed that much?

'No, listen,' Mick urged, 'I talked to her. She's definitely up for it. But she told me to bring you along.'

They heard a galloping of hooves, and the girl rode up behind them.

'You came, then,' she said to Mick. 'And you brought your brother.'

Paul's jaw dropped.

'Uh, yeah!' Mick was flustered. 'This is my brother, Paul. Paul, this is Mary.'

Paul's shoulders slumped. He flashed a weary smile at the girl on the horse.

'Best come on, then,' she said and, spurring the horse, jumped the wall and cantered to the stable.

'You heard her,' said Mick, starting to climb the wall.

'Hang on,' said Paul. 'What's all this brother shit?'

'She asked if you were my brother,' said Mick. 'She likes doing it with brothers. It was the only way . . .'

'OK, OK,' snapped Paul. 'Just this once, I suppose.'

'Cheers, mate!' beamed Mick, slapping him on the back. 'It'll do you good. You been banged up too long.'

Paul watched Mick as he opened the stable door and slipped inside. They did look a bit alike, he supposed: same dark, foreign skin and thick head of black hair. He followed him inside.

The girl was dismounting from her horse. She tugged at the saddle straps.

'You know, I had my first orgasm riding a horse,' she said. 'I must have been about eleven.' She lifted the saddle from the beast and placed it over a horizontal wooden rail. Matter-of-factly, in exactly the same way she'd just unsaddled her horse, she began to undress. She removed her T-shirt, her bare breasts cascading forward, and unbuttoned and removed her jeans. She wore no pants underneath. Her dense brown bush glistened slightly with the sweat of her ride. 'Well?' she challenged, tossing herself back on to a square bale of straw.

Mick was already undressing. He dropped his trousers and pants and stood posing in front of the reclining girl. His hard cock, long and dark – longer and darker than Paul's – bobbed in front of him as he flexed his biceps and pectorals. The girl laughed.

Paul undressed more modestly. He noticed Mick sneaking a look at his hard prick, and the girl staring openly. She beckoned to him to come forward, and spread her legs. Mick watched, a little taken aback, as Paul approached her. She tossed him a condom, which he caught automatically. He opened and discarded the packet, and rolled the rubber down over his cock.

He shot a glance – half-apologetic, half-mocking – at Mick, and began running his hands along the inside of the girl's thighs and up into her bush.

Not disheartened, Mick scampered around to the other side of the bale, his cock bouncing as he moved, and pulled the girl's head back. He angled his cock downward and pushed it into her mouth. Paul followed suit, and slid his prick easily between her cunt-lips.

He fucked her more out of a sense of curiosity than anything else. He concentrated on sensations he hadn't felt for months now. He'd grown quickly accustomed to wanking with his fellow inmates; he'd made the jump to fucking arses. He supposed, under duress, he was even getting used to being fucked himself.

He felt somehow as if he was experiencing this at second hand, or observing it from far away. He watched the girl's breasts jiggling as he and Mick pumped their cocks into her. He watched the bob of the girl's throat as she gobbled on Mick's long cock. More and more he concentrated on Mick's cock itself. It was much like his own – a little bigger, perhaps, but essentially the same coffee colour, with a neat foreskin and a good-sized head.

Mick caught Paul's eye. He smiled and raised an open hand. Automatically, Paul smiled back, raising his hand in response. Palms clashed and clasped in midair over the writhing girl: twin cocks, hard and dark, pumped in perfect synch.

They kept their hands clasped until they came, shuddering to orgasm together, palms tight, fingers squeezing hard as each experienced his orgasm.

They pulled out of the girl, and Paul peeled off the condom and tossed it to the floor. Idly, the horse licked and sniffed at it.

The girl licked her lips. 'Brothers, eh?' she said.

Paul smiled furtively. She got to her feet and placed a hand around each of their softening cocks, pulling the lads towards her. All three stood, naked in a tight huddle. The girl put their twin cocks together and began rubbing them. A final droplet of sperm oozed from the head of Paul's cock-head and oozed over Mick's bulb. The girl rubbed it into the swelling helmet.

'So let's see what brothers get up to,' she said, smiling wickedly.

Both lads looked confused. The girl led them by the cock to the saddle, and sat on its cross beam. She slapped the hard brown leather. 'Up you get,' she said. 'Both of you.'

Mick obeyed without question, vaulting up on to the beam and settling his bare arse in the hard leather bowl.

'Now you,' she said to Paul, and gave his cock a hard tweak. 'Face him.'

Feeling foolish, Paul climbed up beside Mick. They sat in the curved, crowded saddle, naked and facing each other, legs dangling in limbo, cocks and balls and knees nudging. Once again, she extended a pale hand and pulled the two cocks together, closing her fist around them. Mick was fully hard again; Paul was getting there. She stroked them slowly and carefully, drawing their foreskins back in unison, then pulling them forward again. She did this several times, then stepped back.

'Well?' she said.

'What?'

'Boys' games,' she said. 'The sort of thing little brothers are supposed to get up to in stables.'

'I think she wants us to –' Mick said.

Paul was way ahead of him. He grasped Mick's pole and began pumping it vigorously. Mick reached forward and grabbed Paul's prick, now hard again, and still sensitive from his recent orgasm. The sensation when Mick started running his hand up and down the pole was intense.

The girl walked round them, watching. 'Brothers,' she sighed.

Smiling mischievously, Paul began running his hand over Mick's chest. Mick shuffled uneasily, and for a moment stopped wanking Paul's cock. Paul guessed this was all getting a little too gay for him. He decided to see how far he could push him. He tweaked Mick's nipple cheekily. Mick was a little more muscular than Paul, and a little hairier. Paul traced the short black curls which bunched around his nipples and threaded their way across his chest and down his belly. He wetted his index finger between his lips and placed it in Mick's bellybutton.

'Mm,' said the girl. Her hand was buried between her legs, her fingers disappearing into her thick brown muff.

Mick shot him a nervous glance. Paul was still working hard on Mick's cock, rubbing the juices that steadily leaked into his cock-head and down his shaft. Mick responded by tightening his grip on Paul's cock and speeding his stroke.

Shooting the girl a wicked look, Paul leant forward and planted his lips on Mick's neck. He drew the flesh into his mouth, clamping his teeth around it hard, biting, sucking, pulling.

'Ow!' shouted Mick. 'Fucking stop that!'

'No,' the girl said sharply. 'Don't.'

Paul slowly released his bite and raised his head. He had left a livid purple blotch on Mick's neck.

Paul jumped as he felt a sharp, stinging blow to his cock-head. Mick felt it, too, and flinched. From somewhere in the stable the girl had produced a riding crop.

'Don't stop,' she ordered. She snapped her wrist, flicking the tongue of the crop across their cock-heads again.

'Fuck off,' said Mick.

'Just wank,' snapped the girl.

Paul grinned. This was obviously more than Mick had bargained for. He reached down and lightly began to tickle Mick's low-hanging balls. Still wanking the Spaniard, Paul ran his fingers under the two heavy stones in their bag, thickly studded with coarse black hair. He gripped harder, squeezing the balls, letting them roll between his fingers.

The girl suddenly turned and vaulted, bareback, on to her horse. As Paul and Mick wanked each other in the saddle, she straddled the horse, holding tight to its flanks with her legs, clinging on to its mane and dragging her cunt back and forth, up and down its muscular back.

Mick's gaze was entirely arrested by the sight of the girl masturbating herself against the horse. Paul's eyes flashed between the girl and their twin cocks, standing close together, straining as each ran his fist with increasing fervour up and down the other's hard length.

The girl came first, crying out in orgasm, her head thrown back, her buttocks shaking against the horse.

Mick was next. He came with a small cry. His seed sluiced lazily from his cock-head and ran down the shaft, pooling and trailing in his pubes, and in Paul's. Paul quickly joined him; he felt his arse clench against the saddle and a familiar wave pass from his belly, from his balls, up his cock. He came; his spunk splashing off their taut bellies and mingling with Mick's juices in the thick jungle of their pubes.

The next day, predictably, Mick wanted to do it again. Paul was less keen. He'd gone to bed the previous night with the memory of the day sloshing round his brain. Already he was having trouble picturing the girl, whereas Mick's spurting cock, and his own, he recalled vividly. Was he turning gay? Or was the memory of what he'd left behind, outside the prison walls – another life, it seemed – just too painful to be revived in this savage, lonely, womanless place?

'Nah,' he said to Mick.

'Come on, man, you got to,' he pleaded. 'She won't do it unless you're there.' He spat on the ground. 'I reckon she likes you better than me,' he said bitterly.

Paul was unmoved.

'I'll pay you,' Mick said. 'Half an ounce of snout every time.'

It was a fair offer. Everything was for sale, in prison. 'OK,' said Paul.

Twenty-One

Business flourished, and the boom brought with it more practical problems for Simon and his friends to contend with. Firstly, a shortage of bottles on the wing quickly became apparent.

'We'll use buckets,' Simon declared. 'Buckets covered with binbags. And we'll charge a deposit on bottles.'

There were cleaning buckets all over the place. They bought extra soap and scrubbed them diligently. They found that the air that inevitably got in where the bin bags were secured actually speeded up the brewing process. Soon they had it down to three days.

They also had to work to overcome the risk of detection. The brewing hooch stank, and the fertile buckets would periodically bubble and belch. They bought joss sticks to cover the smell; and a radio played constantly in the laundry now.

It was only a matter of time before Spalding paid them a visit.

He arrived with Jock and Ant one morning, all smiles, when Simon and Tim were alone in the laundry.

'I hear you're the boys to see about the hooch,' he said.

Simon shrugged, hoping he looked more confident than he felt.

'So how much of this stuff do you make?' asked Spalding casually, his eyes scanning the room for evidence of brewing.

'What's that to do with you?' Simon asked, trying to stop his voice from trembling.

'Well, I need to know,' said Spalding, leaning close to him, a razor-edged sweetness in his tone, 'so that I can decide how much to take.'

'We're not paying you any tribute,' said Simon. 'You can fuck off.'

Spalding grabbed Simon's face in a vicious pinch. 'Just because you're fucking choir,' he hissed, 'don't think I won't get you if you try and fuck with me. I will. I promise.' He released Simon. 'We'll be back tomorrow,' he said coolly. 'Be a good boy and think about this. I'd hate to have to carve you up.'

The trio of thugs left.

Tim collapsed against one of the machines, breathing hard. 'What the fuck did you do that for?' he demanded. 'He's a psycho. You saw what he tried to do to that nonce – that vicar bloke.'

Simon was silent. He felt angry – a cold, calm fury he'd never felt before. Spalding had taken everything from him since he came in here. His dignity, his hope . . . Within days of his arrival, Spalding had reduced him to subhuman status. He wasn't going to let Spalding ruin this.

'I'm going out for a bit,' said Simon. 'There's someone I've got to see.'

It didn't take him long to find who he was looking for. He returned briefly to the cell, picked up his towel and soap, and headed for the shower room. When he got there, he stripped naked and stepped into the steaming jets.

He crossed the deluge to the indistinct figure at the far end. Gary, the huge Texan, was standing with his back to him, soaping himself. Simon watched as he worked the soapy bubbles through his crew-cut hair and across his face, into his goatee beard, then over his broad neck and massive shoulders, and down the twin granite columns of his back.

Simon stepped forward, soaping up his hand. He ran it around the small of Gary's back. Gary tensed, but didn't turn around. Simon ran his hand slowly down over Gary's arse-cheeks, and finally plunged his fingers down the Texan's crack and into his tight hole.

Gary turned.

'You!' he exclaimed. 'Well, I didn't expect you, boy.'

'I've got a proposition for you,' said Simon. 'Business.' He removed his finger from Gary's hole.

Gary looked at him steadily for a moment. 'Shoot,' he said.

'We need protection,' said Simon. 'You and Louie.'

Gary already knew about the hooch operation – Simon had seen him pissed on the stuff only the day before. In return for a ready supply of the stuff, he agreed readily. 'Spalding's a faggot runt,' he said. 'Me – I'm a faggot, but Spalding's a pissy little runt. I can handle him and his gang of losers. You won't get any trouble from them.'

Simon smiled. He looked down at Gary's prick. It was hard, of course – thick and long and slightly bent. He reached forward and put his hand around it. 'Just to show there are no hard feelings,' he said. 'About the past.' He sank to his knees and licked around the soapy-wet bulb, mopping up the suds with his tongue. He nuzzled the distended head of Gary's cock with his lips and tongue, and bit it with his teeth. Gary groaned and gripped the sides of Simon's head, clutching tight at his hair, pressing his mouth slowly down over his throbbing shaft. Simon felt Gary's big, curved cock fill his mouth. Gary began rolling his hips, sliding his cock in and out of Simon's mouth.

Simon scrabbled for the bar of soap and began rubbing it hard against the underside of Gary's heavy balls, running it back along his perineum and into his arse-crack. He ran it up and down the wet, slippery cleft, then pressed it hard against Gary's hole.

Gary was bucking hard with his hips now. His breath came out in short, deep grunts.

'Oh, boy,' he gasped, between thrusts. 'Oh, boy.'

Simon pushed the bar of soap up, into Gary's arsehole. He felt the other man's sphincter yielding, and the soap slipping inside. He twisted the bar against the sphincter's walls, making Gary gasp.

Gary was coming. He pressed Simon's face into his thick pubes. His cock lodged itself hard against the roof of Simon's mouth. His buttocks clenched – and his sphincter closed on the bar of soap. His cock was erupting in Simon's mouth.

Simon swallowed the hot, salty fluid.

'I guess that kinda clinches our deal,' Gary grinned as he pulled his cock from Simon's lips.

Spalding and his gang returned in force the following morning – Ant, Jock, Vince and Blue, Rob.

Gary and Louie were waiting for them.

'You got no business here, Spalding,' Louie said flatly. 'These boys got nothing to say to you.'

Simon, Tim and Sanjay stood and watched, nervous and exhilarated at the same time.

Spalding regarded them coolly. 'Sanjay, you Paki piece of shit,' Spalding said. 'Get over here.'

'Fuck you, honky,' said Sanjay. 'You fucking albino freak.'

Spalding raised a finger.

'Try it, boy,' Gary said in a voice of dreadful quiet.

Spalding turned to face Simon. 'You think you can be daddy here, you disgusting nonce?' he snarled.

'I'm not interested in being daddy,' Simon replied. 'You can go on playing king of the castle as long as you like – I don't want to play, that's all. You can just leave me and mine alone.'

'You do that, Spalding,' said Gary. 'Or Louie'n me'll be paying you a call.'

Spalding stared murderously at the huge Texan. For a moment, Simon was unsure what the albino was going to do. At last, Spalding turned on his heel and walked out. His gang scurried after him.

Sanjay let out a whoop. The three friends hugged each other ecstatically.

'Christ, that felt good,' said Tim.

'He won't be back,' said Gary. 'He's a piece of chicken shit.'

He and Louie left, both of them clutching a bottle in each hand.

Simon planted an exhilarated kiss on Tim's lips. Then he did the same to Sanjay. The three of them nuzzled faces together, noses rubbing, tongues extended. Simon could feel Sanjay's hand on the outside of his trousers, squeezing his hardening cock. He was doing the same to Tim.

Tim loosened his belt and dropped his trousers to the floor. He unhooked his hard cock from the elastic of his pants, then they too fell to the floor. Sanjay was also dropping his pants. His cock sprang out, thick and long, with its collar of thick dark hair. Tim and Sanjay wanked each other slowly. Simon scrabbled to free his own cock. Soon all three stood, trousers and pants around their ankles, stroking one another's stiff cocks.

Sanjay dropped to the floor and rolled on to his back. He kicked off his trousers and pants, then took a condom from his trouser pocket and tossed it into the air. In a flash, Tim reached out and caught it. He pulled it from its packet and smiled at Simon. Reaching forward, he rolled it down over Simon's cock. Simon was a little taken aback. Below him on the floor, Sanjay raised his legs, and spread them, grinning broadly. Simon smiled back. He squatted down in front of him, leant forward and began licking and nuzzling at the Indian lad's hairy balls and perineum, running his tongue wetly along the backs of his raised thighs, pushing it into his dark arsehole. The taste of Sanjay's sweat and musk was intoxicating. Simon glanced up at Tim. He was watching, smiling; wanking as he watched.

Simon licked slowly up the length of Sanjay's hard cock, tickling the head with his teeth. He dragged his wet tongue up Sanjay's belly, lingering in his navel, moving up towards his breast bone, his chest, his neck, covering Sanjay's body with his own. He pressed his latex-covered prick against Sanjay's hole and pushed, feeling his friend's arsehole close tightly around his cock, hugging his helmet and shaft as he bored into him. He sank his cock into Sanjay to the hilt, then arched his back, lifted his head erect and began to fuck him.

Buttocks raised, Sanjay lay back, smiling from ear to ear, enjoying being taken. He reached for Tim's cock, grabbed it and pulled it towards him. Tim kicked one leg free of his trousers and pants and allowed Sanjay to steer him into position over his face. Facing Simon, he stood astride Sanjay's hair-dappled chest. Sanjay drew him downward, manoeuvring Tim's arse over his face, planting Tim's hole on top of his mouth. Simon saw his tongue extend as Tim's buttocks closed over it.

Tim's fist played frantically over his circumcised cock as Sanjay's tongue wetly worked his hole. Simon fucked Sanjay hard, shivering with pleasure at the hug and suck and pull of the Indian lad's arsehole on his cock as he slid it in and out of him. Beneath them, Sanjay was masturbating himself quickly, his hand drawing his foreskin rapidly across the dark purple globe beneath. His hips shuffled in time to Simon's cock-strokes. His mouth still kissed and nuzzled at Tim's hole.

Tim raised himself slightly and shuffled backward. Gently, he eased Sanjay's head back. Sanjay opened his mouth in anticipation and Tim, bending his cock as far down as it would go, stuck his cock between Sanjay's lips and sank it deep into his throat. He began fucking Sanjay in the mouth, keeping time with Simon's smooth thrusts into his arse. Simon and Tim leant forward, across Sanjay's recumbent body, and kissed wetly. Sanjay – taken, arse and mouth – wanked himself furiously.

Sanjay was the first to come. The three were juddering together like some old out-of-control engine, threatening to shake itself apart. The Indian lad's hip movements became frantic, his hand flew, and his cock spurted its load in a long jet which sailed through the air and splashed off Tim's chest. Tim himself was driving down into Sanjay's mouth. Sanjay's head jerked, and Tim's cock leapt from his mouth, shooting a volley of seed into his face and hair. Grinning, Sanjay licked his lips.

Simon felt his balls tighten and his buttocks clench, and a great wave passed through his belly and balls and along the length of his cock. It spasmed and spat, disgorging its load into the rubber dam, deep inside Sanjay.

'Boy, that was great,' gasped Tim. Breathless, Simon could only nod in agreement and pat Sanjay approvingly on the buttocks as he pulled his softening cock from Sanjay's hole.

'Working for Spalding's taught me a few tricks,' said Sanjay. 'I promised my mum I'd learn a trade while I was inside.'

Twenty-Two

J esus spent forty days and forty nights in the wilderness. John
Williamson had sat in the darkness for . . . how long? He no
longer knew. He vaguely recalled a visit from the boy, Paul. It
seemed long, long ago.

He passed his time in contemplation – meditating, praying, but
most of the time just listening. Listening to the guards shuffling
around outside the door; listening to the harsh clang as they slid
his meals through the flap; listening to them belch and fart and
rustle their newspapers in the corridor outside his cell – listening
mostly to the silence when they left. And, in the silence, listening
to God.

He dreamt vividly, both awake and asleep. He could no longer
tell with any certainty when he was in the one state, and when
the other. He dreamt that the door to his cell opened and outside
the door was a land flowing with milk and honey. Toby was
there, waiting for him. They wandered beneath cool green trees,
lingered in sun-drenched meadows, swam in fast, clear, cool-
flowing streams, basked in riverside mud. They fished and hunted
for their food, children at play in the Garden of Eden. Their
clothes disintegrated and fell away from them. They lived naked
as the first men, clothed only in cool, dry mud. Mud caked their

skin, their faces and bodies; it matted their hair and clung around their genitals.

They made love day and night in the open air, Toby's small cock swelling and cracking the dried mud that coated it, rising like a pink flower. He would go down on John's mud-crusted organ, his saliva dissolving the dirt, revealing the hardening flesh beneath. In John's dreams, Toby was forever hard, forever hungry for his cock. They would lay and suck each other for hours, experiencing ever-new heights of intimacy and ecstasy. It was a kind of revelation for John. Forbidden fruit. The fruit of the tree of knowledge.

Paradise lost.

Some nights, they lived a whole lifetime together.

Other visions, other dreams, came to him – awake or asleep, he didn't know.

Sometimes, he had no sense of the narrow walls which enclosed him. In the darkness, he could see a great plain, stretching endlessly in all directions. He walked barefoot, or crawled on his hands and knees, across hard-packed desert soil, the baking sun on his back. There was something just up ahead, he was sure. Just over the horizon. If only he could reach it . . .

And he was there in the wilderness forty days, tempted of Satan –

Sure enough, Satan came to John in his benighted cell. At first, John thought it was just another dream – a voice from the past, haunting him.

The voice was different to the way he remembered it – deeper and older – but unmistakable.

'Ah, yes, the solitary block,' the voice said. 'I haven't been down here in a long time. Anybody held at the moment?'

'Just one, governor,' a guard replied. 'A vicar, actually.' The guard sounded a trifle embarrassed. 'A nonce, sir.'

'How terrible; how terrible,' the voice said. 'It is a sad indictment of my former profession that so many . . . fall by the wayside. We should pray for them.'

'Yes, governor,' the guard said.

John crawled across the floor to the door. He hammered at it with his fists. The men beyond the door ignored him. He picked up his plate, sweeping the uneaten food to the floor, and clanged it against the metal door. He began to shout.

'Ross!' he cried, quietly at first, then louder. He hadn't spoken in so long: it felt strange. 'Ross!' he shouted. 'It's me! John Williamson!'

'He seems a bit excitable today,' the guard said, apologetically.

'Open the door.' The voice sounded strange now. Anxious.

The key turned and the door swung inward. Sprawled on his knees, John looked up into the face which regarded him with a mixture of contempt and pity. It was him: it was Ross. Those piercing eyes, that pale, Celtic complexion and thick head of black hair. His face was lined now, and his hair betrayed hints of grey, but there could be no mistake.

Ross. John's first teacher, and first love.

'Don't you recognise me?' he whispered. 'The seminary. I loved you . . .'

'Poor creature,' Ross sighed. 'His mind is gone.'

He turned to walk away. John felt a desperate, lurching need inside him. He toppled forward and flung his arms around Ross's legs, clinging tight and sobbing uncontrollably.

'Get him off me!' Ross barked, kicking at John as he tried to disentangle himself.

The guard grabbed John by the collar and flung him back into the cell. 'I'm terribly sorry about that, Governor Keating,' he said.

'How long is this man in for?' Ross demanded.

'A hundred days, sir,' the guard replied.

'Make it two hundred,' Ross snapped. 'Give him time to come to his senses.'

The cell door slammed, and John was plunged into darkness once again.

He lay on the floor, shaking with the revelation. His descent into hell had started decades ago. When practically still a child, secure in the bosom of the Lord and the arms of the church, he had been seduced by the Prince of Darkness. He had followed a false path ever since – worshipped the false idols of fame and admiration and lust.

And here, in the ninth pit of hell, he had come face to face once again with his cloven-hoofed seducer.

As a priest, he had known nothing of the world. Now he knew. He had been sent here to discover the truth for himself, and he had stared it full in the face: the mission to save had failed. The world was irredeemably corrupt. The antichrist was victorious.

He wandered the wilderness of his mind's eye ceaselessly in the days that followed – weeks . . . months. He walked until his feet bled; when he couldn't walk, he crawled. And all manner of demons came to him, and he welcomed them. They cavorted on the fiery sands of the desert, naked and drunk with lust. They took him with abandon, and he let them – their bestial pricks pumped foul seed into his mouth until he thought it would drown him. Wicked, naked imps nibbled at his balls and sucked his cock dry. Wild beasts of the desert sodomised him.

And he danced and sang with them, crying out his ecstasy and his agony, until the darkness took him.

Twenty-Three

With Gary and Louie behind it, the hooch business really boomed. Demand for the stuff far outstripped supply, and Simon, Tim and Sanjay began to build up a hefty private stash – tobacco, phone cards, hash, soap, tinned goods. They even accepted money.

'It's time to expand,' said Simon. 'The operation has outgrown the laundry.'

'So?' queried Tim.

'All the cells have got a sink,' said Simon. 'Have you noticed the panelling underneath it – around the water pipes? It's similar to the ones on the washing machines. The same key should open them.'

'So?'

'So it's time to start franchising.'

They now had a clientele of nearly fifty customers. And how many of them were selling the stuff on, Simon couldn't begin to guess. With Tim's help, he made a list of how many of them he thought he could trust – and came up with a surprising dozen.

All agreed to take the stuff.

Over the next few weeks, they issued each with a couple of buckets, a cheap radio – if they didn't already have one – and some joss sticks. Then Simon employed twenty more people who agreed, in return for a small stipend, just to burn joss sticks in their rooms. None of them knew the reason, but they agreed willingly. It was easy money.

'Decoys,' Simon explained to Tim, back in Tim's big cell. 'Somebody'll suss out what the joss sticks are for, sooner or later.'

Tim shook his head in admiration. 'You're not so green, any more,' he said.

'This is easy,' said Simon. 'The power of the pink pound.'

Tim was right – Simon wasn't so green, any more. It surprised even him, the amount he'd learnt in this place without being conscious of learning anything. It troubled him slightly: was he starting to think – and act – like a con? Like Paul used to? Like Spalding?

One night, returning to the cell, he found Paul lying on his bunk, the lower one.

'What's up?' he asked.

'Nothing,' said Paul. 'Only you're the daddy, now. You should have the top bunk.'

'I'm no daddy,' said Simon, but he climbed up on to the top bunk anyway.

He felt a warm, slightly cruel sense of pleasure – of revenge, even – as he lay back on the thin mattress. Paul had had his shot and blown it. Simon was on the up and up.

That night, he dreamt of Mehmet. He dreamt of the beach at Eilat. They lay together in the surf, loving as the waves lapped over them, their bodies warm and close. Mehmet took him lovingly as the waves splashed over them, pressing his hard body against Simon's back, his cock filling Simon's hole, penetrating him deeply.

Gentle, loving Mehmet. So different from the harsh world he inhabited.

The blissful stillness was suddenly shattered by the sound of gunfire raking the dunes.

'Soldiers!' Mehmet whispered frantically.

The Israelis were coming. Mehmet leapt to his feet and began running along the beach. Simon could see the soldiers now, swarming out of the sea. Except they wore the uniforms of prison officers. Each of them held a gun in one hand, and a length of chain in the other. And, bound by the neck to the end of each length of chain, baying and snarling like dogs, he saw his fellow prisoners. Many crawled on all fours through the surf. All strained at their leashes.

Someone blew a whistle, and the screws released the dogs. The rabid prisoners swarmed up the sand towards him. There was another round of gunfire, and he saw Mehmet fall in a pool of blood. It was the last thing he saw before the pack overwhelmed him . . .

Simon awoke sweating, his head throbbing. He thought of gentle Mehmet. He made up his mind to act.

He was late getting to the laundry, that day.

'I've been thinking,' he said to Tim. 'We've made a huge stash out of all this. It's time to change tactics.'

'What d'you mean?' asked Tim, cracking open a bottle.

'I mean, it's time to fuck up the prison economy,' Simon said. 'We're going to start giving the stuff away.'

Initially, Simon's decision was greeted with incredulity on the wing. Paul assumed some cynical motive, but couldn't work out what it was. The inmates, to their credit, rapidly adjusted to the new situation. The impact was immediate. Already the wing blared with the music of radios in cells. Already it bathed in the perfume of dozens of perpetually burning joss sticks. Now just about everyone on the wing was permanently drunk. The result was a sort of carnival atmosphere – an air of celebration. For the first time, inmates passed joints back and forth freely, lent their soap or their phone cards. The contraband ingredients for the brew came free from the kitchens now. The hooch kept flowing.

Spalding hated it, Paul could tell. Paul could see the albino's power slipping away by the day. The punishment beating of a fraggle, performed publicly by Spalding and his gang in the canteen, one evening over dinner, resulted in the broad mass of inmates – all drunk, of course – getting to their feet and pelting the gang with food, plates and cutlery. Spalding was spoiling the party.

The guards had to wade in and pull the gang out. Paul smiled. Even Spalding couldn't put the fear of God into two hundred people at once. Spalding knew it, and he hated it.

One evening, Spalding summoned Paul to his cell. He was waiting for him there, alone. 'It's got to stop,' he said. 'All this free booze. It's fucking everything up.'

'Nothing to do with me,' said Paul.

'No – but it's got everything to do with your blond bum-chum. That nonce you share a cell with.' He leant close to Paul. 'I'm prepared to grant you an amnesty,' he said quietly, 'if you can find out where they're keeping the stuff.'

'An amnesty,' said Paul. He could sense an anxiety underlying Spalding's sinister calm. 'Right now, an amnesty from you isn't worth shit,' Paul suddenly spat. 'You've fucking lost control out there. That nonce cell-mate of mine's toppled you!'

Spalding hissed malevolently. He looked about to spring. Paul almost wanted to – weeks spent chopping logs had left him fitter than he'd been in years – but he knew Spalding wouldn't risk a one-to-one scrap with him.

'I'm going for a drink,' he said to Spalding, walking from the cell. 'You can go fuck yourself.'

All the way back to his own cell, Paul was waiting for the inevitable attack. It never came.

Later that evening, Donald Craigie took a stroll through the wing. He'd heard murmurings from his junior officers – something was up on the wing. They'd been vague about exactly what was going on, and Craigie knew the futility of getting any information out of them. The officers never saw half of what passed under their noses. Craigie was a realist; he knew that to try to control the day-to-day business of the wing was futile. He far preferred to let Spalding get on with it.

He crossed the recreation room and made for the corridors of cells. There was laughter and music, and perfume in the air. Something was definitely amiss.

He made at once for Spalding's cell. Spalding and his drones were lounging about, smoking cannabis. At the sight of Craigie, they scampered for the door like frightened rats.

He was alone with Spalding. The albino looked defensive.

'What's going on, Spalding?' Craigie asked.

'I don't know what you mean,' Spalding said. He looked furtive and defensive.

'I think you do,' said Craigie. 'My officers inform me there was practically a riot on the canteen the other day. They told me they had to pull you and your brat pack out of there for your own safety.'

'That's not true,' Spalding snapped. 'They steamed in. I could have handled things.'

Not for the first time, Spalding's combination of petulance and arrogance infuriated Craigie. He bore down on Spalding, and struck him hard across the head. Spalding lurched into the wall.

'Don't fuck me about, you little piece of shit,' Craigie hissed. 'There's something wrong here, and I want to know what it is.'

Spalding was silent for a while. 'Couple of fraggles,' he said at last. 'They've been brewing booze. They've made tons of it – it's everywhere. Everyone's pissed all the time.'

'A couple of fraggles,' Craigie repeated. 'So where's your problem?'

'They've got protection,' Spalding sulked. 'And besides, they're choir.'

Craigie was thoughtful for a moment. 'I hate alcohol, Spalding,' he said at last. 'It's a social evil. It makes men mad. I don't want it on the wing.'

'I don't know where they're hiding it,' pleaded Spalding. 'Once I find out, I'll put a stop to it.'

'*If* you find out,' snapped Craigie. 'You've disappointed me, Spalding. You've failed.' He paced about the cell. 'Big cell, this,' he observed. 'For just one prisoner. I'll have to see about that.'

Spalding didn't respond.

'Choir, eh?' Craigie mused. 'All right, I'll deal with this. Alcohol – it's a potentially hazardous situation. For the good of our beloved inmates, I think maybe it's time to impose a bit of martial law.'

Out of sight, just around the corner from Spalding's cell, Tim was listening. He didn't like what he heard. He hurried back to his own cell, where Simon was waiting for him.

'I've just heard Spalding talking to Craigie,' he said. 'He's narked on us. Craigie's going to do something. I think it might get rough.'

Twenty-Four

After their first meeting with the girl, Paul and Mick visited the stable just about every day. Mick boasted endlessly to the rest of the work detail about it. Kev was bitterly jealous of their trysts.

'Wow!' he had exclaimed, that first day. 'That's a hell of a lovebite she gave you.'

'Uh, yeah,' Mick had replied, looking anxiously at Paul.

Paul had just smiled.

Kev badgered Mick to let him in on the act, but Mick point blank refused. 'She's a goddess,' he explained. 'She won't be wanting to fuck a moose like you.'

In his broken English, Tomi told Paul that Kev had taken to following them to the stables, and spying on them. Paul glimpsed him, more than once, standing in the crack of the open stable door, watching them and wanking his thick, stubby prick, tugging at his balls until he came over the front of his trousers. Mick never saw him, and Paul never told.

But the girl remained the exclusive preserve of the 'brothers'.

Paul began, out of pure devilment, to take pleasure in making their sex games ever more gay. It rattled Mick. One day, Mick was lying on his back, naked on the straw-covered floor, and the

ROBERT BLACK

girl was sucking his cock, drawing it deep into her mouth. Mick's eyes were closed; he was grinning from ear to ear. In the doorway Paul saw Kev, watching. Tomi was with him. They were both wanking themselves as they spied.

The girl lost control of Mick's cock for a moment; it popped from her mouth and bounced against her lips. Winking at her, and shooting a swift glance at the spectators in the doorway, Paul eased the girl to one side and spread his lips over Mick's purple bulb. He copied the girl's action, drawing Mick's cock slowly, deeply, into his mouth. Mick moaned with pleasure. Paul increased the speed of his rhythm, and pushed a snaking finger between Mick's clenched buttocks. He located his arsehole and drilled his finger into it, wiggling it about, feeling the give of his walls.

Mick shuddered to orgasm, clutching the sides of Paul's head with his hands, pushing him hard down on to his cock. Only then did he realise all was not as he thought. Opening his eyes and seeing Paul, he swore.

It was too late. His cock was pumping its load down Paul's throat. The girl was laughing.

Mick refused to speak to him – or to anybody – for the rest of the day. Tomi and Kev smirked quietly among themselves. Paul enjoyed the silence.

Regular, straight-ish sex was doing nothing to enhance Mick's moods. Far from it; the formerly talkative Spaniard was becoming noticeably sullen and withdrawn.

Paul soon found out the reason why.

'I can't stop thinking about her,' Mick said, quite out of the blue, one morning. 'I only fucking love her, don't I?'

'Don't be daft,' Paul replied. 'Just make the most of it, while it lasts. And you owe me an ounce and a half of snout.'

'While it lasts,' Mick said bitterly. 'It's over, mate.'

It was true, of course. Paul knew it only too well. The farmer – knowing nothing of the goings-on in his outhouses – had finally had enough of the wanking parties outside his daughter's window

204

and had complained to the prison authorities. They were just clearing their stuff up today; they'd been recalled. The experiment was a failure. Tomorrow, Paul would be permanently back on D wing, at the mercy of Spalding and his gang all fucking day.

'I've got a plan,' said Mick. 'I've talked to Mary, and she's in. I just need you.'

'What d'you mean?' asked Paul suspiciously.

Mick slung a loose canvas sack over his shoulder and stomped off towards the stable. Paul trotted after him. 'It's simple,' said Mick. 'Everyone knows – even the screws – what we're up to in there. They won't come looking for us.'

'I'm not sure I understand,' said Paul darkly, fearing he understood only too well.

'I want to be with her, Paul,' pleaded Mick, stopping in his tracks. 'And she wants to be with me. She's got a car. She'll drive us anywhere we want to go. Anywhere in the country. Then we just lie low for a bit –'

'You want to fucking escape?' Paul was incredulous. 'How far d'you think we'd get?'

'I was thinking maybe we could get across to Ireland, the three of us. You don't need a passport to go to Ireland.'

'You're mad,' said Paul. 'You elope with your girlfriend if you want to. I'm going back. What d'you need me for, anyway?'

Mick sounded sheepish. 'She'll only come if you're coming,' he said quietly. He continued his walk.

Paul ran after him. 'This is mad,' Paul pleaded. 'She won't do it – she's just fantasising. You both are.'

They had reached the stables. Mick entered, followed by Paul. The girl was waiting for them. She was naked, and sitting backward, astride her horse.

'What kept you?' she demanded. 'Christ, I've never been so horned up in my life.'

'We haven't got time for that,' Mick snapped. 'We've got to go.'

'First, we fuck,' she replied. 'Then we go. Now get naked.'

Swearing, Mick hurriedly stripped off his clothes. In spite of his anxieties, his prick was hard. He scrambled up on to the horse, facing her, and they kissed.

'You, too,' she said to Paul, breaking Mick's embrace for a moment.

Paul hesitated for a moment, then began to undress. He figured Mick might calm down after a good, hard sex session. He removed his shoes, his socks, his trousers and pants. He stroked his cock to hardness as the girl watched.

She reclined, clinging to the beast's flanks, and thrust her cunt forward. Mick wriggled along the horse's back and clumsily inserted his cock inside her. He began thrusting.

'Paul,' she gasped. 'Get up here.'

With an increasing sense of unreality, Paul mounted the horse behind Mick. The girl tossed him a condom, which he rolled on to his cock. He watched the pair fuck frantically, breathlessly, Mick's back flexing and arching, his buttocks shuffling backward and forward along the horse's muscular back, the girl rolling her hips, rocking forward on to his big prick, then back again, faster and faster.

There was practically steam coming out of their ears. They came quickly and loudly. Mick tried to grab the girl to him; she threw herself back and clutched at the horse's flanks as she climaxed.

Spent, Mick slumped forward. The girl rolled to one side and dropped to the ground.

'Whew,' she said. 'OK, Paul, your turn.'

Paul made to dismount from the horse.

'No,' the girl said. 'Not me. Fuck him.'

Mick sprawled across the horse in front of Paul, his bare arse exposed.

'Fuck your brother,' the girl ordered.

Paul grinned evilly. The girl grinned back.

'Come on, bro,' Paul said.

'What?' Mick tried to turn and see what was going on.

Paul pounced forward, arms extended, and pinned him to the horse's back.

'Fuck off!' Mick shouted. He tried to move, but Paul held him fast.

'I shouldn't struggle,' said Paul. 'A fall from up here – you could break your neck.' He slid forward along the horse and pushed his hard cock between Mick's arse-cheeks. 'Open up,' he said.

'No fucking chance,' said Mick. 'No – ow!'

The girl had the riding crop in her hand. She had lashed Mick sharply across the shoulders. 'Do it!' she growled. Then, 'Do it for me, honey,' she whispered.

Paul nudged his cock, inch by inch, into Mick's tight hole.

'Ow!' shouted Mick again. 'Fuck!'

'Relax. You'll enjoy it,' Paul whispered to him, leaning forward on to Mick's brown, muscular back. 'Nearly there.' He felt his balls slap against Mick's cheeks, and started rocking his hips, drilling Mick's arse with fluid strokes.

Gradually, Mick's protests stopped. Gradually, he started moving his hips in time with Paul's rhythm, pushing them back on to his prick. Beneath them, the horse's mighty muscles flexed and shifted deliciously.

They were interrupted by shouts.

'Mick!' It was Kev. The stable door opened, and he and Tomi entered. 'Mick, you've got to come now,' Kev cried. 'We're leaving. The screws are right behind us.'

'What – no.' Mick tried to rise.

Too late – Paul couldn't stop. He was coming. He gripped Mick's shoulders and slammed his cock into him, feeling his cock-head spasm and shoot its load into the condom, high inside Mick.

The stable door opened a crack, and Kev entered. His jaw dropped as he saw Paul and Mick, naked on the back of the charger, with Paul coming inside the Spaniard.

'Shut the fucking door,' snapped Mick.

'I –' It took a moment for Kev to gather himself. 'They're looking for you,' he said.

Tomi slipped through the door behind him, an anxious look on his face.

Mick wriggled out from beneath Paul and dropped clumsily to the ground. 'We're not going back,' he grunted.

There was another voice outside. 'Vasquez –' one of the screws '– Travis. Put your cocks away and come on out. We're going!'

The voice seemed to galvanise Mick. He dropped into a squat and fumbled in the canvas sack he'd brought. 'We're not coming out!' he shouted.

Paul, still naked, stepped forward. He still wore a condom on his softening cock. 'Don't be –' He stopped. Mick had pulled a long knife from the bag.

Naked, Mick pointed the knife at Paul's throat. 'We're not going back with you!' Mick shouted. 'I want a car – and some money – I don't know – twenty thousand quid!'

Paul closed his eyes. This was pathetic. Pathetic and dangerous.

'Oh, now, hang on.' Mary sounded pissed off. 'No one said anything about –'

Mick swung the knife to her throat, and grabbed her by the hair. 'I've got a hostage!' he shouted. 'The farmer's little bitch!'

There was silence for a while, then the screw's voice came again, nervous and uncertain. 'Now, don't do anything stupid, Vasquez.'

Paul knew the voice. A young, inexperienced officer called Monroe.

'Let me talk to Travis,' he said.

'I'm here,' called Paul.

Mick glared furiously at him. Paul ignored the glare.

'Are you in on this, Travis?' the guard called.

'No, I'm fucking not,' Paul called back. 'Mick's lost it. He's got a knife.'

'Is there anybody else in there with you?'

Mick made frantic slashing motions with his knife hand.

'Kev and Tomi,' Paul called.

'Right . . . uh . . . don't do anything stupid, Vasquez,' the guard called. 'I'll be back.'

They heard his footsteps receding.

Kev sprang forward. 'What's happening, Mick?' he asked excitedly.

'We're escaping, that's what's happening,' Mick replied. 'Me and Mary and Paul.'

'Not me,' Paul interjected.

'Nor me,' said Mary. 'You're a fucking fruit-loop. If you think I'm going anywhere with you –'

'Shut it, bitch,' Mick snapped, pressing the knife hard against her throat. He kissed her gently on the cheek. 'You'll thank me when this is all over, darling,' he whispered into her ear.

'What about me?' Kev demanded. 'You always said you'd take me with you, Mick. You promised.'

Mick looked at him thoughtfully for a moment. 'All right,' he said. He kicked the canvas sack towards him. 'There's an axe in there,' he said. 'If anybody tries anything, let them have it.'

They waited. Mick, distracted, still naked and clutching the knife, paced the length of the stable, muttering to himself. Every so often, he turned to the others. 'They'll be here soon,' he ejaculated, or 'Where the fuck are they?'

Kev stood guard, thick-set and dumb, hefting the axe. Paul, Tomi and Mary sat huddled among bales of straw at his feet. Paul and Mary were still naked. The condom dropped from Paul's shrunken cock and lay on the straw, leaking.

'Why didn't you tell me your brother was a fucking loon?' Mary hissed.

'I didn't know,' said Paul. 'And he's not my brother.' He tapped Kev on the leg. Kev jumped to attention. 'Can I at least get my clothes?' Paul asked. 'Get dressed. They're over there.'

Kev looked suspiciously at Paul's discarded clothes, then back at the group. 'Nah,' he said. 'You might have a knife or something. Sorry, mate.'

'Kev,' Paul pleaded. 'You can see he's lost it. This is fucking crazy. This'll only get you into shit.'

'You shut it!' Mick snarled. 'You –'

There was another voice outside the door. 'Vasquez – listen to me.'

It was a voice Paul didn't recognise, though the authority – and the caution – in its tone were plain to hear. 'Give this up now, you hear me,' the voice said, 'before you get into even more trouble.'

'Where's my car?' Mick shouted. 'And the money?'

'Think about this, Vasquez,' the voice said. 'How far d'you think you'd get? Every police force in the country would be after you. You'd be hunted down.'

'Just get me a fucking car!' Mick ranted.

'I'm afraid we can't do that,' the voice said. 'No deals. No car. You come out here now.'

Mick darted across to the stall where the captives were huddled, grabbed the girl by the hair and yanked her to her feet. He dragged her across the stable and pressed the knife against her throat. 'I've got a hostage!' he snarled. 'I swear I'll cut her!'

The girl screamed. The voice from outside shouted. And Paul made a frantic dive past Kev, lunging for Mick.

Kev swung the axe down. Paul rolled desperately, and the blade clanged off the stone floor. With a dull roar, Tomi threw himself on Kev, and the two crashed to the floor.

Paul scrambled to his feet and stood facing Mick. The Spaniard threw the girl to one side and looked at Paul along the knife blade. Naked, the two inmates circled each other.

'Why are you doing this, Mick?' Paul asked in a low, threatening voice. 'Is it for the girl? You reckon you love her, do you? Holding a knife to her throat – threatening to kill her . . .'

'I'll make it up to her,' Mick growled. 'When we're away from here.'

'For fuck's sake – she's not interested in you,' Paul snarled. 'She never was! It was me she fancied. You said yourself, she wouldn't go along without me! She was never that interested in you.'

'You fucking . . .' Mick lunged forward, thrusting with the knife. Paul swung to avoid the blade, which whistled past his face.

210

He grabbed Mick by the arm and twisted. The knife clattered to the floor and the two of them rolled together, wrestled, their muscles straining, their naked bodies locked together, cocks mashed beneath clashing walls of muscle. Behind them, Paul could see Tomi and Kev also rolling around on the floor.

He was barely aware of Mick groping for the fallen blade. By the time he had hold of it, it was too late for Paul to do anything. He tried to roll from its path, but too late. Mick's arm flashed up, then down. Paul felt a searing pain between his ribs. The stable began to spin. Everything behind his eyes went red, then black.

Twenty-Five

Tim's fears proved prescient. The day after his meeting with Spalding, Craigie rolled his troops in. The canteen, over breakfast, was crowded with screws. They lined the walls, truncheons in their hands, an edgy look in their eyes.

Dave stepped forward. 'When you've finished, go straight back to your cells,' he ordered. 'All work is suspended until further notice.'

'Lockdown,' Tim whispered to Simon. 'We won't be able to see each other.'

They clasped hands under the table and squeezed.

'They might try and put pressure on us,' Tim said. 'Force us to tell them where we're hiding the stuff.'

'I won't tell them anything,' said Simon with steely determination.

'Nor me,' said Tim.

Sanjay looked apprehensively at the table.

They returned to their cells. Simon was alone – Paul hadn't returned from his work party, the previous night. He lay on his bunk and waited, hour after hour, for the approaching footsteps and creak of the door which he knew would come.

It came late in the afternoon. Simon sat bolt upright and

dropped to the floor, ready to fight. Two screws, truncheons in their hands, marched into the cell.

'Where's your radio?' one of them barked.

'What?' Simon was confused. 'Why? I'm entitled to have it.'

'We're confiscating all radios,' the screw said, scanning the room and grabbing the little transistor off the window sill. 'Mr Craigie's orders.'

'It doesn't work, anyway,' said Simon.

The guard grinned, hefted the little machine, and slammed it against the wall. It fell to the floor in pieces.

'It doesn't now,' he said.

And they left. Annoyed, Simon returned to his bunk. He suddenly noticed the silence of the block. No music, no voices.

The first thing Paul was aware of was the godawful, burning pain in his side. Then, slowly, his vision came into focus. He was in the infirmary. A nurse was standing nearby.

'Nurse,' he called, 'what's been going on?'

'You were stabbed,' the nurse said. 'You lost a lot of blood. You're lucky. Try to rest.'

She bustled off. Paul felt his side with gentle fingers. It was wrapped in bandage.

'Welcome back,' a voice from the next bed said. 'I understand you had a lucky escape. If you'd call it lucky.'

It was John. He looked awful – his eyes were red, his hair was uncut and matted, and an untidy beard hung from his chin.

'What happened to you?' Paul asked. 'Is your time in solitary up?'

'Prematurely curtailed,' said John. 'They tell me I had some kind of attack. Some kind of psychotic episode.'

'And did you?'

'Did I go mad down there?' John rubbed his face thoughtfully. 'Perhaps,' he said, 'Perhaps. But, as a greater man than I once said, if to be mad is to see God, who would be sane? I went on a journey, Paul!' He leant from his bed, suddenly intense. 'A marvellous journey. I walked in the footsteps of our Lord. I wandered the galleries of hell – I was taken by demons . . . ravaged . . . they ate the flesh from my bones. They burnt me – purified me! I . . .'

He seemed to sag, and slumped back on to his pillow. 'I'm sorry,' he said. 'You must think me quite mad. They all do. Yesterday I had to see the prison psychiatrist. I've given him something to think about. He wants to see me again, today.' A thought seemed to occur to him. 'Of course,' he said, 'he'll now have to decide whether I really am ill – in which case I suppose he'll send me back on to the wing, with some sedatives – or if I'm just putting it on to try and avoid going back to solitary – in which case, back I go.' He smiled.

'I see – so you're fooling them,' said Paul, slightly relieved.

'What do you think?' said John, grinning widely.

'All right, John,' the nurse said, bustling over. Paul could see she had a syringe concealed in her hand. 'Time for your chat with Dr McGregor. Come along now.'

'They all talk to me as if I'm mad,' he said, getting out of bed. He wore only a pair of boxer shorts. Paul could see that his hands and feet, and his knees and elbows, were badly cut and grazed. John padded off down the ward.

'You have a visitor,' the nurse said to Paul, interrupting his reverie.

Paul turned. Tomi, the big Finn, stood in the doorway.

'Don't be shy,' the nurse said, and he shuffled across the floor. 'This young man is a bit of a hero,' said the nurse. 'You nearly died. This fellow saved you.'

'What happened?' Paul demanded agitatedly as Tomi pulled a chair up next to the bed. 'The last thing I remember is fighting with Mick.'

It was difficult to get the facts out of Tomi, on account both of his overwhelming modesty and his appalling English. Eventually, Paul managed to piece together the story. It was simple – the mighty Finn had overpowered first Kev, then Mick. The police had broken in, Mick and Kev had been carried away in handcuffs, and Paul had been brought here.

'I reckon I owe you my thanks,' said Paul. He gave Tomi a manly pat on the thigh.

Smiling, Tomi reached forward and eased the bedclothes back. He lightly touched Paul's bandages, then gradually moved his hand down Paul's belly, beneath the blankets.

Paul was wearing a pair of godawful, stripy prison pyjama-bottoms. Beneath the blankets, he felt Tomi's big, clumsy hand fumble with the elastic. His cock was hard, and poking up through the piss-slit in the front of the pyjamas. Tomi's fist closed around it and began working Paul's foreskin up and down over his bulb, squeezing as he did so, with his characteristic heavy stroke.

Paul quickly glanced about the ward. The nurses were all preoccupied, further down the ward, and most of the patients seemed to be asleep or dead.

He reached for Tomi's lap and grasped the great pole that bulged beneath his prison trousers. Paul crushed the tight material around Tomi's cock and began rubbing him through his trousers. Tomi drew back at first, then relaxed and allowed Paul to unzip him and wrestle his huge prick free of his pants. Tomi was attractive, but in a curiously crude and unfinished way. Raw-boned good looks. His cock was the same – big and rough and wayward, with a loose, untidy foreskin over a huge, bloated bell-end. He drew the foreskin up, tight around Tomi's helmet, then back to reveal the pink bulb beneath. He fell into a steady, brisk stroke. Beneath the bedclothes Tomi tugged hard on Paul's prick.

The blankets fell away as the Finn's hand pistoned up and down. With his free hand, Paul hitched his balls out of the piss-slit in the striped pyjamas and hooked them over the seam. As Tomi roughly wanked him, Paul rubbed and squeezed his own balls, rolling them between his fingers, never losing his stroke on Tomi's prick.

They came together. Paul's cock spasmed and his seed showered down over bedclothes and bandages; Tomi's great prick heaved in Paul's hand and his thick spunk splashed dully out and ran between Paul's fingers.

No one had heard them. They used Paul's bedclothes to wipe themselves dry of their creamy juices.

'I go now,' said Tomi, glancing at the clock on the wall.

Paul took his hand. 'I don't know when I'll see you again,' he said. 'You're back on B wing, and I suppose I'll be sent back to my cell on D wing, soon.'

'You can go back tonight,' the nurse interrupted. 'Just come back every couple of days to get that bandage changed.'

Paul smiled at Tomi. 'This is it, then,' he said. 'For now.'

'For now,' grunted Tomi.

'Take care of yourself, yeah?' said Paul.

'You too,' said Tomi.

Paul returned to the cell that night. There were screws all over the block.

'What's up?' he asked Simon.

Simon told him. Paul felt an instant wave of relief. At least lockdown meant Spalding couldn't get at him.

'Looks like we're stuck here, then,' he said.

Simon dropped from his bunk and fished under the sink. He extracted two small bottles of hooch.

'Drink?' he said.

They drank in friendly enough silence. Paul's thoughts were still dominated by Mick and Tomi and the farm. He suspected Simon was otherwise preoccupied.

'Worried about your bloke?' he asked gently.

'If they do anything to him . . .' Simon said quietly.

'He'll be all right,' said Paul. 'I doubt they'll do anything. They probably just want to smoke us out. Get someone to nark.'

'Maybe you're right,' said Simon, smiling weakly. Paul could tell he didn't mean it for a second.

Later, they heard a distant commotion. It grew louder as the night went on. It was coming nearer. Soon, they could make out what the sounds were – cells were being opened and forcibly searched. And, from the sound of it, that wasn't all. They could hear shouts of anger and cries of pain. People were being beaten up, raped –

There were footsteps outside the cell. The key turned and the door was kicked inward, clanging against the wall. Four screws piled into the cell.

'What the fuck do you want?' demanded Paul, rising from his bunk, wrapping his blanket around his waist to conceal his nakedness. Above him, Simon was sitting up in bed.

'These'll do,' one of the screws slurred – a cruel-faced guy with black, curly hair worn too long over his uniform. He sounded drunk. 'They're a pretty pair.'

'What do you want?' asked Simon.

'We're looking for alcohol,' the screw said with exaggerated politeness. 'We've found quite a bit stashed up in the cells.'

His colleagues giggled.

'And very good stuff it was, too. But we still haven't found the main stash, or where they brew it.' He turned to his colleagues. 'You two, search,' he ordered. 'It's my turn again. Mine and Jimmy's.'

'Haven't you had enough yet, Frank?' asked one of the others. 'I'm surprised there's anything left of your prick.'

'Which one?' the screw called Jimmy asked.

His colleague pointed at Simon.

'You want him, you come through me,' Paul growled.

'Thinks he's a tough kid,' Frank said, pleased. 'You two . . .'

The other two screws closed around Paul. He was pushed back on to his bunk, a truncheon held across his throat so that he could hardly breathe. He could only lie there and listen as the screws took their vicious pleasure from his cell-mate. He listened to the blows which rained on Simon, to the slap of flesh as the two screws fucked him in turn.

'Suck me!' one of the screws barked. Paul could hear Simon gagging on a plunging prick.

He struggled against his bonds, but felt the truncheon, hard on his throat. Another screw grabbed him hard by the cock and balls.

ROBERT BLACK

'You don't want to try anything, mate,' the screw hissed. 'Feels like you've got a good set of tackle in there. I could rip it off.'

He unbuttoned Paul's trousers and pants and dragged them down. Paul's cock was limp and loose. He brought his baton up and plunged it between Paul's legs. Paul felt its cold hardness against his balls and buttocks. The screw was trying to penetrate him with it. Paul's sphincter yielded, and the screw forced the baton inside him. Paul felt his hole stretched beyond endurance. The pain was exquisite. He was getting hard. The screw twisted the baton inside him – plunged it in and pulled it back, plunged and pulled. One hand reached into his uniform and pulled his hard cock free. The screw wanked himself as he buggered Paul with his truncheon. His partner still held Paul to the bed, his truncheon pressed against Paul's windpipe. Paul was barely able to breathe. Below him the bed creaked and flesh slapped. Simon whimpered slightly in the darkness.

The orgasm Paul experienced was as intense as it was unexpected. The room spun. He felt himself blacking out. His arse throbbed with the pain of the black wooden baton. He was vaguely aware of the screw coming into his own hand, and then, from nowhere, a great trembling seized him. His heart pounded – he thought perhaps it was giving out on him – and his whole body seemed to surge. His cock erupted over his belly in a series of violent volleys.

The truncheon was pulled from his arsehole – his sphincter collapsing back into place – and the screw put his come-sticky cock away.

'I don't think there's any booze in here,' the screw said. 'Pity – maybe we'll have to come back. Search again.'

Twenty-Six

Simon found Tim early the next morning. He stopped him in the corridor on the way to breakfast.

'Did they?' Simon whispered.

He knew the answer from the look on Tim's face.

'I've had plenty of practice in the choir,' said Tim, forcing a smile. 'What about you?'

Simon nodded.

'I didn't tell them anything,' said Tim.

'They didn't ask me anything,' said Simon. 'They were drunk by the time they reached our end of the wing.'

They filed into the canteen. Once again, the walls were lined with screws — more, if anything, than yesterday.

The room was crowded. It seemed as if the whole wing was in there. Some sat; most stood. The doors at the far end were locked.

'Something's happened,' said Simon. He saw Sanjay pushing his way through the crowd towards them, a look of anguish on his face.

'Guys,' he said. 'I fucked up. I should have told you yesterday.'

'What d'you mean?' asked Simon.

'They day before yesterday — we brewed too much,' Sanjay replied. 'I had a couple of buckets just sitting in my cell. I tried all the usual people, but every sink was full. I even tried some new people.'

'So what did you do?' Simon asked with a mounting feeling of alarm.

'Guys,' Sanjay pleaded. 'Yesterday morning I waiting till Spalding had left his cell for breakfast, and –'

Simon's alarm was turning to dread.

'– and . . . I opened his sink panel.'

'You did what?' Simon whispered, appalled.

'Then, when they started this lockdown, when they sent everybody back to their cells, I couldn't . . .'

Sanjay was beginning to cry. Tim slipped an arm around him.

'He's bound to have found it by now,' Sanjay sniffed, 'the noise it was making.'

'Let's just see, shall we?' said Simon. He looked at Spalding, seated as usual with his gang around him, smiling and talking animatedly. He didn't think he'd ever seen Spalding in such a good mood. It terrified him.

The atmosphere in the canteen the next morning was so thick it could have torn. The screws had gone round every cell, that morning, pulling people out, herding them like cattle. The whole wing was crowded into the canteen.

There wasn't enough room to seat everybody at once, and prisoners stood angrily about, eyeballing the screws.

From where he stood, Paul looked about the room. Spalding and his gang were seated in their usual place. The gang looked unusually ill at ease. Spalding, on the other hand, made a point of particularly enjoying his breakfast.

Hardly anybody else in the room was eating.

Paul spotted Simon, standing with his boyfriend and Sanjay, Spalding's linen-boy. He pushed his way over and tapped Simon on the shoulder. 'What's happening?' he asked.

'Listen!' hissed Simon.

From out on the wing came a series of dull, metallic thumps, harsh and rhythmic. Sounds of hammering, and rending metal.

'They're smashing the panels off the sinks,' cried Tim. 'They've rumbled us.'

A murmur of protest ran around the canteen. The hooch was found. A nark, somebody said. Others took up the cry. The hammerings grew louder. The murmur of the crowd grew to a roar.

A harsh whistle cut across the cacophony. Dave the screw stepped forward. 'All right,' he called. 'Settle down.'

The roar became a murmur again – a series of muttered conversations.

'No!' a voice suddenly bellowed from the near-end door.

John was standing there, shaggy, unwashed and terrible to behold. His eyes held a look of dull thunder. 'Will you let these agents of Satan do this to you?' he growled. 'They treat you like animals – and you let them! They treat you worse than animals – they beat you up, they sate their foul lusts on you . . .'

The hall was silent, amazed, listening. John padded into the room. The crowd parted like the Red Sea before him. He was shouting, now. 'And you – you're all too busy squabbling and ripping each other off to notice the injustices heaped upon you! Man was not meant to live like this! They tell you to settle down – I say no!' He snatched up a plate and hammered it down on the table. 'No!'

He hammered it again. 'No!'

Other prisoners began picking up their plates, beating the table in time to his voice, chanting his mantra. 'No! No! No! No!'

Breakfasters rose from their places. Practically the entire room took up the chant. Paul looked at Spalding's table. Ant was on his feet, chanting along with the crowd. Spalding sat, thunder-faced, watching.

John snatched up a chair and brandished it above his head. 'Let us drive the money-changers from the temple!' he bellowed, and charged the line of screws.

The crowd surged after him. A hail of metal chairs rained across the room. The screws, their backs to the wall, could only cower, and protect themselves as best they could. Paul saw Dave go down early.

After the battery of chairs came the inmates themselves. They kicked and beat the screws savagely. Many succeeded in wresting the screws' truncheons from them, turning the weapons against their masters, clubbing them to the floor.

Paul heard a hammering from the kitchens. Some inmates had broken into the cupboard where the knives were kept. He saw Jock leap on to the serving hatch, a tartan teatowel tied around his waist, a carving knife in each hand and a mad grin on his face.

Dave was on his feet again.

'This way!' he shouted, and began pulling screws out of the mêlée, towards the door. They broke into a run. Chairs, knives, pans rained down on them as they scurried like trapped mice towards the door.

Jock charged after them, roaring. Others followed.

The room gradually quietened down. There was an air of exhilaration, laced with latent fury.

Spalding got slowly to his feet. He stepped from the table and walked slowly up to John. 'You . . . nonce!' he barked. 'You walk in here like the Lord fucking Jesus . . . I should have done a better job on you before. Someone should do all your kind, you disgusting, cock-sucking nonce!'

'Oh, limb of Satan,' growled John.

Spalding whipped something from his pocket. A toothbrush, melted at the end, with a razor blade stuck in it. Vicious, and often lethal.

'You need a shave, Jesus,' he purred, stroking John's beard with the blade.

John held him in his gaze.

Paul had had enough of this. He felt suddenly, overwhelmingly angry. He wished he'd done a better job on Spalding before. He'd have to finish it now. He stepped forward. 'Leave him alone,' he said to Spalding.

'What?' Spalding spat, turning to face Paul. 'Oho! Well, look who's standing up for the nonce. Of course, what everybody else probably doesn't know but I know is that this is the bloke who narked about the hooch. How do I know? Ask him who his cell-mate is. This bloke shares a cell with the lanky streak of piss who brews the stuff. He must have let something slip to the nark here –'

'Shut it, Spalding,' said Paul.

The inmates were muttering and grumbling among themselves. Their mood was darkening.

'What did you say, nark?' Spalding smarmed.

'No!'

Paul looked round. Tim, Simon's little boyfriend, had stepped forward.

'You're lying, Spalding,' Tim said. 'You're the one who narked on us. I was listening outside your cell. I heard you narking to Craigie, the night before he sent the screws in. It was you who sold us out.'

'You little choirboy piece of . . .'

Spalding spun to face Tim. He advanced on him, brandishing his makeshift weapon. He held the razor blade only inches from Tim's face.

'Spalding!' Paul called.

Spalding smiled horribly at him. 'Oh, I'll attend to you,' he purred. 'Just as soon as I've carved this piece of shit up.'

He took a step nearer to Tim. The canteen was silent. Paul saw Tim swallow hard.

'Spalding!' The deep, thunderous voice of John Williamson reverberated around the hall. Arms outstretched, he strode up to Spalding and embraced him, taking him by the back of the head, forcing their mouths together in a long kiss.

Spalding's arms flapped helplessly. The razor blade weapon hung, forgotten in his hand.

John released him, and he staggered back. The whole room looked at him, silent, disgusted. Gradually the chant arose. *Nark . . . Nark . . . Nark . . . Nark . . .*

Spalding backed away, looking frantically around him.

Ant was chanting, along with the rest of the room. The remains of the gang stood, silent and nervous. None would meet Spalding's eye.

Some of the inmates were again arming themselves with chairs.

Spalding suddenly turned and threw himself through the doors and into the corridor. A hail of chairs followed him.

Anarchy reigned for the rest of the afternoon. The screws hadn't had time to reach most of the hooch before the tidal wave of hysterical convicts had driven them from the wing. Tim ran from room to room, unlocking panels, freeing the spirit.

They spent the afternoon lounging in his cell — Simon, Paul and Sanjay. John came in to see them.

'You did good out there,' Paul said to him. 'But you know they'll be back, don't you?'

'Oh, I'm depending on it,' said John.

He spent most of the afternoon striding about the wing, organising the defence force. Many listened to him. Others charged about the corridors, drunkenly smashing everything in their path, or just lolled about the cells and communal areas, drinking and laughing. When Simon and his friends had left the near-deserted canteen, one group of old lags had sat down and begun breakfast.

One by one, the revellers drifted off, until only Simon and Tim remained, lolling on the bed.

'I can't believe this, man,' said Tim softly. 'This is like . . . the sixties, or something.'

Simon pulled Tim to him and planted a hungry kiss on his mouth. Their tongues wove wetly around each other. They struggled out of their clothes. Their arms and legs twisted and tangled around each other; their bodies strained together. Tim's hands ranged across Simon's body, tweaking his nipples, stroking and pinching his soft skin. He turned on the bed, nipping at Simon's hard cock, sucking his balls one by one into his mouth, playing them between his teeth. Tim's cock stood proud before Simon's face. Eagerly, Simon took it into his mouth and sucked. He felt Tim's mouth close over his own cock. They blew each other quickly and eagerly, shooting into each other's throats, laying there long after they'd come, their cocks leaking and softening in one another's mouths.

Tim pulled out and reached for a condom.

'Fuck me, darling,' he whispered, stroking Simon's wet cock to hardness again.

He rolled the latex sheath down over Simon's tall, elegant shaft and turned on to his stomach, raising his buttocks into the air and pulling his cheeks apart with his fingers. Simon lowered his head to Tim's arse-crack and smeared it with his saliva, pushing his tongue into the tight hole. He let the head of his cock skid up and down Tim's crack before nesting it in his taut pucker and pushing deep into him.

'I love you,' gasped Simon as he fucked his friend from behind, beginning slowly, with long, smooth strokes, gradually gathering speed, growing in intensity and passion. Tim gripped the bed-frame with one hand: the other reached back and took hold of Simon's balls, pulling them towards him, pulling Simon's cock deep into him with ever-increasing fervour. Simon reached around his waist and gripped Tim's cock, squeezing the circumcised head, stroking and kneading it hard.

Simon nuzzled Tim's loose brown curls, kissed his neck, and bit down hard on his lightly freckled shoulders as he approached his second orgasm.

They came together, Tim splashing the bed and Simon's hand, spunk curling around his own pubes; Simon shot his load deep inside his lover, his spunk oozing warmly around inside the condom, while Tim continued to cling tight to his balls.

They collapsed together in a sweating, giggling heap on the bed.

'Gee, hope I ain't interrupting anything.'

Gary stood in the doorway. Simon and Tim scrambled back into their clothes.

'Just came to see how you was doin',' Gary drawled. 'I can't stay long. Mah duty calls. Gee, it's good to be in action again.'

'Stay and have a drink,' said Simon, groping around for a bottle. They were running low.

'There's still a batch in the laundry,' said Tim. 'I'll go and get it.'

Tim trotted off and Gary sat and glugged on a bottle.

'Where's Louie?' asked Simon.

'Goddamn!' said Gary. 'Can you believe that damn preacher man done made him a lieutenant? And me just a goddamn nothing? Shee–it!'

John Williamson stood at the barricade they'd built and waited for the legions of the enemy to appear. This was the front line. Ten yards ahead of him was the double security door – the airlock – through which the attack must surely come. They'd blocked all other means of access, but these were sliding metal doors. There was no way to hold them shut.

Until today, their barricade had been one of the long canteen tables. He didn't expect it to hold for long. There was another one ten yards back, and others beyond that. The barricades were just there to weary the armies of Satan and to split them up – and, above all, to trap them when they tried to get out.

The doors slid open. John smiled. It was as he'd hoped – as he'd prayed. Craigie stood at the head of his horde, a flak-jacket over his uniform, his whistle in his mouth, his truncheon in his hand.

He blew a piercing note, and the screws charged.

John's rag-tag army was ready for them. A barrage of bottles, snooker balls and batteries rained down on the screws. They began to fall back.

'Come on!' yelled Craigie, and charged forward. His men followed him.

John had instructed Louie to organise men to fill buckets with bleach, the nearest thing they had to boiling oil. Now he ordered their use. They were swung high, jetting their contents into the faces of the advancing guards.

Craigie covered his face and bellowed his rage. Putting his head down, he charged the barricade. Again, his men followed.

'Fall back!' John called. 'Don't engage in hand-to-hand combat! Fall back!'

His horde retreated to the next stage in their fortifications. There they repeated the procedure – an artillery bombardment which sent the officers reeling, followed by a strategic withdrawal.

Craigie was still bellowing orders to his men, urging them on. John smiled – like flies into a spider's web. Just beyond the next barricade was an intersection with another corridor. Once beyond that barricade, the screws would be vulnerable to attack on both flanks.

He watched Craigie with divine loathing in his heart. He had given his men strict instructions – there was to be no killing. It was not an injunction he himself intended to obey.

It took Tim an age to reach the laundry. Parties of drunken inmates kept waylaying him – dragging him into their cells to drink his health. They were heroes, man. He was swaying by the time he reached the laundry door.

He tottered inside and groped in his pocket for the key. He tripped the catch, and the metal plate fell to the floor with a clang.

'I suppose this is where it all started.'

The voice was like an electric shock to Tim. He jumped to his feet and spun around.

Spalding stared, unblinking, at him. His red eyes blazed malevolence. 'Ingenious.'

There was a rising column of smoke behind Spalding, and an acrid, burning smell.

'Spalding,' Tim said, his mouth bone dry. 'There's a fire.'

'I know,' said Spalding. 'I started it. I've also lit fires in the classrooms and the chapel. This whole place is going to go up.'

Tim felt his brain capsizing. He mustn't panic. He began to edge towards the door. Spalding circled him like a big cat preparing for the kill. He closed the door and wedged a chair beneath the handle. Just the way Tim used to, before he and Simon made love . . .

Spalding took his weapon from his pocket.

'I had this wing in the palm of my hand,' he snarled, 'until you and your nonce boyfriend came along and fucked it all up.' He advanced on Tim. 'So now I'm going to fuck you up.'

Tim made a mad run. He dodged around Spalding and threw himself at the door. The chair was wedged fast. He waited for Spalding to pounce.

Above his head, and throughout the block, the fire bells started to ring.

Twenty-Seven

Now they really had run out of booze.

'Where the hell's Tim?' asked Simon. 'How long can it take you to get from A to B in a prison?'

Gary chuckled deeply.

Outside the cell, a fire bell began to clang sharply. Simon sprang to his feet. 'Jesus, that made me jump,' he said.

People were milling about in the corridor. Simon wandered out.

'There's a fire,' somebody said. 'Over at the far end of the wing. By the laundry.'

Simon felt a shiver of cold dread pass through him. 'Tim!' he cried, and started running down the corridor.

Gary sped past him. 'Way ahead o' you, buddy,' he said as he sprinted forward.

Simon caught him up at the laundry door. Gary was charging it with his shoulder.

'Something's wedged,' he said, crashing into the door. It gave with a sickening shriek.

Simon followed Gary into the room, which was fast filling up with smoke. 'Tim,' he called.

Gary was frozen like a statue in front of him. He suddenly

229

spun round and grabbed Simon, hugging his face to his huge chest.

It was too late – Simon had seen. He let out a wail of anguish and despair.

'Why, you . . .' Gary snarled.

Standing in the smoke was Spalding. He was grinning. 'Some fucking protection you were,' he sneered.

Within a second, Gary had crossed the room to Spalding. He grabbed Spalding's blade hand and smashed it into one of the washing machines. Spalding let out a shriek. Gary gripped Spalding's face in his huge hand and pistoned his arm out like a shot-putter. Spalding's head hit the wall with a sickening crunch, and he sank, limp, to the floor.

It was over in a matter of seconds.

Simon felt Gary's strong arms wrap themselves around him. Gary lifted Simon off his feet and gently carried him back through the door.

'No!' wailed Simon. 'I'm not leaving him!' He kicked at Gary's legs and pummelled his back with his fists.

Gary kept moving.

Simon could see flames breaking through the door of one of the classrooms. Somewhere, a window shattered. All he could think of was Tim. Tim – lying there in a pool of his own blood, his face . . . his face . . .

This was chaos. Glorious chaos. John Williamson looked upon what he had created, and he saw that it was good.

He watched as Craigie stormed about the corridors like a captive bear. A general, baton in hand, shouting orders to his nonexistent army. He was cut and bruised. Blood poured from a wound on his head. His men were scattered across the wing, alone and defenceless. Some had fled. Others lay, injured, dead or dying.

The fire alarms were going berserk. John passed the chapel, and a blast of heat nearly knocked him to the ground.

A door to a storeroom toppled forward, and flames belched out from inside. Craigie staggered back, coughing. John could see him looking frantically about for a means of escape. The corridor was rapidly becoming a tunnel of fire.

John stood, motionless, and stared at Craigie through the flames. He stepped forward, through the curtain of fire.

'You!' Craigie spat.

John smiled. He'd hoped to attract the attention of the governor. Ross Keating. His first love. Craigie would have to do.

'You did this!' Craigie snarled. 'You!'

Behind him, a window shattered. Craigie seemed suddenly galvanised. He tried to push past John.

John stepped into his path.

'This is no time to fuck about,' Craigie snarled. 'The whole fucking place is about to go up! We've got to get out of here.' He tried again to pass John.

John gripped Craigie's shoulders and thrust him suddenly backward. 'You're not leaving,' he said.

'The fucking prison's on fire!' Craigie yelled.

John smiled, enjoying the warmth. 'We're in hell,' he rhapsodised. 'These are the infernal fires. The purifying flames which burn out the evil from men's souls . . .'

He leapt forward and threw himself on Craigie. The two fell to the floor, rolling among burning debris. Craigie lashed out with his truncheon, catching John a vicious blow to his cheek. John heard the cheekbone shatter, but felt nothing. Craigie scrambled past him and attempted to regain his feet. John hurled himself on him again. Craigie lurched and twisted, and crashed through the doors of the chapel.

The place was a temple of flame. The Lord, crucified, burnt above the altar. The altar itself burnt. Pulpit, pews: everything was on fire.

'Jesus,' Craigie spat. 'D'you want to die? What do you want?'

'To complete my mission,' John replied. 'I might not be able to hack off the head of Satan, but I can put out his eyes and amputate his foul limbs!'

He leapt at Craigie a third time, driving him back, back towards the Lord's table. Craigie swung again with his truncheon, catching John in the chest. John didn't flinch. His hands closed around Craigie's throat and he thrust him back on to the burning altar. It collapsed beneath them. John's hands remained tight around Craigie's throat, squeezing, squeezing.

Craigie's eyes were wide and bulging. He flailed at John with his truncheon. John ignored the blows. He pressed down with his thumbs on Craigie's Adam's apple, crushing his windpipe. Craigie's blows became slower and feebler. The truncheon dropped from his hands.

There was a rending, crashing sound above them. The skies were opening. The Lord was returning. John raised his eyes in ecstasy. The huge, flaming cross, bearing the Saviour, descended on them.

Simon was barely aware of being carried by Gary. Smoke and tears blinded him. Gary ran back and forth, coughing and swearing. The heat was sweltering.

At last, Gary put him down. 'There's no way out,' he gasped. 'We're going to have to make a run for it.'

The words meant nothing to Simon. Dimly, he felt his legs give way beneath him, and he collapsed to the floor.

'Shit,' said Gary. 'OK, little buddy.' He picked Simon up and slung him over his shoulder. 'Here goes . . .' He plunged forward, head down, feet pounding on the corridor floor. The smoke grew thick around them. The air was hot.

'I can't see,' Gary spluttered. He was slowing down.

Simon's lungs burnt with the smoke. His head spun.

He felt Gary collapse beneath him. Simon seemed to float to the floor.

Darkness descended.

Panic spread across the wing faster than the flames. The fighting ceased. Prisoners and screws milled about in confusion. The security doors had been sealed behind the advancing guards.

They couldn't get out.

Paul found Louie, his eyes wide, a bottle of hooch clutched in his hand.

'This is chaos!' Paul shouted. 'We've got to do something!'

'We've got to find a way out, man!' Louie shouted back.

Paul's mind raced. He began to run along the corridor.

'Not that way, man!' Louie yelled. 'That's where the fire is!'

'The door into the exercise yard!' Paul yelled.

'It'll be locked!'

'We'll have to break it down or something.'

The door was steel: his plan sounded desperate. Impossible.

He was running against the crowd, pushing past waves of panicking people. He reached the door, and tugged vainly at the handle. It was hot. He could feel his hands burning. The corridor was already on fire. It was difficult to see through the smoke.

'It's no good, man!' Louie shouted.

Paul looked desperately around for something to try and break down the door with. He spotted a screw, badly beaten up, lying insensible on the floor.

'His keys!' Paul yelled. He ran to the body and groped inside the screw's pockets. He located the big bunch of keys and searched for the right one. Gritting his teeth against the pain, Paul unlocked the door and heaved it open.

'You try and get everybody out!' Paul shouted to Louie. 'I'll do my best to keep the flames back.'

'Yo!' shouted Louie, and disappeared back down the corridor.

Paul picked the screw up by the shoulders and dragged him through the door and down the metal steps into the yard below. Gasping urgent lungfuls of cold, fresh air, he plunged back into the burning building.

There was a fire-hose on the wall, securely locked behind a door marked FIRE-HOSE. Paul fumbled through the bunch of keys until he found the right one. He rapidly uncoiled the hose, and gunned it into life, swept its ferocious jet in an arc, driving the flames back.

Behind him, people were starting to jostle and fight their way through the door and into the stone-walled yard beyond it. Paul advanced down the burning corridor, into the inferno.

Through the wall of smoke, he could just about make out two prostrate figures.

'Shit,' he muttered, and threw down the hose. Holding his breath, he ran through a halo of flame towards them.

He stopped. It was Simon and Gary. Neither moved. He gripped Simon by the arms and began dragging him back down the corridor. He dumped him just outside the door, hoping he wouldn't be trampled in the rush.

Spotting Sanjay, he called to him. 'Take Simon! I've got to go back in!'

Sanjay looked scared – confused. He moved as if in a trance.

'Take Simon!' Paul shouted again.

Sanjay seemed to come to. He hauled Simon to his feet and half carried him down the stone steps.

Paul pushed his way back into the building. The fire-hose jetted its payload across the floor, writhing like a dying snake. The flames were advancing again.

Paul leapt through them and ran to Gary. The huge black man was heavy. Groaning with his weight, Paul dragged him backward.

The ceiling was on fire. It began to collapse around him. Coughing, choking, Paul tried to shield himself from the flaming debris. He felt a sudden, cold douche, a ferocious jet of water. Louie, wielding the fire-hose, advanced towards him.

'Help me!' Paul shouted. 'He's too heavy for me!'

'Holy shit!' yelled Louie, dropping the fire-hose. Between them they dragged the prostrate bulk of Gary towards the door. They heard voices they didn't recognise – calm, commanding voices. Half a dozen firemen ran past them. Two of them picked up the hose and trained it again on the flames.

Paul staggered out of the door and down the steps into the yard, breathless and coughing. His head was swimming. The yard was packed with inmates, standing, entranced, watching their prison burn.

★

It took the firemen well into the night to vanquish the fire. The chapel, the laundry, the canteen – one whole section of the wing was destroyed. Eighteen people, apparently, were missing: six officers – including Craigie – and twelve prisoners. John Williamson and Spalding were among them.

So was Tim.

The fire never reached the cell blocks. By one in the morning, the prison population was safely under lock and key again.

Simon was ghost white, wide eyed and shaking uncontrollably. He stood rigid, clinging to the bed-frame for support.

'Are you all right?' asked Paul lamely. 'Come on.'

He had to prise Simon's hands from the metal frame. Slowly, Paul managed to get him to climb on to his bunk, then lay on the bunk below him, not knowing what to say.

The lights suddenly went out. Simon gave a little cry.

'Bastards,' Paul whispered. 'You'd think, tonight of all nights –' He stopped. He could hear Simon, in the darkness above him, sobbing softly. He slipped on to the top bunk next to Simon and hugged him tight. Simon was shaking, clinging to Paul, pressing himself against him. His hard cock nestled in the hairy hollow of Paul's groin. Paul felt it beginning to move as Simon rubbed himself against him. He curled his fingers around the hard pole; Simon's stroke grew firmer. He was sobbing as he rubbed himself off against Paul. Paul kissed him hard on the head and neck and shoulders, biting slightly. They lay together, gently rubbing and nuzzling, kissing and biting. Their skin grew hot as they held each other; their hard cocks kept up a gentle rhythm against one another's groins and bellies.

It was the gentlest sex Paul had ever had, and the most intense. Denying themselves movement meant that the sensation was somehow concentrated, focused on the points where their bodies met – mouths, chests, feet and, above all, hard, needful cocks. They clung and they rubbed and they nuzzled and, by the faintest of motions, inched themselves down the long, delicious road to orgasm. Simon's cock-juices were leaking over Paul's belly and groin, a slippery bowl around which his cock slid deliciously. Paul could feel his own cock getting slippery, too, as it snaked and skidded minutely up and down his friend's belly.

Their mouths joined in an endless kiss, tongues gently touching, lips nuzzling. Their legs entwined; their chests pressed together; their cocks mashed and slipped against each other. They brought each other off that way, barely moving, containing their passion in a straightjacket of gentleness. Their orgasms, when they came, were intense, channelled. They shuddered against each other, kissing, clinging tight in an embrace that neither wanted ever to end.

Epilogue

Governor Keating couldn't cover this lot up. There was a scandal. A public enquiry. The governor was dismissed, then arrested: charges pending.

A new firm was brought in to run the prison. Things were better, so far.

Paul Travis was commended for his role during the fire. It stood him in good stead when he came up before the parole board. He'd paid his debt to society: a date was set for his release.

He and Simon talked until dawn, the night before Paul's departure. They talked about Tim – and about Mehmet.

'I don't suppose I'll ever see him again,' said Simon.

'You'll be out of here, soon,' said Paul consolingly. 'A year at the most, I reckon. Then you and him can be together.'

'Maybe,' said Simon. 'Maybe. So much has happened in here – I'm not even sure I'd know what to say to him any more. To anybody. I'm not the same person I was, Paul.'

'I don't think any of us are,' said Paul. He smiled weakly. 'I suppose that means the prison system works.'

Simon smiled. 'What will you do?' he asked.

'Out there? I don't know,' Paul replied. 'I might look Tomi

up – the Finnish guy I told you about. Rotten fucking English. He got out last month. Sent me a letter. Practically unreadable, of course. First I want to go back down south, though. Visit my old stomping grounds, just once more. There's someone I want to see.'

'A girlfriend?' asked Simon.

'No,' said Paul. 'The cunt who shopped me – put me in here.'

'Paul,' said Simon gently, 'is it really worth it?'

'Don't worry,' Paul replied. 'I'm not going to touch him. He's not worth it. He's a coward, and I never want to see him again. I just want to tell him that.' Paul clambered from his bunk and vaulted up next to Simon. He lay close and put his arms around his friend. 'I don't like leaving you here,' he said.

'Don't be daft,' said Simon. 'I'll be all right. I've got Gary and Louie, for starters – and besides, I've got respect. I'm a legend in my own prison sentence, darling.'

They fell asleep curled up together, and were woken like that in the morning. The smirking screw was there to escort Paul out.

Unashamed, Paul kissed Simon on the lips. 'I'll write,' he said.

Simon nodded, and smiled.

Paul allowed himself to be led from the cell. He collected his street clothes – not worn in nearly a year – and put them on. Last year's fashions, he reflected. Everything would probably have changed. He'd probably look a twat.

The screw shook his hand at the main gate. 'Good luck, son,' he said. 'Keep your nose clean.'

Do they learn this stuff from a phrasebook? Paul wondered.

The screw opened the gate, and Paul looked out through it. The Blackcastle Moorlands sloped away in front of him. The great wide open.

He stepped through the gate. The bus stop was just down the road. There should be one along eventually.

The gate closed behind him. He started to walk.

IDOL NEW BOOKS

Also published:

THE KING'S MEN
Christian Fall

Ned Medcombe, spoilt son of an Oxfordshire landowner, has always remembered his first love: the beautiful, golden-haired Lewis. But seventeenth-century England forbids such a love and Ned is content to indulge his domineering passions with the willing members of the local community, including the submissive parish cleric. Until the Civil War changes his world, and he is forced to pursue his desires as a soldier in Cromwell's army – while his long-lost lover fights as one of the King's men.

ISBN 0 352 33207 7

THE VELVET WEB
Christopher Summerisle

The year is 1889. Daniel McGaw arrives at Calverdale, a centre of academic excellence buried deep in the English countryside. But this is like no other college. As Daniel explores, he discovers secret passages in the grounds and forbidden texts in the library. The young male students, isolated from the outside world, share a darkly bizarre brotherhood based on the most extreme forms of erotic expression. It isn't long before Daniel is initiated into the rites that bind together the youths of Calverdale in a web of desire.

ISBN 0 352 33208 5

CHAINS OF DECEIT
Paul C. Alexander

Journalist Nathan Dexter's life is turned around when he meets a young student called Scott – someone who offers him the relationship for which he's been searching. Then Nathan's best friend goes missing, and Nathan uncovers evidence that he has become the victim of a slavery ring which is rumoured to be operating out of London's leather scene. To rescue their friend and expose the perverted slave trade, Nathan and Scott must go undercover, risking detection and betrayal at every turn.

ISBN 0 352 33206 9

DARK RIDER
Jack Gordon

While the rulers of a remote Scottish island play bizarre games of sexual dominance with the Argentinian Angelo, his friend Robert – consumed with jealous longing for his coffee-skinned companion – assuages his desires with the willing locals.

ISBN 0 352 33243 3

CONQUISTADOR
Jeff Hunter

It is the dying days of the Aztec empire. Axaten and Quetzel are members of the Stable, servants of the Sun Prince chosen for their bravery and beauty. But it is not just an honour and a duty to join this society, it is also the ultimate sexual achievement. Until the arrival of Juan, a young Spanish conquistador, sets the men of the Stable on an adventure of bondage, lust and deception.

ISBN 0 352 33244 1

TO SERVE TWO MASTERS
Gordon Neale

In the isolated land of Ilyria men are bought and sold as slaves. Rock, brought up to expect to be treated as mere 'livestock', yearns to be sold to the beautiful youth Dorian. But Dorian's brother is as cruel as he is handsome, and if Rock is bought by one brother he will be owned by both.

ISBN 0 352 33245 X

CUSTOMS OF THE COUNTRY
Rupert Thomas

James Cardell has left school and is looking forward to going to Oxford. That summer of 1924, however, he will spend with his cousins in a tiny village in rural Kent. There he finds he can pursue his love of painting – and begin to explore his obsession with the male physique.

ISBN 0 352 33246 8

DOCTOR REYNARD'S EXPERIMENT
Robert Black

A dark world of secret brothels, dungeons and sexual cabarets exists behind the respectable facade of Victorian London. The degenerate Lord Spearman introduces Dr Richard Reynard, dashing bachelor, to this hidden world. And Walter Starling, the doctor's new footman, finds himself torn between affection for his master and the attractions of London's underworld.

ISBN 0 352 33252 2

CODE OF SUBMISSION
Paul C. Alexander

Having uncovered and defeated a slave ring operating in London's leather scene, journalist Nathan Dexter had hoped to enjoy a peaceful life with his boyfriend Scott. But when it becomes clear that the perverted slave trade has started again, Nathan has no choice but to travel across Europe and America in his bid to stop it.

ISBN 0 352 33272 7

SLAVES OF TARNE
Gordon Neale

Pascal willingly follows the mysterious and alluring Casper to Tarne, a community of men enslaved to men. Tarne is everything that Pascal has ever fantasised about, but he begins to sense a sinister aspect to Casper's magnetism. Pascal has to choose between the pleasures of submission and acting to save the people he loves.

ISBN 0 352 33273 5

ROUGH WITH THE SMOOTH
Dominic Arrow

Amid the crime, violence and unemployment of North London, the young men who attend Jonathan Carey's drop-in centre have few choices. One of the young men, Stewart, finds himself torn between the increasingly intimate horseplay of his fellows and the perverse allure of the criminal underworld. Can Jonathan save Stewart from the bullies on the streets and behind bars?

ISBN 0 352 33292 1

CONVICT CHAINS
Philip Markham

Peter Warren, printer's apprentice in the London of the 1830s, discovers his sexuality and taste for submission at the hands of Richard Barkworth. Thus begins a downward spiral of degradation, of which transportation to the Australian colonies is only the beginning.

ISBN 0 352 33300 6

SHAME
Raydon Pelham

On holiday in West Hollywood, Briton Martyn Townsend meets and falls in love with the daredevil Scott. When Scott is murdered, Martyn's hunt for the truth and for the mysterious Peter, Scott's ex-lover, leads him to the clubs of London and Ibiza.

ISBN 0 352 33302 2

HMS SUBMISSION
Jack Gordon

Under the command of Josiah Rock, a man of cruel passions, HMS *Impregnable* sails to the colonies. Christopher, Viscount Fitzgibbons is a reluctant officer; Mick Savage part of the wretched cargo. They are on a voyage to a shared destiny.

ISBN 0 352 33301 4

THE FINAL RESTRAINT
Paul C. Alexander

The trilogy that began with *Chains of Deceit* and continued in *Code of Submission* concludes in this powerfully erotic novel. The evil Adrian Delancey has finally outwitted journalist Nathan Dexter – and – Nathan Dexter is forced to play the ultimate chess game, with people as sexual pawns.

ISBN 0 352 33303 0

WE NEED YOUR HELP . . .
to plan the future of Idol books –

Yours are the only opinions that matter. Idol is a new and exciting venture: the first British series of books devoted to homoerotic fiction for men.

We're going to do our best to provide the sexiest, best-written books you can buy. And we'd like you to help in these early stages. Tell us what you want to read. There's a freepost address for your filled-in questionnaires, so you won't even need to buy a stamp.

THE IDOL QUESTIONNAIRE

SECTION ONE: ABOUT YOU

1.1 Sex (*we presume you are male, but just in case*)
Are you?
Male ☐
Female ☐

1.2 Age
under 21 ☐   21–30 ☐
31–40 ☐   41–50 ☐
51–60 ☐   over 60 ☐

1.3 At what age did you leave full-time education?
still in education ☐   16 or younger ☐
17–19 ☐   20 or older ☐

1.4 Occupation _____

1.5 Annual household income _____

1.6 We are perfectly happy for you to remain anonymous; but if you would like us to send you a free booklist of Idol books, please insert your name and address

_____

_____

_____

_____

SECTION TWO: ABOUT BUYING IDOL BOOKS

2.1 Where did you get this copy of *Hard Time*?
    Bought at chain book shop ☐
    Bought at independent book shop ☐
    Bought at supermarket ☐
    Bought at book exchange or used book shop ☐
    I borrowed it/found it ☐
    My partner bought it ☐

2.2 How did you find out about Idol books?
    I saw them in a shop ☐
    I saw them advertised in a magazine ☐
    I read about them in _____
    Other _____

2.3 Please tick the following statements you agree with:
    I would be less embarrassed about buying Idol
    books if the cover pictures were less explicit ☐
    I think that in general the pictures on Idol
    books are about right ☐
    I think Idol cover pictures should be as
    explicit as possible ☐

2.4 Would you read an Idol book in a public place – on a train for instance?
    Yes ☐   No ☐

SECTION THREE: ABOUT THIS IDOL BOOK

3.1 Do you think the sex content in this book is:
    Too much ☐   About right ☐
    Not enough ☐

3.2 Do you think the writing style in this book is:

      Too unreal/escapist ☐   About right ☐

      Too down to earth ☐

3.3 Do you think the story in this book is:

      Too complicated ☐   About right ☐

      Too boring/simple ☐

3.4 Do you think the cover of this book is:

      Too explicit ☐   About right ☐

      Not explicit enough ☐

Here's a space for any other comments:

SECTION FOUR: ABOUT OTHER IDOL BOOKS

4.1 How many Idol books have you read?

4.2 If more than one, which one did you prefer?

      _____

4.3 Why?

SECTION FIVE: ABOUT YOUR IDEAL EROTIC NOVEL

We want to publish the books you want to read – so this is your chance to tell us exactly what your ideal erotic novel would be like.

5.1 Using a scale of 1 to 5 (1 = no interest at all, 5 = your ideal), please rate the following possible settings for an erotic novel:

      Roman / Ancient World   ☐

      Medieval / barbarian / sword 'n' sorcery   ☐

      Renaissance / Elizabethan / Restoration   ☐

      Victorian / Edwardian   ☐

      1920s & 1930s   ☐

      Present day   ☐

      Future / Science Fiction   ☐

5.2 Using the same scale of 1 to 5, please rate the following themes you may find in an erotic novel:

Bondage / fetishism ☐
Romantic love ☐
SM / corporal punishment ☐
Bisexuality ☐
Group sex ☐
Watersports ☐
Rent / sex for money ☐

5.3 Using the same scale of 1 to 5, please rate the following styles in which an erotic novel could be written:

Gritty realism, down to earth ☐
Set in real life but ignoring its more unpleasant aspects ☐
Escapist fantasy, but just about believable ☐
Complete escapism, totally unrealistic ☐

5.4 In a book that features power differentials or sexual initiation, would you prefer the writing to be from the viewpoint of the dominant / experienced or submissive / inexperienced characters:

Dominant / Experienced ☐
Submissive / Inexperienced ☐
Both ☐

5.5 We'd like to include characters close to your ideal lover. What characteristics would your ideal lover have? Tick as many as you want:

Dominant	☐	Caring	☐
Slim	☐	Rugged	☐
Extroverted	☐	Romantic	☐
Bisexual	☐	Old	☐
Working Class	☐	Intellectual	☐
Introverted	☐	Professional	☐
Submissive	☐	Pervy	☐
Cruel	☐	Ordinary	☐
Young	☐	Muscular	☐
Naïve	☐		

Anything else? _____

5.6 Is there one particular setting or subject matter that your ideal erotic novel would contain:

_____

5.7 As you'll have seen, we include safe-sex guidelines in every book. However, while our policy is always to show safe sex in stories with contemporary settings, we don't insist on safe-sex practices in stories with historical settings because it would be anachronistic. What, if anything, would you change about this policy?

_____

_____

SECTION SIX: LAST WORDS

6.1 What do you like best about Idol books?

_____

6.2 What do you most dislike about Idol books?

_____

6.3 In what way, if any, would you like to change Idol covers?

_____

6.4 Here's a space for any other comments:

_____

_____

_____

_____

Thanks for completing this questionnaire. Now either tear it out, or photocopy it, then put it in an envelope and send it to:

Idol
FREEPOST
London
W10 5BR

You don't need a stamp if you're in the UK, but you'll need one if you're posting from overseas.